The
FIRE EATERS

The
FIRE
EATERS
A Novel

WILLIAM COBB

W. W. NORTON
& COMPANY
New York · London

Copyright © 1994 by William Cobb
Printed in the United States of America
First Edition

The text of this book is composed in Goudy Old Style
with the display set in Bernhard Modern.
Composition by PennSet Inc.
Manufacturing by Courier Companies, Inc.
Book design by Charlotte Staub.

Library of Congress Cataloging-in-Publication Data

Cobb, William, 1957–
    The fire eaters : a novel / William Cobb.
        p.   cm.
    I. Title.
PS3553.O198F57   1994
813′.54—dc20   93-11534

ISBN 0-393-03581-6
W. W. Norton & Company, Inc.
500 Fifth Avenue, New York, N.Y. 10110
W. W. Norton & Company Ltd.
10 Coptic Street, London WC1A 1PU

1 2 3 4 5 6 7 8 9 0

for Fernande,
and my brother, Tommy

Contents

This book is the winner of the Associated Writing Programs Award for the Novel, 1992. AWP is a national nonprofit organization dedicated to serving American letters, writers, and programs of writing. AWP's headquarters are at Old Dominion University, Norfolk, Virginia.

The
FIRE EATERS

Prologue

As a child, I remember reading a Chinese fairy tale about a man who swallowed the ocean. After he swallowed it the sea was empty. Starfish, sea horses, and octupi flopped around on the muddy ocean bed. The Chinese man's head was shaved except for a ponytail on the very back. His eyes were slanted. He held the entire sea in his mouth, his cheeks puffed out, his eyes bulging, sitting beside the shore. There were illustrations. Starfish in the foreground, pagodas in the background, the ribs of a sunken ship exposed in the now empty harbor.

The Chinese man had an enormous belly.

I wondered how he could do this, hold the sea in his mouth, the entire sea, for so long. Long enough for the villagers to gather the flopping fish from the ocean floor. Long enough for his family to pry pearls from the mouths of giant clams.

Looking at the picture, I knew that eventually he would have to let it go.

1
The Ear
in
the Jar

For many years when I was growing up, if you had asked me where my father was, I would have shown you a shoe box beneath our kitchen sink. In this box was a glass fruit jar. In the jar, lightly coated with salt, was a piece of my father's ear. It was a small half-moon of gray dried flesh, and if you held it in your thumb and forefinger, it felt as light as a communion wafer. For many years, this piece of ear was his only presence in our house.

My father died when I was too young to see it or hear it, or to know how it happened, but I always believed that he died in his sleep. This was a disturbing thought for me, especially at night. Our family lived in an old wooden house, and because I had insomnia, I often lay awake in the middle of the night, in the bunk bed below my older brother, Louis. As I lay there in the inky, fluid darkness, with amoeba shad-

ows of our fig tree leaves pulsing across the window, I wondered if I too could die in my sleep. If my father did it, why
not me? It seemed like a peaceful way to go, like slipping
your head into the warm water of the bathtub. But even if
I considered entering it peacefully or willingly, eternal noth-
ingness was like the bottom of the sea. Murky. Distant. A
place I could never clearly imagine. My mother told me,
"One day, your father just didn't wake up." We had a space
heater in our room, and mother warned us to turn it off
before we went to sleep, or the blue flames might burn off
all the oxygen in the room.

"You wouldn't want to wake up dead, would you?"

We seldom talked about my father when I was growing
up. That was how we dealt with our tragedies, by not talking
about them. Ignore the subject. With five kids in our family,
it was easy to do. Being noticed was sometimes the hardest
thing. It seemed that if we didn't talk about a problem, it
would evaporate and vanish. "Mom?" I asked. "How do you
die in your sleep?" She would look in the oven, or at the
book she was reading, or anywhere but at me, and say, "I
don't want to talk about it."

"But why not? Why don't we ever talk about him?"

"He had a lot of bad habits. I don't want to talk about
it," she said.

Once, while we were eating dinner, I told everyone, "I
saw my father in the living room last night."

"Oh, right," they said.

"He was wearing a black tie and a white shirt. He had on
cufflinks and a black coat with buttons on the sleeves."

My brother Louis slapped the bottom of a Heinz ketchup
bottle and we all watched, wincing, waiting for it to explode

into a shower of thick red droplets. Louis frowned and slapped the bottle, but no ketchup came out.

"My father looked good in his suit and tie, and he said that one day we were going to find a million dollars in the backyard. He said it's out there right now, if only we knew where to look."

Mother snatched the ketchup bottle from Louis's hands and stuck a butter knife up its mouth. She wiggled the knife back and forth until the ketchup started to flow. "Your father never wore a black tie in his life."

"Was he skinny? He looks skinny when I see him at night."

"He had some bad habits."

"Was he tall? Am I going to be tall? I want to be tall."

"I'm not tall," said Louis.

"Yes you are."

"He was tall," said Mother. We looked at her. "He was so tall we had to knock out the doorframe so he wouldn't have to stoop. He was so tall we all looked up to him."

"You're pulling our legs," said my sister Lizzie.

"Last night," I said, "when I saw him in the living room, in his suit and tie, he was so tall he had to bend over."

"What were you doing in the living room? Are you sleepwalking again?"

"I needed a drink of water."

"When you saw your father last night, how many ears did he have?"

"Ears? What do you mean?"

"Ears. You heard me. How many?"

Everyone turned to look at me. My sister Melody turned her suffering martyr eyes on me and stared.

"Two," I said. "Two. Like everyone else."

Mother shrugged. "Must have been somebody else, then. Your father only had one ear."

Melody nodded, and Louis didn't seem surprised.

"Who else would it be?" I asked.

"I don't know. Maybe a burglar. Maybe the ghost of some- one who used to live in this house. Besides, your father never lived here. He probably doesn't know where to look if he wants to haunt us."

"Why don't we ever talk about him then? Why'd he only have one ear? Everybody's got two ears."

"He had some bad habits."

"I want to know!"

"Listen," said Mother, setting down her fork. "Listen. I'll tell you one story about your father. One story only. It was nine years ago. We were living in Texas City then, and he worked at the Union Carbide plant. You don't remember Texas City. It's all refineries and chemical plants. The air smells like burning oil, and at night you can look out the window and see the roaring flames of the refineries burning off excess gas. We lived so close to one of those I could hear the sound of the flames if the wind was in the right direction." She sat there calmly, like a gypsy telling our fortunes, watch- ing our rapt faces. "It sounded like sheets on a clothesline. Sheets, on the clothesline, popping in the wind. But it was flames.

"Your father hated his job at Union Carbide, because he couldn't get along with the foreman. And that was a problem. Your father had his good side, but he also had some bad habits. He was a drinker and a gambler and he didn't lie when he should have. If he didn't like a person he wouldn't ignore them or be polite to them or act phony and shake their hands and smile at them. He'd go up and look them

The Fire Eaters

in the face and say, 'I don't like you,' or, 'You know, just looking at you makes me sick.' That's the way he felt about his foreman. And it made his job a bad one.

"Every morning, when he left for work, I prayed that he would not get fired or take a pipe wrench and bash in the head of the foreman on his loading dock at Union Carbide, because he hated that man with a hatred so thick and hard that he would lie awake in bed at night, telling me how he was either going to kill him or die trying. I'd try to calm him down. But it wasn't easy.

"And the foreman was a lot like your father. Cut from the same cloth. A big drinker and gambler. At first they tolerated each other, although they were never really what you'd call pals. Until he fired one of your father's friends. And that was that.

"I told him to just forget about it. But he couldn't do it. He said some things you can't forget. And I guess he was right. I guess he *is* right."

The food on our plates, the meat loaf and the gravy, the ketchup, the creamy corn and the mashed potatoes, was getting cold, but none of us lifted our forks to eat.

"The first day of every month was payday. In October, I was busy taking care of Melody and Louis, weak with Lizzie on the way, and we were broke at the end of the month. Or before the end of the month. For a few days there, I had to sit around the house in the daytime, praying that Danny wouldn't be fired or kill the foreman. And as I sat there praying, all I could hear was the sound of those flames of the burn-off, sounding like a high wind buffeting the house.

"I was sick of it. Sick of everything. Not that this was the first time we were broke, but this time I remembered thinking it was getting old, not having money to buy a pound of hamburger meat or a half gallon of milk. So when the first of November arrived I was so happy we were getting another paycheck. And your father hadn't been fired or killed the foreman.

"I put on my favorite dress and got out my purse. I waited for him to come home after five o'clock when he got off work, so we could cash the check at the supermarket and buy food for dinner. I decided to fix his favorite dinner of smothered steak and onions, potatoes au gratin, and chocolate meringue pie." She paused for a moment, smiling at the memory, and shook her head.

"But six o'clock came and went. Then seven o'clock. Eight, nine. No Danny." She took her fork and drew lines in her mashed potatoes with it. "We were hungry and broke, and on payday, your father decided not to come home." She stared boldly at our faces, and we were anxious by then, and waiting. "He cashed that paycheck and joined a poker game after work. He said he felt so lucky that day. That he had to win something.

"He came home at three in the morning, stinking of beer and cigarettes. And he wouldn't even look at me. I asked him where he'd been all night and he told me he didn't want to talk about it. I asked him where his paycheck was and he didn't answer me. I wanted to hit him or scream or something, or just walk right out of the house, but I didn't.

"He'd lost the entire paycheck to the foreman in a poker game.

"Three weeks later the foreman was shooting his mouth off on the loading dock about a flat-bottomed fishing boat he'd just bought because he had some extra money that month, and your father jumped on him. The other workers formed a circle and cheered him on, since everybody hated

The Fire Eaters

the foreman. They cheered him on, and they didn't try to break it up. As your father's life was going down the toilet, they stood there and cheered. I always appreciated that. Afterwards, I just wanted to go up and thank each one of them personally for that." For a moment Mother looked at us, a twisting smile on her face.

"But the foreman was a big, heavy man, and in the middle of the fight, he bit off most of your father's ear. The foreman ended up with a concussion from having his head pounded against the concrete floor. He stayed in the hospital for a while, because of that. And your father lost his job.

"He wouldn't let the doctors touch him because we couldn't afford it, and drove home in that old blue Chevrolet we had, his work clothes covered with blood, getting it all over the upholstery. After he was cleaned up and his head was bandaged he rummaged through his filthy clothes, and he reached in his pants pockets and took out the piece of his ear the foreman had spit out on the loading dock. He filled one of my mason jars with salt and preserved that hunk of skin. Later, whenever one of his friends would joke about his having only one ear, he'd say, 'I still have two ears. Only one's in a jar.' "

Mother grinned at that, and looked around the table at the somber and shocked faces of the children who didn't know this story, and Louis and Melody, the oldest, who vaguely knew about it, but had believed that it was forbidden ever to be mentioned, even they were probably shocked that mother had told the story. And that was it. We went back to not talking about it. We finished dinner, but as I ate my mashed potatoes and creamy corn, and covered my meat loaf with ketchup, I thought about my father's bloody ear, what he must have looked like as he walked through the front door that afternoon after the fight with the foreman. How, even though Mother must have seen it coming, how she must have been sick at the sight.

A week later Melody said, "Okay, I'll show you. But you can't tell anyone else. Especially not Mama."

"Promise."

She made me stay in my bedroom while she went to get the mason jar from its hiding place, then she came back with one of the small brown paper lunch sacks we put our sandwiches and apples in every day, to take to school. She took the jar out of the sack and handed it to me. "That's your father's ear. So show some respect."

It was a heavy glass mason jar with a brass cap used for making preserves and storing fruit, but inside was a withered half-moon of an ear, the curved top half. The skin was wrinkled and gray, covered with clean white salt. The piece of flesh seemed small and insignificant. I wished that we had more of him. A bigger part. Like a foot. Or a hand. Or his heart, the size of my fist.

2

Gun and Bone

Besides his ear, the only souvenirs we had of my father's existence were a double-barrel twelve-gauge shot-gun and the disembodied bill of a sawfish he caught in the blue water of the Gulf of Mexico, off Galveston Island, in 1949. Gun and bone. Along with his ear, these leavings somehow defined the lingering effect my father's broken life had on my brothers and sisters and me, and my mother. He had been a hunter. The wooden house we lived in for most of these years had an attic with rats in it. Now and then I could hear their muffled scamperings above me in the middle of the night, as I tried to fall asleep. I remember imagining their thick pink tails dragging over the boxes of old clothes, faded letters and envelopes, and cartons of old photographs from the 1940s. Most of the boxes and photographs contained some memory of World War Two.

Up there, in the dusty stillness, there were photos of soldiers my mother had gone to high school with, photos of Quonset huts in the Pacific, a snapshot of a scared and very young-looking boy in a sailor's uniform, about whom my mother said, "He didn't make it back," as if he were lost in a forest.

Photos of my mother on roller skates, my mother clowning with a soldier in someone's front yard. My mother in a beautiful full-skirted evening gown at her debutante ball, 1944. Sometimes all that remained of the war was the shadow of a sailor in uniform, cast by the sun on a sidewalk, which the photograph seemed to freeze in an otherwise silly snapshot of my mother and her best friend, Jenny Stapleton, striking sultry Betty Grable pin-up poses for their beaux in battle.

My mother had long ago quit gazing at these scalloped-edged photographs, taken with her old Kodak Brownie, but they fascinated us children as if they were snapshots of Eisenhower, Patton, and Hitler himself. There were only a few photos of my father. In one he looks very young and is wearing a brown private's uniform. It resembles a retouched photo, hand-colored, with the same effect as in a colorized version of a classic movie like *It's a Wonderful Life* or *Casablanca*. His eyes seem startlingly, unusually blue, and my eyes are the same color. Mother always said, "You've got your father's eyes."

Gun and bone. There are several photos of my father in hunting and fishing poses. Besides the soldier snapshot, these are the only images I have of him: my father proudly holding up a string of five-pound redfish on a black-and-white Gulf Coast beach, wearing rubber waders that encased his entire body, fastened at his shoulder like wet rubber overalls, his open-faced saltwater reel big as a coffee can, the rod reaching well over his head. His handsome face stubbly and dark with a baseball cap on his head, a Clark Gable smile, and a cigar clenched in his teeth.

We handled these photos so much they became curled and smudged from our grubby children's fingerprints. The cardboard boxes that they were stored in, which dated from the 1950s, were dusty but remarkably stiff and strong. Some of the photos must have come from the developers in paper mini-albums, while others—the World War Two photos— had been placed in embossed leather binders with stiff, thick black paper pages. Sometimes the photos fell out, but generally, and especially when I was alone, I turned these pages with care and reverence. Gazing at these hunting and fishing photos in the dusty and remote silence of the attic, I wanted to jump inside that world and join those adventures. My own existence seemed dull and commonplace compared to these images of my father's manhood, and much more active than my afternoons of watching TV and doing homework.

But I didn't need to go as far as the attic to find mementos of my father's existence. We kept the sawfish bill in the back of our closet in the boys' bedroom, behind the footballs, sneakers, chess and checker set, Monopoly and Life games. And the sawfish bill was as fascinating as the photos, yet with an earthier sense of reality. It was a pale yellow bony snout about three feet long, with a vicious row of teeth on either side; I was obsessed with this bill, with its yellowish teeth, intrigued that such an absurd creature could exist. There in the closet of the boys' bedroom, where my brother Louis and I slept, it was close at hand. I took it out so often to look at and play with that some of the teeth fell out. Before long it resembled a monstrous broken comb.

After my father died, he developed the bad habit of swimming through the air of our living room late at night, in the form of a huge, speckled sawfish. Many nights I watched him swim slowly through the ocean of our living room, his long sharklike tail sweeping side to side, almost grazing the bookshelves, the lamps, the seascape painting that hung above our sofa.

I wasn't supposed to be up at this time of night. My mother scolded me for it, thought I would ruin my mind with lack of sleep. She implied it was more of a voluntary act than it was. "You can't stay up so late, Damon! Get some sleep! How will you ever grow to be strong and healthy if you stay up all night?" But she was tired herself, working all day long at her eight-to-five job as a bookkeeper in downtown San Gabriel. She was usually fast asleep by ten-thirty. On weekends we were allowed to stay up after the ten-o'clock news to watch horror movies, but on weekday nights, on school nights, we were supposed to be in bed by ten. I wasn't in regular school yet, but mother dropped me off at a crummy kindergarten on her way to work.

At night, I would lie in bed with my eyes open, listening to the wind outside or dogs barking or any sound in the world. And the house was never completely quiet. My sisters' voices and the sound of running water from the bathroom closest to their rooms were eventually replaced by the creakings of the house as it settled.

Louis had explained these noises. "It's the wood of the

house expanding or contracting as it settles for the night, as the air cools down."

"If you ask me, I think the house is haunted," said Melody.

To some extent, I believed Louis about the house settling, although I developed an image of the house itself as being alive, expanding, shifting, loosening its belt, puffing out its chest. And some of the creakings sounded like a foot stepping onto the weak boards in our living room, dining room, or hallway. A sharp snap. A drawn-out creak. The muffled sounds drawing closer and closer towards me, the only one awake in the house by midnight, my mind fully, nearly insanely alert, my nerves stretched tight, my senses spread out radially from the pinpoint of my forehead or some nexus between my ears to the many rooms and hallways of our five-bedroom house. I could sense a floorboard creaking by the china cabinet in the dining room, a lampshade being grazed by an invisible hand or fin in the living room, the soft whoosh of the hot water heater bursting into life near the kitchen, the blue flames casting shadows out from the louvered wooden slats of its small door near the dry-goods pantry, in the tiny closet that held only that huge white cylinder and a litter of half-burned wooden kitchen matches.

After everyone was asleep I would sneak out of my bed and slow-glide down the hallway to the living room, wearing my quilt like an Indian blanket around my shoulders. There, on the living-room couch, I watched for my father, close enough to the front windows to see the dark globs of the oak trees in the front yard. I would curl into the sofa, using one of the couch cushions for a pillow. Just being in the living room made me sleepier and less anxious. The pressure was off. The pressure to sleep. Immediately I relaxed, breathing in the familiar smells of the couch cushions, a mix-ture of house dust and upholstery, slipping my hand in between the cushions just far enough to touch the Bic pen that had slipped down there and had never been retrieved, the feel of it somehow comforting, knowing that I too could slip away and no one would notice, no one would raise a fuss.

All this filled me with a furtive peace. The entire living room seemed as if it were underwater, with the television, china cabinet, coffee table, and couch like the ceramic cas-tles, arched bridges, and tiny Poseidon-with-trident that sat at the bottom of Lizzie's aquarium on a floor of bright orange coral.

It was here, in this atmosphere of liquid air, this ocean floor of our house, that my sawfish father would swim by, his shiny black eye hard and solid as a marble, not seeming to look at me, not seeming to notice me. The speckled sides of his body would flex and sway, the tail fin sweep-ing him forward like a shark. I could never tell, the next morning when I remembered this, whether I had been awake or asleep when I had seen him. And I could never quite remember when I actually slipped into sleep, but could only remember the image of my sawfish father swimming by.

My mother didn't want me sleeping in the living room and tried to keep me in bed with threats of spankings. But it wasn't enough to stop me. So I took to waking up every morning in the living room, blanket wrapped around me. I was intensely grateful to her for allowing me to sleep, for not rousing me off the couch. I would lie there in the cocoon of warmth created by my blanket, looking out at my mother and brother and sisters walking by, waiting for the last pos-sible moment before getting ready for school. Eventually my family gave up nagging me and accepted my eccentricities as a weird symptom of my being the youngest.

And I wasn't alone in weirdness. Melody had a stuffed life-size Winnie-the-Pooh bear that she took everywhere with her and spoke to constantly. My mother felt the strain of these eccentricities and blamed it on our lack of a father. The quirks were particularly numerous at the dinner table —Lizzie couldn't sit next to Melody during dinner, and Sonia, the youngest sister, was morbidly afraid of monosodium glutamate after learning that it destroyed brain cells and caused cancer in lab rats; she read the labels of all food to find the lurking MSG.

"You kids are going to be the death of me!" Mother would say. "We need a man around here to straighten you up. Look at my hair. It used to be much darker than this. Now look at it. And my hands. And I've got wrinkles under my eyes.

"I feel like I'm drowning," she would say. "I feel like I'm underwater and can't breathe."

3

Apparitions in the Water

My mother remarried on a windy day at Breckinridge Park in San Gabriel, with a hired justice of the peace performing the service. Although we were Catholics, my new father didn't particularly believe in anything, so they couldn't do it in the church. On the way to the wedding, he and my mother argued quietly but fiercely. The car was crowded, because along with all of us he was bringing two sons and one daughter from his first marriage. Now there were eight children. My new brothers, Tony and Leland, sat in the back. Leland was Louis's age, Tony two years older than me. And my new sister Agnes was several years older, almost the same age as Lizzie. My mother was jammed against my stepfather on the bench seats of the station wagon, with Lizzie and me sitting next to her, my right arm pinned against the car door, my left side cushioned by the warm weight of Lizzie, who wore a yellow dress and had a white veil pinned into her dark hair.

"Maybe we should just call the whole thing off, Barry," said Mother. "Maybe this isn't a good idea to begin with."

We were driving to the park in a new green station wagon Barry had borrowed from the car dealership where he worked. "Don't put smudge marks on the seats," he had told us when we clambered into the car. "Don't touch anything, if you can help it. This car isn't ours. You get it? If it comes back dirty, I could lose my job."

Since our real father had had his bad habit of losing jobs, we knew what it was like to live without money for a long time. We wanted to avoid that fate if at all possible. We paid attention to Barry's warning.

"You should have told them you needed a car for the wedding. They might have let you borrow one. You don't know. What were you thinking?"

Barry pushed in the cigarette lighter and, keeping his eyes on the road, fished in his sports coat for a pack of cigarettes. "Would you just shut up?"

"Don't tell me to shut up."

"Would you calm down?"

"No, I won't calm down and I won't shut up. Maybe you should stop the car right here."

"Clara."

"Stop the car. Kids, we're getting out of the car and walking home."

Melody said, "Mom . . ."

"If you don't stop the car we're all going to jump out while it's moving, and you'll have that on your conscience. I'm not marrying a man who tells me to shut up. How would you like me telling you to shut up? Shut up, shut up, shut up. How do you like that?"

"There's not going to be any problem with the car," said Barry. "I'll take it back tomorrow and no one will ever be the wiser."

"You can't go through life just taking things when you want them," said Mother. "What are the children supposed to think?"

Barry blew a cloud of smoke at the windshield and shook his head. "Maybe you're right," he said. "Maybe we should call this off."

For a moment we sat there, holding our breaths, wondering if Barry was going to stop the car and we were going to walk home, if the wedding was off or not, but mother quit complaining, Barry finished his cigarette and flicked it out the window, and we continued rolling in the borrowed green station wagon down Alameda Avenue, towards downtown. It was a Saturday afternoon, and as we drove through the curving lanes of Breckinridge Park, we passed families eating fried chicken at picnic tables, saw teenagers playing softball games, and, at an intersection, had to wait for a miniature train full of children to pass by. The adults on the train looked like giants. Their arms and legs hung out of the small lemon-yellow and cherry-red train cars. We passed a little girl feeding Fritos to a tame deer. I wanted to get out and pet it, but they said no, we didn't have time for that. Maybe later.

The justice of the peace was a heavy man in a dark blue suit who looked like he was late for something and wanted to get this over with as soon as possible. He was taken aback when we pulled into the parking space and eight children got out of the car, along with my mother and Barry. When my mother told him the children would be witnesses to the wedding, he seemed offended for a moment, as if we were breaking the rules. The wedding took place in one of the numbered, marked picnic areas. We parked in the shade of two gray cypress trees, and between the trees, there were a metal barbecue grill, a picnic table, and a wire litter basket full of beer bottles and red-and-white boxes of Kentucky Fried Chicken.

I sat on the picnic table and deciphered what was written on it: RAMONA LOVES LUIS. VICTOR -N- GRACIE. EAT ME. Into the worn brown wood someone had carved a large heart.

"Don't get your suit dirty," said Louis.

There were cigarette butts beneath the picnic table, and ants crawling on the bench seats. The spot chosen by my mother for the ceremony was a picnic area on the San Gabriel River next to the zoo. We could hear the peacocks crying on the other side of the fence, and on the leaf-speckled green water of the river floated a flock of enormous white geese. Beyond the picnic table was a small waterfall over the concrete dam that made a pool in the river. There was a young couple standing on the dam, their pants legs rolled up to their calves, the water rushing over their ankles as they threw pieces of bread into the dark green water of the river for the huge white geese. The geese had large yellow beaks. Over the cries of the peacocks and the honking of the geese, the justice of the peace began reciting the memorized conditions for matrimony. The sickness and health. The richer and poorer. The death do you part.

The young couple finished throwing bread to the geese and stood there, watching us. Louis, being the oldest boy, was the best man. He held the ring. The rest of my brothers and sisters stood in a group behind our mother and Barry as the justice of the peace married them. The stiff wind made the sweeping branches of the cypress trees along the river-bank sway in the wind, and upset my mother's white pillbox hat so she had to hold it on her head with one hand.

The wedding took less than five minutes. Someone clapped as Barry kissed my mother. The justice of the peace drove away as soon as it was over, and we stood there awkwardly, staring at the two of them. Barry looked into our young faces and said, "Well. That's that."

We unloaded our picnic basket of fried chicken, potato salad, and Cokes. Barry ate one drumstick, then went off under the branches of the cypress tree to smoke a cigarette. Mother told us not to bother him. I threw bits of fried chicken down to the ants crawling on the exposed roots of the cypress tree beneath the picnic table. We ate with plastic forks and paper plates. The paper plates sagged, as we held them in our laps, from the weight of the potato salad, the chicken. Mother passed out the food, trying not to get anything on her clean hands. She seemed afraid to sit down on the rough wooden benches in her wedding dress, and stood there beside the table, eating carefully.

"Be sure to share the white meat and not hog it all to yourself, Louis," she said. Louis didn't like the dark meat. Lizzie complained that it was hot and there were ants every-where. "Hush," said Mother. "A few little ants aren't going to hurt you."

"But what if we get bitten? I might be allergic."

"You're not allergic to anything. Don't be so squeamish."

Leland said, "She thinks she's being a lady."

Lizzie made a face at him and said, "What do *you* know, stepbrother?"

"Lizzie. That's not a nice thing to say."

"Well that's what he is."

"I don't care. I want all of you to get along. So don't let me hear you saying that again."

When we were finished, we tossed the chicken bones into the river. Up from the dark green water rose the whiskered faces and fins of catfish. They moved sluggishly at first, then they flashed in the water, fighting each other for a piece, while across the pond the white geese flowed toward us on the surface. In the murky green water I saw the speckled fins and heavy beating tail of my sawfish father, but I didn't point and shout, and said nothing to the others.

I had learned to keep quiet when Father swam by.

4

What's Eating Barry?

At first I liked Barry because he took us to see *101 Dalmatians* and bought us popcorn, Cokes, and red-hots. I told him I wanted puppies just like the ones in the movie, and he nodded.

"I'll see what I can do," he said. But the puppies never arrived.

Barry was tall and had dark wavy hair. He smoked Pall Malls, read the paper every evening, and didn't seem to enjoy talking. What's more, he began to get irritated with us kids. In the middle of dinner one night, when we were arguing about who got to choose what TV shows we were going to watch, he threw down his knife and fork and said, "What are you kids always jabbering about? Can't you keep quiet for just one goddam second?"

"We're just talking," said Leland. Barry was his father, so he could speak up to him.

"But you never *say* anything. All you do is gab gab gab. A person can't even hear himself think in this goddam house."

"They're just being kids," said Mother. Barry glared at her and got up from the table.

"Thanks for the support," he said.

He brooded. Mother would say, "Something is eating Barry." Or she would say, "I wonder what's eating Barry?" This was in the first few months, when we were getting used to living together. No one seemed to know what was eating Barry. I wondered about it, too. At night, I pictured an invisible creature attached to his body, a dark and slimy leech attached to Barry's spine or in his armpits, eating away at him as he sat there, reading the newspaper or watching television or just staring into space, sometimes shaking his head as if he were arguing with someone inside the reaches of his mind. In the first few months he did almost seem to have something physically eating him, something invisible and relentless, as he lost weight, grew pale and moody, and brooded.

After Barry brought his two sons and one daughter to live with us the house seemed to swell with the collective breath, voices, arms, legs, and fingers of eight children. The bathrooms were never empty. The phone was always in use. We were a sixteen-armed creature, divided by factions of age, blood, order of birth. I was the youngest, the smallest, the easiest to push away when I fought for attention. The three new brothers and sister looked different from my blood brother and sisters. Their faces were wider, their bodies

What's Eating Barry?

broader. Agnes was almost fat. They didn't have our blue eyes. "You've got your father's blue eyes," my mother had told me.

It soon turned out that Barry was a failure and an alcoholic. We never said he had caught a "disease," but we recognized that he drank so much it was scary. We nicknamed him the It Monster. He was always in a bad mood when he came home from work. He drank bottles of Jim Beam and Old Crow and worked as a car salesman, but was in a perpetual slump. Once he told us, "I couldn't sell a car if my life depended on it." That night he stumbled and broke a wall mirror as he got up from the table to fix himself another drink.

"Oh, great," he said. "Another seven years' bad luck."

We were having meat loaf, mashed potatoes and gravy, and squash. Barry's eyes were bloodshot and angry. I watched my mother's face and could tell she didn't like him making another drink. When he got drunk sometimes he hit us. We cringed and held our breath when he came back to the table.

"How did I ever get myself into this goddam mess?" he asked.

I asked what was for dessert. "Oranges," said my mother.

"You're not getting dessert until you eat everything on your plate," said Barry. I looked at my food and avoided his face. I knew Barry hardly ate anything on *his* plate. Why should I have to? "It's a double standard," said Melody. Barry's breath stank from the whiskey.

A large pool of squash sat on one side of my plate. It made me sick just looking at it. "You're not leaving this table till you eat that," said Barry. My lips trembled and I started to cry, because I knew if I ate the squash I would throw up.

"You're scaring him, Barry," said my mother.

Barry leaned back from the table and lit a cigarette. "If he doesn't shut up I'm going to give him something to cry about." Mother picked me up and took me to the bedroom. She tucked me in, and we stayed there together, while the rest of the family ate dinner and we watched the light come through the crack at the bottom of the door. I liked the smell of my pillow and curled into it. I put my thumb in my mouth and sucked happily after she left. Barry would have slapped me if he had seen that.

"You have to grow up!" he often shouted.

But my mother never seemed to mind my doing it. She came in afterwards with an orange wrapped in her apron. I peeled the rind off in one piece as Melody had shown me, keeping it whole, in one round shape. It looked like a map of the world.

Our dog Pepper liked to chase cars and bark at their wheels, which seemed to be a constant problem with the dogs we owned—they were always chasing cars and coming to some tragic fate. Pepper was barking at Barry's car when he pulled into the driveway one day and the bumper smacked Pepper's head, knocking him several feet into the flower bed. His legs scrabbled in the black dirt, trying to get up, but he couldn't raise his head. He pushed his nose into the ground and his pink tongue got covered with black dirt. Barry climbed out of his car. His suit was rumpled and he had dark patches of sweat under his arms. His tie was loose.

"I told that dog to stay out of the way," he said.

My mother came out onto the front steps, wiping her hands on a yellow checkered apron. "What happened?" she asked.

Pepper lay under the branches of a hibiscus bush, some of

the pink flowers bent beneath him. Thick red blood dripped out of his wet black nose. Mother pulled the dog's body out from the bush and laid his head on her apron. Barry kept saying that it wasn't his fault, that he hadn't even seen the dog. "I warned you that something would happen if that mutt didn't stop chasing cars. And now this." Then he walked away, shaking his head. Mother didn't say anything, although she let me keep petting Pepper long after he quit breathing. She brushed the hair out of my eyes and told me everything was going to be all right. The two of us carried the body around the side of the house to the backyard, where she had Louis dig a grave. When we arranged Pepper's body outside his small doghouse, Mother took the apron out from under the body and opened it up, with the bloodstain multiplied by each fold like a paper cutout of dolls. Then she laid the cloth over Pepper and tucked him into the dirt.

After this, we started talking about how much we hated the It Monster, how disgusting he was when he was drunk. And at some point we realized that there was only one It Monster, but there were eight of us. Nine, counting my mother.

One afternoon while Barry was away my four sisters and three brothers and I took his bottles of Jim Beam and Old Crow out of the pantry in the kitchen, carried them in our arms to the firepit in our backyard, emptied them, and smashed the bottles. We smashed them with rocks and red bricks. The air was full of the charred smell from the deep ashes in the bottom of the pit, where we burned our paper garbage and put the ashes from our fireplace in winter. There were burnt and blackened tin cans in the bottom, from canned vegetables and Campbell's soup, with their labels burned off. At the edge of where we usually built the fire, wisps of burned newspapers floated up like black butterflies. The garbage pit in our backyard reminded me of the old campfires we sometimes found in a ring of white stones by the railroad tracks not far from our house, campfires that Louis said were made by hoboes who had nowhere else to go, no family, no job, no friends. Later in my life, I connected these hobo campfire rings to the garbage pit in our backyard and the afternoon we burned the It Monster's bottles. Louis cut his finger on a sliver of glass, but we kept at it until there was nothing left but a shining pile of clear shards. The paper labels on the bottles held some of the bigger pieces together.

"This is going to teach him a lesson," said Louis. After spotting some bricks with droplets of blood, Louis took off his T-shirt and wrapped it around his bleeding hand. Bare-chested, he looked skinny and frail, though his skin was the color of pecans.

When Barry returned home my sister Sonia and I hid in the treehouse in the oak tree in our backyard. Melody and Louis stood by our old car, Louis's hands—the cut one now bandaged in gauze—clenched in fists. From the treehouse we heard Barry shouting at our mother, doors slamming. The air crackled as if in a thunderstorm. Soon afterwards we heard the engine of his Rambler racing in the driveway until it sounded like it was going to explode, and then he screeched into the street.

That was the last we saw or heard from Barry for over a year. He was gone, and we quickly adjusted to this. It was easy not to be afraid.

That night after he left, as I was going to sleep I faintly heard my sisters singing the Wizard of Oz song.

"Ding! Dong! The witch is dead!
Which old witch? The wicked old witch!
Ding! Dong! The wicked witch is dead!"

I heard their laughter through the thin walls, and Louis saying clearly, "If he ever comes back here, he'll be sorry!" A few minutes later my mother told them to hush, to calm down. They had to get some sleep.

They were making enough noise to wake the dead.

5

Keeping a Secret

My mother's mother was a lovely black-haired woman whose family had emigrated from Ireland in the 1880s, and who died of leukemia when she was twenty-three years old, two years after my mother was born. On our living-room fireplace mantel sat an old-fashioned studio photograph of her mother—my grandmother—dressed in a Roaring Twenties outfit of slinky black dress with thin straps, fringed shawl, and small hat with a feather in it.

My mother's father was a black saxophone player in a jazz band. Like my father's death and reappearances, this was another thing we did not talk about. The only souvenir we had of my black grandfather's existence was a Civil War saber that hung on a pair of nails in the boys' bedroom. The story went that our grandfather's grandfather found the sword after the battle of Vicksburg. He was a young boy then, and had sneaked onto the battlefield to collect weapons to sell or trade for food. The saber was all that remained in our family of this trade of dead men's weapons for food, and all that remained of my mother's black father. His grandfather supposedly had found the saber standing upright in the gory field, speared through the rib cage of a gray-suited Confederate soldier, and when my great-great-grandfather pulled it out, the wound made a sucking noise, and the blade was covered with rebel blood.

The saber hung on the nails against the faded white walls of our bedroom, reminding us of the black blood in our veins. Once I asked my mother why we didn't have a photograph of her father on the mantel. She was making dinner, and I sat on the floor, playing with a toy tank. She stopped making dinner and took me outside to the picnic table in the backyard, where no one else could hear us. "Now Damon, I want you to understand one thing very clearly. Who your grandfather was or what he looked like is no one's business in the world. I want you to swear to me that you will never, ever, *ever*, speak about your grandfather to anyone except your brothers and sisters."

"But I was just asking why we didn't have a photograph of him."

"Because he's a secret. Do you understand? It's important that you understand this, Damon. Your grandfather is a secret and a secret is something you hide, not something you put on the mantel to tell all the world about. No one else in the world needs to know about your grandfather. He's not *their* grandfather. He's your grandfather. He's not something you share, but something you keep to yourself, something you keep close to your chest so no one else can see and meddle with it. So they can't take it away from you."

After Mother married Barry, the Civil War saber simply disappeared. The spot where it had hung on the wall was whiter at first, like a photo negative shadow, although in time it became as dingy as the rest of the wall. When I asked mother what had happened to it, she said, "Hush up about that sword. It's a dangerous weapon and you shouldn't be playing with it anyway." It was whispered through the walls of our house that Barry was not to know about our black grandfather. And we were all told not to tell Tony, Agnes, or Leland about it either. It was another reminder that they were totally separate from us. But Agnes found out, and she later used it against us.

In the year after Barry left, the mere mention of his name became taboo. We soon found out he had left San Gabriel, quit his job at the car dealership and hightailed it out for greener pastures. He didn't write or call Tony, Leland, or Agnes, and it was easy to treat him as someone no one wanted anything to do with, since he wasn't bothering to contact his own children. At first there was no talk of Mother getting divorced, but we must have somehow expected it. She supported us as best she could with her job as a bookkeeper, although she was always worrying we would end up in "the poor house." The It Monster became a family legend and took on even more monstrous qualities than he'd actually been guilty of. We, the children, ruled our house, and it seemed to work. Now we had control, and since Mother didn't seem to mind, we laughed and smiled much more than we used to, didn't seem to mind that we had so little money, didn't seem to mind that the house was so crowded with all of our voices, our wants and needs. We watched TV in the afternoons after school and loafed around the house as much as we wanted to, threw our clothes on the floor, played Canasta at the dinner table while we were eating. Now and then someone said, "If the It Monster saw that, he'd kill." And we'd smile among ourselves, the expression of victory.

By the next fall, when the school year was well under way and it seemed that somehow we were going to make ends meet, our mother relaxed and was happy. Even though she was working hard and we hardly had enough money for food, we didn't have Barry breathing down our necks. We didn't have to fear his coming home. The world seemed a beautiful place. The autumn sky was white, and the leaves of the sycamores and maples turned yellow and orange along Olmos Creek, where it crossed Sunburst Road not far from our house.

In the cool days my brothers and sisters and I walked into the woods to collect fallen branches for our fireplace. Winter came one day when we were collecting wood and it began to snow. We had a fire in the fireplace and the air outside smelled of wood smoke because the cloud poured out the chimney and hung low over the front yard. My breath puffed in the air and I held out my tongue to catch the fat white snowflakes. The ground was covered with snow, the oak trees in our front yard white with it. We hurried to collect wood so we could see more and more of the falling snow and smell the wood smoke as it drifted down. That night we threw a powder in the fireplace that made the flames turn ruby, emerald, and cobalt. When Louis and I went out to get more wood from the woodpile, the air was crisp and the sky had cleared, now cold and full of stars. Louis and I stood out there for a moment, looking up at the Milky Way.

He said he wished the It Monster would never come back.

We put up our Christmas tree on December 20th that year, which was my real father's birthday. The It Monster wasn't mentioned much around the house anymore, but if we did talk about him, even my mother called him the It Monster, and not Barry, as she had when he still lived with us. When the rest of the house was dark and I was supposed to be asleep, I watched the Christmas-tree lights flashing on the wall. The living room seemed dominated by the nativity scene on top of our television, whose clay figures of sheep, camels, wise men, Joseph, Mary, and baby Jesus were hollow. If you turned them over and looked from the bottom, they were cool and curvy as the inside of an ear. The baby Jesus slept on a cotton ball. That first Christmas without the It Monster was happy. We all seemed to get the presents we wanted. We weren't afraid of anything.

One night the phone rang and Melody answered it. She cupped her hand over the mouthpiece and told Mother, "It's long distance." Mother talked quietly into the phone and laughed, although when we asked who it was she waved at us to go into the other room. When she got off the phone her hands were trembling. She lit a cigarette and smiled oddly.

"Who was it?" asked Louis.

"Oh, that was Barry," she said. She told us he was coming to visit the night of Christmas Eve. "And I don't want any of you making ugly comments. Understand?"

We spent the morning cleaning up the house, without having to be asked to do it, and when Mother got off early from work on Christmas Eve she came home to find us still cleaning. She asked what had gotten into us. When we explained that the It Monster would be mad if he came home and found the house in a mess, she was angry and upset with all of us. She said that we would never clean up the house for her but we would for the It Monster, even though he never did anything for us. She said we didn't appreciate the fact that she loved us and fed us and took care of us. She ended up crying in her room until Louis and Melody told her we were all sorry, that we loved our mother very much and hated the It Monster. I offered to make a mess and my mother started to laugh, wiping the tears off her cheeks with the backs of her hands, hugging me and saying, "Oh, you."

He never arrived that night, and we never saw him alive again. His three children became part of our family. Mother got official custody of them because Barry was judged incompetent. He didn't even show up for the court hearing. I think he was in Florida then. He apparently went on drifting across the country, drinking in bars and struggling to make a living, until he died of liver failure. He never wrote or telephoned Agnes, Tony, or Leland, his flesh and blood, and somehow we weren't surprised.

But that Christmas Eve was tense as we waited for him. My brothers and sisters watched television. Melody taught me how to play Canasta. No one spoke very loudly. Mother sat in the living room with us, smoking cigarettes and reading, with her cat's-eye reading glasses on. It took her forever to turn the pages. If a car passed by, everyone looked up to see if it was pulling into the driveway.

6

Stealing Milk

For a long time after the It Monster left, I couldn't get enough to eat. What I really wanted was candy bars. My fantasies were filled with blue-white coconut and thick chocolate, caramel and nougats. My dream world was filled with Almond Joy. But even potatoes and syrup were hard to come by. As soon as I woke up in the morning, I started thinking about ways to get more food. One of these was to fake being sick, stay home, and eat like a madman while my brothers and sisters were in class. I was the youngest, and the others, who were taller and older, would hold the food out of my reach when they were home, above my head, saying, "Gosh, this is good." They danced around the kitchen, keeping the food above my outstretched arms. They chewed with their mouths open. They laughed as I pummeled their thighs.

On Saturdays my mother would go to the supermarket to buy all the food for the coming week. It was exciting and festive in the house when we unpacked the paper sacks. The shelves of our refrigerator filled with colorful packages and shiny wrappers. Cartons of orange juice. Bottles of cola. Bags of apples. Syrup. Oleo. Whole chickens. Cold cuts. Hamburger meat. Ham. Bacon. The doors of the refrigerator filled with eggs, mayonnaise, mustard, olives. Whole packages of hot dogs were stacked on the bottom shelves, like overgrown Vienna sausages wrapped in cellophane. In the pantry we placed the white bread, Pop-Tarts, peanut butter, jams. For dessert we had plastic bags full of Hershey bars, vanilla wafers, ice cream. It always seemed as if there was all the food you could imagine, on Saturdays.

That was when my brothers and sisters would start gorging themselves, holding food over my head, teasing me. They locked me outside, on our concrete back porch, and waved at me from the kitchen windows, Leland horsing around with a drumstick in one hand, a glass of milk in the other. Hercules and Fritz barked as I pounded at the door, shouting that I wanted some food too, but it didn't do any good. The others ate too fast. Mother warned them about this.

"Now remember," she said. "That's all you get."

But she didn't stop them.

By Tuesday, every week, the Hershey bars would be gone. The ice-cream container would be folding in on itself, and the only way you could get anything was if you licked the thick paper tongues of the half-gallon carton. The refrigerator would get a vacant look. It lost its color, so that when you opened the door it looked white and empty inside. The wires of the stainless-steel shelves would be distinct, noticeable.

I kept a spoon hidden behind the electric can opener, and

when no one was in the kitchen, I opened all the jars and gobbled mouthfuls of whatever I could find. Some things were sweet, like the thick imitation marshmallow sauce. Some were tart and chunky, like the pickle relish. This was how I got hooked on the barbecue sauce. I started by eating spoonfuls of it on Thursdays, when we were always out of food, but after a while I couldn't stop myself. Once Louis caught me screwing the lid back on the barbecue sauce, with the spoon in my hand. All my brothers crowded around me. "We're going to teach you a lesson," they said.

They stripped me and tied my ankles and wrists. Then they carried me to the other side of the house, where the girls were curling their hair and talking on the phone. They dropped me in the hall and locked the door, and the girls came out as I flopped there on the ground, screaming and crying. They surrounded me, tickling my sides until I was laughing so hard I couldn't breathe.

Everyone had a good time, except me.

But I used this to my advantage. When I was untied and dressed, Lizzie let me eat the leftover macaroni and cheese.

"I thought we were supposed to have that with dinner tonight?" said Melody. They were looking at each other as if there was going to be a fight, so I ate faster, in case the macaroni was yanked from my hands.

"We'll live," said Lizzie.

Melody grabbed me by an ear. "Don't eat so fast, you."

One morning I got up quickly, before the others, and sat too close to the gas heater. It was a dull red, maroonish rectangular metal box connected to the floor by curly copper tubing. Along the front of the heater was a row of holes through which you could see the blue flames. Mother stood by the heater with her dress hiked up, warming her bottom before she went to work. You could see the dark bands at the top of her hose. Her lips were bright red. Even for work, she always dressed as if she were going to a party. My face glowed with heat, as red as the electric wires that throbbed to life in our toaster. I liked the dark, mysterious heart of hot things, of toasters and heaters, of hair dryers and ovens.

"I don't feel very good," I told Mother, as she was on her last before-work cigarette. In the ashtray there were three filter-tipped cigarette butts. Each of them had a pink print of her lips.

Another time, after I said this, she felt my forehead and looked worried. It was as if she had forgotten me among the many arms and legs of the eight children in the house, as if I had suddenly reminded her that I was alive, that she had brought me into the world, that she was somehow responsible for me. And on that morning, she tucked me in under the blankets, and stayed home with me. The house was peaceful and eerie without my brothers and sisters there. It was as if I were an only child, and could eat anything I wanted. Mother fried bacon for my breakfast, and let me sit at the table in my flannel pajamas. The bacon smell filled the kitchen and dining room, so that I closed my eyes in anticipation. My mother was singing a little song, and I was filled with a happiness beyond words or meaning.

We watched soap operas. She changed into her robe and slippers and we wrapped ourselves in blankets, and Mother asked me, "Can you believe these people?" They were all crying.

I couldn't hold it in anymore. I raced around the house

yelling, "I can't believe them! I don't believe them!" shaking my head back and forth with my tongue hanging out.

"Calm down, buster," said Mother, laughing. "I thought you were supposed to be sick!"

The next time I told mother I didn't feel good, she snapped her purse shut and said, "Don't give me that. What do you think I am, stupid?"

Melody said, "He's been trying that sit-by-the-heater-trick again, hasn't he?"

"I think I'm going to throw up," I told them.

Mother shook her head. "It's been done."

Our bus stop was at the end of Moonlight Lane, where it ran into Huebner Road. Hercules followed me to the bus stop, even though he was not supposed to. Hercules looked like a Labrador retriever, although he wasn't pure-blooded, and wasn't as big and square-faced as Labs usually are. He was sleeker. More like an otter. Like Pepper, he had a bad habit of chasing cars. We would scream at him and spank him when he came trotting back, tongue hanging out, tail half-wagging, but it never seemed to do any good.

I tried to reason with him. "You could have been killed," I told him once. "Is that what you want?" He licked my hand.

When he chased cars he ran close to the ground, almost sideways, snarling and barking at the tires. It seemed as if he saw something in the tires that we didn't. Something in the whitewalls. It seemed as if he saw the enemy.

The blond clay dust on Moonlight Lane held the footprints of raccoons, skunks, rabbits. Ahead of the others, Hercules and I slipped into the woods, and I squatted beneath an oak tree to hide. Hercules sniffed for the trails of the animals that left their prints on Moonlight. Here I ate the peanut butter sandwich, apple, and crackers that were meant for my lunch. A mockingbird sang somewhere above me. I couldn't see it, but it changed its tune every few seconds. The trunks and branches of crape myrtles twisted and writhed before me, the bark fleshlike, smooth as gray skin, the branches curving and voluptuous as the naked arms and legs and bellies of my sisters after showers. The crape myrtles were scattered among the rough-barked limbs and drooping leaves of mesquite trees, so that the thicket in front of me became a hybrid of the two. I was the only thing out of nature there. My Spider-Man lunch box glowed red against the dark brown leaves on the forest floor. But the branches of the mesquite tree were covered with thorns, and tangled as the crown of Christ were the upper reaches where the pods held seeds of new trees, new thorns, new, naked limbs.

It was a quiet morning at school. I wasn't hungry at first, and when I sat in Miss LeClaire's class, I tried not to think about lunch. When the year began our teacher had been Mrs. Christiansen. She was old and weak. I could tell she ate very little. She seemed bloodless. To touch her skin would have been like stroking an iguana. Rough, leathery, wrinkled. The day President Kennedy died we were studying Africa.

"In the Sahara Desert," she said, "the nomads use camels for transportation, like we use cars. And sometimes, when they are tired and thirsty in the great wilderness of sand dunes, they imagine lakes—"

Interrupting her, our principal's voice broke into the classroom, over the PA system. It was crackly and difficult to hear at first, and because of this, he repeated himself. His voice was weak, but the second time we understood what he was saying. Our president had been assassinated in Dallas that morning. The principal asked for a moment of silence.

Mrs. Christiansen stared at our faces. We were six years old. She was sixty-two. She twisted her fingers together, watching us. "They imagine great cities," she said, "but . . . these mirages . . ." She stumbled almost, wavering before us, before the map of Africa that was pulled down, blocking the blackboard, and as Penelope Dupnik rushed to get her a glass of water, a dark spot appeared on the ruffles at the throat of Mrs. Christiansen's white blouse. She tried to cover up her face, and looked completely lost, as if she didn't recognize us anymore. Her nose was bleeding violently by then, uncontrollably. Nurse Edwards arrived and led her away. In the silence that followed, the class listened as Mary Beardsley sobbed.

Mrs. Christiansen left after that. In the week after the shooting she seemed to shrink. She would often forget what we were supposed to be studying, and on the blackboard she would draw birds and horses, square houses with peaked roofs, a squiggly line of smoke rising from the chimneys. We took to playing hide and seek in the cloakroom, to climbing out the lower windows and escaping to the playground early for recess and lunch.

Then one day a beautiful woman walked into our class in a pink sleeveless dress. She was slender. She wore silver bracelets and black high-heeled shoes. "My name is Miss LeClaire," she said, and wrote it in graceful, slanting cursive letters as beautiful as italic type. Miss LeClaire had dark hair parted in the middle, a faint mustache, and long fingernails like the talons of a bird. She was from Montreal, and had a face like Joan of Arc. When she called on me, I could not speak. I stared at her, smiling, dumb, ga-ga.

"Come, Damon. Tell me. What is boiling point of water?"

"Hot," I told her. "Really hot."

The class giggled.

"Two hundred and twelve degrees Fahrenheit," said Penelope.

"And what is normal temperature of healthy boy?" asked Miss LeClaire, brushing her hair out of her face with both hands, her shaven, grayish underarms visible for a moment.

I was dizzy, and couldn't answer.

During lunch that day, my stomach was tight and hollow as the classmates all around me ate meat loaf, cherry Jell-O with fruit cocktail inside, mashed potatoes. Most of them had rich families. Most of them had fathers. We were so poor that we had to share each other's clothes sometimes, and once my sister Sonia didn't have any clean underwear to wear, so she borrowed a pair of my mother's.

At recess, while Sonia was playing, Mother's underwear fell around Sonia's ankles, and everyone laughed and pointed at her. She wouldn't go to school for a week, and finally Mother had to skip a day of work and forcibly take her to class.

Most of the other kids in school had parents that gave them lunch money. They bought month-long passes, and the cafeteria ladies used a hole puncher to mark their days. I watched these cards enviously. I wanted their cards, their lunch boxes, their spiral notebooks. I felt like an oaf around them. Even my shoes were old and ugly.

The lunchroom refrigerator that held the half-pint cartons of milk was appliance-white, about three feet high, with doors on top that folded back. There was a gray rubber boot that sealed the cold air in when the doors were folded down. You reached in to the cartons stacked on their sides, row on row, red-and-white for white milk, black-and-white for chocolate.

You paid by dropping a nickel in the cigar box. They trusted you would only take what you had paid for. I dropped in a nickel, keeping my fist over the coins so no one could tell what I had put in. But they could hear that I had put in something. It was as if a choir were singing—these voices filled my ears, this roaring I could not stop, pushing me onwards.

I took two cartons of chocolate milk. I could have been buying for a friend.

It was a new experience, drinking stolen cartons of chocolate milk, concentrating on my hunger, wishing it away. I knew I should not steal. It was a mortal sin. When I knelt in the shadowy chilliness of the confessional, when Father Benavidez pulled back the sliding door, I would have something to talk about.

Miss LeClaire was on duty, and as she was walking down the aisle between the long cafeteria tables, carrying her own lunch tray, she saw me sitting quietly, now twirling an empty milk carton on its straw.

"Where is your tray, Damon?"

I explained that my mother made lunch every day, and that I liked it better that way, because I didn't want to tell her we were too poor to afford the cafeteria food. I was afraid, looking up at her; I thought she might somehow know that I had stolen the milk. She asked where my sack lunch was.

"I ate it at the bus stop."

"In the morning?"

"Uh huh." Her tray was piled high with adult servings of Jell-O, corn bread, potatoes, and, because it was Friday, fish sticks. Miss LeClaire must also have been Catholic. She would have been beautiful in church, a white veil on her dark hair, her white gloves, black satin purse, and smoky dark hose. Did she wear her sleeveless dresses in church? Sitting across from her, with her tray of food between us, I could see the dark moles on her arms. They were like constellations in the night sky, only reversed, with her pale skin as the black sky, her dark moles, the stars.

When I looked up, she was watching me. She wiped her hands on her napkin and said, "Come, Damon. You must eat."

She led me to the stainless-steel counter of the cafeteria food line, with her warm, damp hand on the back of my neck. While I slid my tray along the rails, she urged the cafeteria women, whose hair was bound in nets and plastic bags, to give me extra helpings of fish sticks, corn bread, cole slaw. They gave me two full squares of cherry Jell-O on two white plates. There was barely room for all of it.

Side by side we ate, and I had to force myself to chew slowly, not to seem a barbarian. I felt singled out by her attention, suffused with warmth from the food I was eating. I knew the other students were whispering about me, but I didn't care. Safe in the center of authority, I listened to Miss LeClaire lecture on the mammals of North America.

"In the Rocky Mountains, we have grizzly bears and badgers. Have you ever seen moose, Damon? They have enormous antlers, like this," she said, sticking her hands out sideways from her ears, wiggling her fingers.

After lunch, Miss LeClaire asked us to take a nap, so that we would not become sluggish and cranky. "It is important to sleep," she said. Each student had a bath towel for this. We unrolled them on the tiled floor beside our desks, and lay on these to sleep. I could see the other students through the legs of the desks, some of them fidgeting, but many of them at rest, at peace. I could not sleep. With our small bodies lying on the cool tile floor, it was as if we were prostrate in the face of some great calamity. I saw the calves of Miss LeClaire as she stood at the windows, closing the lower ones with the window crank. The panes were painted a dull green on the outside, which did not let in light, so that the room was darkened when they were closed, although the windows above were still open, letting in a cool light that shone down on all of us. I saw Miss LeClaire's high heels, the hem of her pink dress ending just below her knees. For the moment, my belly was full. I imagined that, out the window, the sun shone on the wintry playground. The night before, the weatherman on Channel 5, who lived down the street from us, had said it would freeze. The cold wind whistled against the closed window panes. The swings on the gray playground must have been swaying in the breeze, as if invisible children were marking time in them.

7
The New
House

Our old house at Moonlight and Sunburst was situated on about three-quarters of an acre of land, with four oak trees, a cactus bed, and a rose garden in the front yard, one side yard with three oaks, the other with a vegetable garden, and a backyard full of peach trees, fig trees, and junipers. It was surrounded by fields of grass and cactus. In these fields grew oaks and junipers, and through the fields and woods ran creek beds of limestone and brown clay that filled with rainwater during the spring and early summer. The fields and woods were full of animals. We often found their skulls, with eye sockets you could poke your finger into, dull white and covered with damp leaves, a pill bug inside, sometimes a bit of fur lingering in the grass beside the skeleton. Sometimes the creatures of the fields wanted inside our house. And sometimes they seemed to invade.

In 1966, we had the greatest inchworm hatch in the history of our neighborhood. They hatched from eggs planted unseen among the oaks and junipers in our backyard. Soon they were eating everything in sight. I remember sitting in the tire swing in our backyard, inchworms crawling under me and clustering on the rotten peaches in the St. Augustine grass. The inchworms were brown, smaller than woolly worms, and smelled. The normally crunchy gravel of our back driveway felt like velvet, it was so thick with inchworms. It was a spicy, sweet smell, with a tinge of bitterness to it, like one of the birthday cakes my sisters baked when they forgot to include some vital and necessary ingredient. As I sat there, my mother swept the inchworms off the back porch, barefoot, while I hung my legs out the other side of the tire swing, holding on to the frazzled hemp rope that was tied to the oak branch above. I breathed in the musty smell of the tire, a smell of parking lots and oil changes, and swung, listening to the sloshy sound of the old rainwater that collected inside the tire and was impossible to get out. It splashed up on my legs as I swung, watching my mother sweep the inchworms off the porch. Our great aunt was in the hospital for a serious illness, and since she was old and wrinkled and feeble, we believed she was going to die. We also believed she was rich.

"How old is Na-Na?" I asked.

"Sixty-three."

"That's pretty old, huh?"

"Not that old. Some Russians live to be one hundred and twenty years old."

"I don't believe that."

Mother banged the broom against the side of the concrete porch, trying to knock the inchworms out of the straw spines of the broom. "Believe what you want to believe," she said. "I read it in *Reader's Digest*."

Inchworms climbed the dark sides of the concrete porch, up from the gravel driveway, and their massed bodies showed in streaks of dark green on the gray concrete. We had stepped on so many of them the porch had a trail of yellow smears in our walking path. At first we tried to avoid them and not squash their bodies, because you could slip and break your neck, but after a while there were so many it was hopeless. We came to take a perverse joy in walking on a slimy path of dead and dying inchworms. Now along with worrying about whether I would wake up dead at night, I took to worrying about the inchworms. They began showing up everywhere, in our clothes, in our car, on the television screen.

I wondered if they could crawl through the window screen at night, hump their way across the floor and up to my bunk bed, and while I was asleep, worm their way into my mouth. There they could plant their eggs, so that even if I woke up and managed to pull them out, dig them from beneath my tongue and peel them off the roof of my mouth, I would still not be rid of them. Weeks or years later they might be triggered to hatch, as the unseen eggs had hatched in our backyard and our juniper trees. Maybe I would be in class or having dinner with my family, and suddenly my mouth would once again fill with inchworms, my screams muffled by their soft and furry bodies. Or maybe they would bore through my nostrils and into my brain, to drive me insane with their drilling.

It was another thing to imagine as I fell asleep at night.

If I listened very closely, and kept perfectly still, hanging in the tire swing, I could hear them rustling through the oak leaves and grass under my feet. It was a gentle, insidious crepitation, but one that my family tried to ignore, because if we concentrated on it too much, we could imagine the inchworms were eating the earth out from under us. We knew they were trying to get inside our house, and that there was little we could do about it.

We had found inchworms in our china cabinet, in the worst of it, eating our lace doilies. Mother was afraid they would squirm their way into my sisters' hope chests.

"There's one on your back," I told her, pointing.

"Hush," she said. She set the broom inside the screen door, then wiped her feet on the welcome mat before going inside. "I wish Irene would call," she said. Aunt Irene was supposed to let us know about Na-Na, who had had another stroke the day before this, and was then in intensive care. She had been in the hospital in Galveston for two months already.

The week before I had prayed for her to die. She seemed very old and unable to enjoy life any longer. Now was the time for her to die, I thought. We would get money from her will. I knew very little about funerals and death, but I had been told by Louis and Melody how we would inherit money from Na-Na. This I understood. Cash.

I imagined buying all the things I'd always wanted at Wonderland Mall. A slip and slide. A Feely-Meely set. A new stamp book for my collection. I had stamps from Madagascar and Hungary. Stamps with Olympics on them, butterflies, trains, and Japanese volcanoes. Mount Fuji, with Japanese characters I couldn't read. I had a two-cent stamp with Benjamin Franklin on it, stamps with Thomas Jefferson, Alexander Hamilton, buffaloes, biplanes. I had special commemorative stamps to celebrate the launching of the Mercury space program, and understood exactly what it meant for us to be in the Apollo program. Louis was always talking about the Apollo rocket launches and preparations. "You wait," he said. "We're going to be on the moon before you know it." I believed him. I sincerely believed we would land on the moon, and that when that happened, when we had traveled the 240,000 miles through dark space to reach the blue surface of the moon, with one-sixth of our gravity, there would be a stamp to commemorate that, too. And I would want that moon-landing stamp for my collection, for my book.

My brothers and sisters also lay awake at night praying for Na-Na to die. They needed money, just like me. They wanted money to buy all the things that would make them happy. I secretly believed that even my mother was praying for Na-Na to die. She wanted the money more than all of us. She had even made an appointment for us to look at a new house, on Sunday after church.

"Are you going to give confession today?" asked my mother that morning. She was standing in the doorway to the boys' bedroom, where I was getting dressed, still in my white Fruit of the Loom underwear, pulling on my socks.

"Yes, ma'am." Mother smiled at me. We could hear Elvis Presley's "Girls Girls Girls" album playing on the living-room phonograph set. The phonograph was a bulky plastic thing that had two speakers attached on the sides, which swung out on doorlike hinges when you wanted to use it and folded back when you wanted to store it away. When folded up, it resembled a piece of furniture, kind of, if you think of fur-niture made from gun-metal-gray plastic. We thought this was a brilliant, modern design: handy and multifunctional. We often placed an entire stack of record albums on the stainless-steel pole, enough for several hours' worth of music. My mother seemed to be listening to the music as she stood in the doorway, smiling at me, wearing a flower print dress and gaudy earrings. "Okay," she said. "We'll be sure to wait for you. And remember to pray for Na-Na's soul today."

"I will."

"And no burping during mass."

To get ready for mass, I shined my shoes until they were black and shiny as purses. I put on a blue suit, inserting the plastic prongs of a clip-on tie into the collar of my white shirt. I wet my hair to keep my cowlick down. Leland splashed on Old Spice and danced in front of the mirror to the Elvis Presley music, which was now "Heartbreak Hotel." He had wavy black hair and a dimple in his chin like Kirk Douglas. Louis had blue eyes like mine, and was shorter than Leland by a half-inch. They were both in high school and looked sharp in their church suits. Leland used a small black plastic comb to touch up the waves in his hair.

"I'm going to buy that Mustang I saw off Wurzbach," he said, without taking his eyes off his reflection in the mirror, combing his hair.

"She might not even die," said Louis.

"Maybe. Maybe not."

"We shouldn't be talking like this." Louis felt closer to Na-Na because he was related to her by blood. Leland was not physically connected to Na-Na in any way, although she did send him birthday and Christmas presents, often money in envelopes. There was always a circle cut into the envelope so that the president's face on the money would show through. You would know how much money you were getting by the president that was in the circle, whether it was Washington, Lincoln, or Andrew Jackson. The best we could ever hope for was Andrew Jackson. And this was still a rarity. That's why Louis told Leland, "We shouldn't be talking like this."

"You're right," he answered. "We might jinx it."

W̅e piled into our white station wagon, which Na-Na had bought for us, to go to church. Melody and Lizzie rode in front with Mother, while Louis, Leland, and Sonia rode in the backseat, and Tony, Agnes, and I were jammed in the rumble seat at the very back of the station wagon, which folded flat when we bought groceries. The dust bunched up behind the car while we drove down Moonlight Lane, which wasn't paved. I told Agnes to scoot over, that she was crowding me with her fat rear.

"My name is Holly."

"Agnes Agnes Agnes."

"Let's all name ourselves after plants," said Lizzie. "Call me Ivy."

Agnes had chosen a new name for herself, Holly, because she didn't like the name Agnes. But none of us would give in and call her Holly. She said Agnes sounded old-fashioned and fat. She wanted a slender, graceful name. She was heavy and thick, and somehow we all thought Agnes was the name that fit her. "Heavy," was how my mother would put it. "Agnes isn't fat. She's just rather heavy."

"Where are we going to look at houses?" someone asked.

"Kings Grant."

"Do they have swimming pools?"

"Wouldn't that be neat? A swimming pool!"

"I want my own room," said Lizzie. "I'm tired of living

The Fire Eaters

with lunatics." She was talking about Melody. They hated each other.

Melody had her life-size Winnie-the-Pooh doll in her lap. She took Pooh everywhere she went. The last time we had been to Galveston, on vacation, visiting Na-Na, Melody had taken Pooh to the Pancake House where we had had breakfast. She made Mother ask for a high chair. She opened little plastic squares of Welch's grape jelly for Pooh's toast. She peeled back the plastic film that covered the dark purple of the jelly, and we watched as she offered it to the stuffed animal.

Under her breath, Lizzie had whispered, "What a wacko."

Melody had carried Pooh into the old people's hotel where Na-Na lived, and we made faces behind her back when all of us were crowded into the wooden elevator. We were supposed to be quiet as mice. The air of the elevator smelled of mothballs and Mentholatum.

In Na-Na's apartment, we tried to sit quietly on our hands during the visit. "Na-Na, this is Pooh," said Melody, holding the bear doll close to Na-Na's face so she could see it. Na-Na's hands trembled as she reached out and stroked the stuffed animal.

"Such lovely fur," she said. "Such loveliness." She had a crystal bowl full of peppermint candies on her coffee table; they reminded me of circular barbershop poles. She offered the bowl to each of us, slowly, with her spotted, trembling hands.

In church I stood beside Leland, who lip-synched "Don't Be Cruel" during the Gospel. He bobbed his head, shaking his leg just like Elvis, and closed his eyes in the emotional parts of the song. I watched his lips move, then knelt and closed my eyes, my hands pressed together, the tip of my nose touching the tips of my fingers. "O heavenly father, please take Na-Na's soul into your heavenly bosom so we can inherit some real money and not be so poor like we always are. Please take Na-Na into heaven and let me buy a tackle box full of artificial lures like my friend Russell Jensen has. He's got a swimming pool too. It's not fair."

We knelt against the pew in front of us, on green felt, like that on the base of the Virgin Mary in our nativity scene on top of the TV during Christmas season. I took holy communion, hoping the priest wouldn't place a bug on my tongue when I stuck it out for the body of Christ. Leland said it happened to him once. He nearly gagged.

"Father Benavidez is a real practical joker," he said.

I thanked God I got the white Christ wafer. The priest's fingers were graceful as he held out the white wafer to my pink tongue. They smelled of cigars. The body of Christ stayed on top of my tongue as I walked back to our pew. I thought of the wrinkled gray piece of my father's ear, and imagined it was the ear that I held on the tip of my tongue. It would have made me gag, except the Eucharist tasted like nothing, and I waited for it to get soggy before swallowing. It reminded me of Stridex medicated pads.

Later, the congregation passed around a silver platter full of coins and dollar bills, and mother gave each of us money to pay for our sins. The teenagers got a quarter, the rest of us a dime. I always had an urge to grab a handful of that money and stuff it in my pocket, but because everyone was looking and it was in the house of God, I never gave in to this temptation. I believed this was a test, a part of the service for poor Catholics like ourselves, to be offered up temptation every Sunday, but to be in the company of our congregation, to have the eyes of everyone in your pew on you and the pews before you and after you, watching what you were doing, aware that you wanted to reach in and grab a handful, but that it was something you had to resist, because it would only cause humiliation and remorse. Sometimes the offering was on a silver platter, as it was on this day, and sometimes it was on a wicker tray. I often calculated mentally how much money that was, passing by me, probably fifty dollars at least, if you were halfway back in the pews, and sometimes more, maybe two hundred, if you arrived late and had to take the last seats, near the ushers in the back, near the white throats of the lilies and eerie stillness of the holy-water basin. It was difficult to imagine what fifty or two hundred dollars would buy, since I had never known that much money in my life.

It seemed as if it would buy a certain kind of happiness.

Often, the priest would make specific requests for the offering, for starving children in Peru or Ethiopia, but I was aware of my own hunger, and found their stories of suffering and famine less than convincing, especially since I was drinking barbecue sauce every Thursday and Friday, breaking out in hives from secret overdoses of it, suffering that plate of money being passed around as if we had all we needed in the world, as if it meant nothing to us.

I realized that to steal from the offering would have damned me to some hideous fate, and figured that I would be punished physically for it, as if I might reach into my lunch box and find a gila monster latched onto the end of my hand, slowly grinding its blunt teeth and viscous poison into me, while I screamed and tried to shake it off. This would be a sin in the house of God. It wasn't like stealing milk from the dairy product containers at the elementary school cafeteria, where you were on your honor not to take any, but with all the arms and hands reaching in to grab the half-pint cartons of milk, and the cigar box in which you dropped the nickels to pay for the milk, who would notice one missing here or there? Did they actually count the half pints of milk sold every day against the number of nickels they took in?

After mass was over, we walked slowly out to the car. Mother once told us, "When you leave the house of God, you have to move with dignity." We walked like the apostles. Leland was especially dignified and graceful, giving each of his steps a little smooth transition, a little kick of his heels, before the next one, as if he were doing a slow and graceful dance to a gospel by Elvis. He held his hands on his lapels, and Melody and Sonia often rolled their eyes at him.

"Where do they buy those wafers?" I asked Mother.

"I don't know," she said, fishing for something in her purse, probably a cigarette, as we settled into the car. "Maybe they get them in Rome, sweetheart. They must come from far away, is all I know."

"Who makes them?"

"Nuns," said Lizzie.

Louis and Leland took off their ties and coats. "Nuns don't work," said Leland. "They're too busy praying. That's their job, to pray for everybody. Like me and you."

"They have a secret recipe," Lizzie whispered.

"They must make a lot of them. Think of all those people eating all those bodies of Christ in all those churches in all the different cities and towns and nowheresville spots in the

The Fire Eaters

world. There must be a factory somewhere, manned by nuns."

"Yeah, I saw pictures once," said Tony. "A whole flock of nuns at a conveyor belt."

"I wonder how much they cost?" I asked. "Maybe that's what the offering is really for, to pay for the bodies of Christ."

"They're free, stupid," Leland said. He wrinkled up his eyebrows and stared at me, his "look," he called it, that meant I must be ignorant, and maybe not part of the family at all.

"You're all a bunch of pagans," said Melody. She put her hands over Pooh's ears. "Don't listen to them."

"They'd be better with sugar," said Lizzie. "The holy communion wafers, you know? I think we should write and tell them that body of Christ sure could taste a little sweeter, and maybe more people would come to church."

"And they could give more of them to us, too, if they were sweeter. I'd go back for seconds."

"We're going to buy a new house! We're going to buy a new house!"

"I hope it has a swimming pool."

"And a sunken living room."

"Do I have to sit next to Agnes again? She smells."

Someone said our old house used to be an army barracks. When it rained we put pots and pans around to catch the drips from the ceiling. The floors were rotten. The septic-tank pipes were often clogged with roots, and twice we had to dig them up and put in new clay pipe. Louis pulled the concrete lid off the septic tank and made us look inside. It was a deep, disgusting pool of dark liquid, full of what we flushed down the toilet. It looked big enough to swim in, big enough to drown in. Leland threatened to throw us in if we didn't help fix the pipes.

An owl lived in one of the oak trees in the front yard, and squirrels lived in the others. The eaves of the house were full of wasp nests. Now and then Louis and Leland made torches out of old mop heads soaked in motor oil and lit the smoky, flaming torches to burn the wasps out from beneath the eaves and in the juniper trees, but they always seemed to come back.

We wanted to move to one of the suburbs they were building close to us. When we had first moved out to that neighborhood, in 1961, it seemed wild and unsettled. We remembered when Colonies North was nothing but fields and a dry creek bed, and there used to be a dairy farm where Shenandoah was built. These new houses were clean and tidy. Their yards were full of new grass. They rolled it out from pickup trucks. Sod. They had sliding glass doors and intercom systems. They had white concrete driveways, dark paved streets. In the evening, you could hear the sound of crickets and sprinklers. We heard that they didn't want black people to move into these new suburbs, and that was another reason to keep our identity secret. We had to lie and hide the truth, so people would not hate us. We had to lie so we could move into a new house if we ever got the money.

We drove to Kings Grant Village, a suburb down Vance Jackson. It was so new the grass wasn't installed yet, and in its place were plots of black soil, muddy from rain. Black dirt striped the white sidewalks. Some of the sidewalks still had the two-by-four supports in place, where they had poured the concrete. Red fire hydrants seemed to rise like stumpy towers from the black earth of the yards. The air smelled like land that had been plowed and readied for crops, for fertile seeds, for something to grow, to be irrigated.

We stopped at one of the empty houses and got out of the car, feeling as if everyone—the real estate people, the home-owners, the builders—were watching us. It had a wooden sign planted by its sidewalk—MODEL HOME! Red, white, and blue triangular plastic streamers stretched from the roof of the garage to stakes in the front yard and fluttered in the wind. There was a family across the street at another house, and they stared at us as we looked around the yard. We felt as if we were doing something wrong. Lizzie made a stink about someone's initials in the concrete of the driveway. Leland and Tony pressed their noses up to the glass of the windows in the garage door. Tony pressed a button by the garage door and it clanked into motion, humming with its electric motor, as the garage door opener folded back the door in sections on its track.

"Be careful to keep your shoes clean," whispered Mother. "These houses all have carpeting."

"Wall to wall!"

"Floor to ceiling!"

"Head to toe!"

The stairs were springy and soft, covered with light green carpeting, tucked under the lip of each step. The house smelled of latex paint and drywall spackle. Leading into the house from the front door was a thin scrap of extra carpeting, so we wouldn't track in the mud. Mother didn't like the looks of the carpeting on the stairs. She argued that it would be too easy to slip and fall, and they should have left it with good clean wood instead of that soft, slippery stuff. "You could break your neck on that," she said.

I skimmed my hand along the rail beside the stairs. The

air smelled of the new linoleum in the kitchen, and there were small piles of wood shavings where something had been drilled on one of the cabinets. The range, refrigerator, and dishwashing machine were brilliant white, and had stickers on them from the manufacturers. You could tell, you could feel, that the people who had built this house were proud of it, because it was new, and clean, and anyone could live there and be happy.

The walls were as white as Styrofoam. It reminded me of the inside of an ice cooler.

Upstairs, there were four bedrooms, connected by a long narrow hallway. "This is going to be my room," said Melody.

She carried Pooh to the huge window pane, which looked out on the naked black yards and the cul-de-sac at the end of the street behind the house. There was a white paper sticker in the center of the pane of glass, advertising the glass company. Pooh looked out the window with his plastic eyes, never blinking. "Only the best families will live in this neighborhood," said Melody.

Mother peeked in the room, running her hand down the door trim as if she were checking for flaws. Her ankles wobbled when she stepped on the carpet in her high heels. "Isn't the air wonderful?" She smiled and looked younger than usual. She was smiling so wide you could see her big teeth, which had tiny red spots of lipstick on them.

"We would never be hot again."

Driving home that afternoon, as we turned onto Orsinger Road, the dust billowed behind our car, catching up with us and filling the car with dust as we slowed at Sleepy Hollow to turn. The pavement ended at Vance Jackson, a quarter mile from our house. We always wanted our streets to be paved. It seemed as if there was something backward about the dirt roads of our old neighborhood, something to get away from. For a time we believed that if our roads were paved our lives would be better, improved, that we would not be losing something but gaining something, that we would be making progress, and becoming something better, something superior to what we had ever been before.

We drove slowly through the water at Olmos Creek, at the low-water crossing, which always flooded in the spring, during the heavy rains, cutting Moonlight Lane in half, so that you would have to go the long way around Sunburst to reach Vance Jackson or Huebner Road and head for school or work. A flood gauge stood beside the road, marked in alternating black and white sections, up to eight feet. Everything in our neighborhood seemed primitive. The fields were full of cactus and meteors, and once, near the train trestle, we found an arrowhead. We wanted to live where the roads were paved, where we could ride our bicycles down smooth streets to the swimming pool, where the water was clean and blue and tasted of chlorine. We wanted to live like everyone else. The only place to swim, then, when we lived at Moonlight and Sunburst, was the rock quarry, a mile's walk down the railroad tracks, where the water was a murky green color, full of frogs. And snakes, eating the frogs.

Aunt Irene called during dinner, and mother went into the living room to talk. Lizzie set her knife and fork down on the tablecloth. Leland closed his eyes and crossed his fingers. There was a long silence, and with my eyes closed, I saw blobs of purple and red on the inside of my eyelids.

"I'm sorry, Irene, but don't blame yourself. You did everything you could. You know we all loved her."

The air above our dinner table felt rippled, vibrant, burst.

"It's probably the best thing that could happen. I understand. I know. We've all been praying for her." Mother listened to the voice on the other end of the telephone line, Aunt Irene's voice from Galveston, telling her that Na-Na had died. But it wasn't until a month later that we learned how small our inheritance would be, how we would not be rich at all, but poorer still, our bank account full of disappointment. But I remember that evening it was so quiet in the dining room that I heard the sound of the Firpos' dog rooting in our morning glories. And an inchworm reared up on my plate, like a bronco, lost in a world without leaves.

8
Making Enemies

Brian Tunch was bigger and slower than most of the boys on the playground, and gradually it became clear to everyone that Brian was not only growing faster than the rest of us, but also becoming misshapen and distorted. Sullen and moody, he took a quiet pleasure in sneaking up behind you and kicking the back of your legs, so that your knees would jerk forward and you would topple to the ground. He had a shock of dry, straight blond hair, oddly pale yellow, that was always hanging in his face, while the sides of his head were cut so short you could see the freckles on his fair skin through the thin spikes of hair. It was in the fall of the year that I noticed something specifically odd about his left hand. It was growing faster than the rest of his body, faster than his right hand and arm, and was becoming larger, swollen, like a gorilla's paw. I noticed this one day while we were on the playground. He was hanging from the gray metal bars of the jungle gym, and I was staring at it.

"What are you looking at?" he asked.

"Your hand."

"What about it?"

"It's weird."

"No it isn't."

"Yes it is. It's bigger than the other one, isn't it? You've got one hand that's bigger than the other one, don't you?"

"Shut up, you."

I told Michael Shapiro, Russell Jensen, and Kit O'Hara about it, told them to check out Brian Tunch's hand when they got a chance, when he wasn't looking, and notice how red and misshapen it was, how the skin was scaly and rough, how he held it beneath his desk in class, so no one could see what he was hiding. Later, they whispered in class to each other, and you could tell they were staring at Brian. Soon everyone else was too. "What are you looking at?" he asked. "Why don't you mind your own business?"

"What's the deal with the paw, Brian?" asked Michael Shapiro. "Show us the paw."

There was a silence in the class as Brian stared at Michael and told him to shut up, but Michael was snide, and not afraid of anyone. He grinned at Brian and said, "Oh sure, whatever you say, monkey man," then made a face at the rest of the class and hunkered over, sticking his left arm out the side of the desk, as if he were a hunchback. Someone snickered but Brian said, "You're gonna get it."

"What's all this talking going on? Brian? Are you trying to disturb the class?" Mrs. Meyers stepped down the row of seats and forced us back to our reading lesson, the SRA reading series where you had to read as fast as possible to get in the highest color codes in class. I was in gold, the second-highest zone in class, while Brian was in purple, one of the lowest. Everyone could see what color you were by your assignment, by the color of the folder on your desk, and everyone always knew Brian was in purple, and would always be in purple. That was as high as he'd ever get. When the class was quiet and we were reading our assignments, I looked up from my page and saw Brian turned around in his desk, staring at me.

"You're gonna get it."

"What'd I do?"

"Damon?" called Mrs. Meyers. "Is that you talking?"

I kept quiet for the rest of the class, watching the circular white clock with black hands and numbers above the green chalkboard at the front of the class. Brian had his left hand beneath his desktop, but now and then he turned back to glare at me. I didn't want the class to end. I didn't want to leave the protection of Mrs. Meyers's room for the terrible freedom of the playground. The fact that everyone liked me would not help with Brian. That only made it worse. That gave him a reason to hate. Why had I mentioned how weird his hand looked? Why had I pointed it out? It had been cruel and vicious of me to do that, and now I was going to be punished. Donna Sullivan tried to pass me a note during the last few minutes of class, but I pretended not to understand, to be absorbed in my reading assignment, which was on the Wright Brothers, Orville and Wilbur, and the first airplane, at Kitty Hawk. I felt as if I was going to throw up. I felt the glands swelling in the sides of my throat.

The bell rang. I loitered at the rear of the class, waiting for everyone to file out into the halls and onto the playground for recess, trying to stick close to Mrs. Meyers, but when we reached the double doors that led outside, she waited as we filed out, then stayed inside. Mrs. Brown was already on the playground with her class, and she was in charge of watching everyone.

The playground had hard-baked earth and crabgrass. In the middle of it was a slide, swing set, jungle gym. On the side closest to the school parking lot was a flagpole. As the children yelled and chased each other, the metal eyelets of the flag tapped against the metal flagpole. On the other side of the playground was the baseball field, and Brian came up behind me and told me, "Walk over there," pushing me towards the baseball field, towards the brick walls of the cafeteria, which was between us and the baseball field and had no windows on one side, so that you could hide from the teachers' eyes there.

I was guilty and deserved to be punished. I walked slowly and reluctantly. When no one else could see us, when we had passed the corner of the cafeteria's brick wall, Brian put his scaly, oversized left hand on top of my head and forced me down on my hands and knees, kicking at the back of my knees to knock my legs out from underneath me.

"Take it back," he said. "Take back what you said about my hand."

I didn't say anything, but twisted my neck against the dull pressure of his huge hand. He pushed my face into the dirt, into the smell of pill bugs and mud. Into the smell of earthworms and beetles, moles and rotting leaves.

"Take it back!"

"I take it back." His hand had my face pushed into the dirt, and I had to keep my lips shut tight to keep out the dirt, to keep out the earthworms.

"How do you like it, huh? What does it feel like?" He

slugged my neck with his fist, a quick, dull thud, then he got off me. I jumped up and looked at him walking away. He turned around, and before reaching the corner of the building, before we'd be in sight of everyone else, said, "I'm not through with you yet."

My stepsister, Agnes, was something like Brian Tunch. She was heavy and slow, and the rest of us children were quicker, more agile than she was. On our walk to the bus stop each day, Sonia and I scampered about Agnes as she lumbered along. It seemed that Sonia could not contain the energy in her body, and ran from sheer excitement, but I often ran just to torture Agnes. As we walked down Moonlight in the cool morning air I paced circles around her to prove how much faster I could walk. We didn't get along. She had brown hair and a mole on her wide face, but her eyes were small and nervous, following my movements with suspicion and resentment. She thought that everything I said and did was to mock and ridicule her, and since she was three years older than me, she used that to punish me and make my life painful.

One morning she crept into the boys' bedroom with her pillow while I was asleep and placed it over my face. I woke as she was trying to suffocate me. She didn't pin me to the bed as fiercely as Brian Tunch had jammed my face into the dirt, but she filled my nose with the peculiar smell of her pillow, filled my lungs with it.

It was as if I awoke with a pungent, spicy food in my nose and mouth and couldn't spit it out, a mixture of ginger, curry, and saliva. I kicked beneath the covers and tried to get my hands free to push her off, but her soft, warm heaviness weighed me down, oppressive and wide, and she didn't stop until Leland said, "Aggie. Cut it out, will ya?"

In the living room at night, while we were watching television, Agnes carried her pillow with her and propped it under her head as she curled up on the couch, or the floor, or in one of the upholstered easy chairs. It was an old down pillow, lumpy with age, sheathed in a dingy white pillowcase faded to beige with use, splotchy with the spots of saliva that escaped from Agnes's wide mouth when she fell into her deathlike slumbers at night. When Agnes slept on her back, with her mouth open, she snored so loudly that Lizzie, who shared a room with her, couldn't get to sleep.

Since Agnes was my stepsister, I thought she was odd and unnatural. She reminded me of creatures I had seen in children's books, illustrations of trolls. Her toenails were long and as curled as claws. Her thighs rippled with fat wrinkles, and when she trudged heavily down the hallways of our house, her feet made a dull thumping sound on the wooden planks. It was as if the floor itself were complaining aloud.

At home Agnes wore old sweatshirts, T-shirts, and shorts, and at night, dressed like this, she came into the living room carrying her splotchy pillow. In the mornings, as we dressed for school and waited for each other to get ready and to finish breakfast, I often noticed the white wisps of feathers that had escaped from Agnes's lumpy pillow. There were feathers on the couch, in the gaps between the cushions, feathers pierced into the web of the living-room rug. I sometimes wondered what my father thought of the feathers in the living room as he was swimming through it at night, if his dark and stonelike eyes caught glimpses of their white quills in the darkness as he flipped his fins above the sofa, the seascape, the rabbit ears of the television set. Maybe he believed we were devouring birds at night in the living room, plucking them as we watched TV. I hoped he didn't know about Agnes, about her odd and unhealthy presence in our house, how she was something the It Monster had left behind as a mark upon all of us.

I became obsessed with Agnes's pillow. I dreamed of its splotched and speckled pattern. I dreamed of a huge sawfish swimming in the mote-filled depths of the sea, and the speckles on its side were the splotches of Agnes's pillow. The memory of this dream further disgusted me. The smell of that pillow. The way she carried it into the living room at night, tucked under one arm, as she trudged to watch another evening of *Sing Along with Mitch.*

Lizzie said it wasn't right, Agnes carrying around the pillow that way. It wasn't hygienic. "What do you mean, not hygienic?" asked Agnes, turning her small, suspicious eyes towards Lizzie.

"Hygienic," said Lizzie. "It's unhealthy, is what I'm saying. It's dirty and full of germs."

"It is not."

Lizzie made a face at the pillow. "It's a sack full of disease."

"It is not!"

"It is too. Maybe it's infecting you. Maybe we should burn it."

Melody, the oldest, said nothing, because she still slept with her zoo of stuffed animals, and still carried on long, multivoiced conversations with her life-size version of Winnie-the-Pooh, even though Pooh was showing signs of wear and tear. He had seen better days. He sat at her feet, watching television with his one remaining plastic eye.

"I vote for burning it," said Lizzie brightly. "We'll purify it by fire."

"I second the motion," I said.

For a moment, everyone turned to consider me, as if a mouse had spoken.

"Leave me alone!" yelled Agnes. "What did I ever do to you? It's my pillow! It's not dirty!"

Mother walked in at that moment. "What is *wrong* with you children?" she said. "Can't I leave you alone for a moment? Can't you be sweet to each other, just once?"

I was thinking so much about that pillow that I faked sick and stayed home from school. While everyone was away I opened a white bottle of Clorox bleach, with its blue label and cap, and poured a cup of the strong yellow liquid into a metal bucket, then pulled Agnes's pillowcase off and stuffed it into the bucket. I stirred the bleach, water, and pillowcase around with the white plastic handle of a spatula, and left it there all day. The smell of the bleach was so strong I couldn't breathe near the bucket. I was certain this would remove the stains.

I had become convinced that the splotches and stains on Agnes's pillow were more than random, that they somehow represented shapes that explained our lives, that they were infiltrating us, that they were some kind of encoded messages relating to our entire family. So I bleached the pillowcase. It would purify the linen, erase the marks, clean the slate. When she got home from school Agnes saw her lumpy pillow naked on her bed, and she stomped through the house searching for the pillowcase until she saw it fluttering on the clothesline like a brilliant white flag. She took it off the clothesline and smelled it. She glared as she passed me in the hall, and as the others learned of what had happened, what I had done, they laughed and joked about it.

"Whatever got into Damie? He must get kind of weird when he stays home from school."

"He's becoming quite the homemaker."

"Well it's not going to be the same anymore, is it, Aggie?" said Lizzie. "It's probably going to be so clean you won't even want to sleep on it."

"Oh, my eyes are hurting," cried Leland, putting his hands up to shield his eyes. "Jesus. You could read by that thing."

"Ha ha. Very funny," said Agnes. But during the evening, while I lay on the floor in front of the television, I could feel her malignant energy focused on me. Before we went to sleep that night she stopped me in the hallway and poked me in the chest with one finger. "You," she said. "You're gonna get it."

"Me? What'd I do?"

"You know what you did," she said. "You think you're too small to touch, don't you? Well, you're wrong."

9

Revenge of Secrets

Brian Tunch continued to grow larger than the rest of us, to push people's faces into the dirt on the playground, and to break out in tears if the teachers punished him. He was moody and erratic, one moment talking loudly and tugging on a girl's long hair, the next moment quiet and brooding, considering the class through his green eyes. His left hand remained misshapen and oversized, and he either kept it concealed beneath the desk or reached with it into the beautiful dark hair of Sylvia Martinez in the seat in front of him. Sometimes he stared back at me as he did this, as if he knew that the thought of that red, scaly, misshapen hand in the softness of Sylvia's hair disturbed me more than anything else he could have done.

One morning while I was sitting at my desk, struggling through a math problem, I noticed that the other students in the class seemed to be whispering to each other, about me. The soft sound of whispered breath was just audible over the scratching of pencil lead on paper, of the people working their math problems, heads bowed, concentrating. Brian whispered to Sylvia, and she turned to look at me with her dark eyes full of pity. Everyone seemed to be glancing at me when I looked up from my desk, and would turn away when I looked back. At recess, conversations stopped when I walked up to people, even my friends like Russell Jensen and Michael Shapiro. When I walked past Brian Tunch he stopped what he was doing and grinned. "Hey look. It's the secret nigger."

"What?"

"You heard what I said. Everybody knows. Everybody's talking about it. You may look white, but you're a nigger. That's what Susan Campbell said. She heard it from her sister in high school, who knows your sister. You were trying to hide it, weren't you?"

"I wasn't trying to hide nothing."

"Yes you were. Well we all know now. We all know all about you, nigger." Brian grinned as if he thought that my being *nigger* was the funniest thing in the world. "Ha. A white nigger. We thought you were just white trash. Now we know you're worse."

"Shut up."

"You know what God said after he made a nigger?"

"Shut up, Brian. You don't know nothing."

"Whoops! Burnt another one!"

I sat down by the flagpole, away from the other kids, and threw rocks into the parking lot. No one came over to talk to me, and afterwards everyone in that school acted differently towards me. Some were nicer. Others acted as if there was something wrong with me. As if I were a mistake some-one had made and would have to pay for for the rest of his life, or her life, or their lives. Or a mistake that I had made without knowing it, that I would have to pay for for the rest of my life. As if this mixed blood were shame itself.

That night I went into Mother's bedroom to say good night. She was reading in her bed, as she did every night, and had her head propped up with pillows, and was wearing her cat's-eye reading glasses, with a silver chain that looped around the back of her neck. I sat on the side of her bed and asked what she was reading. It was a science fiction novel about another planet where the world is covered with water, and a group of warriors sail from one island to the next, defending themselves against other warriors and de-fending the islands that pay tribute to them and attacking the ones that don't, and the sea is filled with creatures that are half man, half sea beast, that devour the bodies of dead sailors and any warriors that happen to fall overboard during battle between the sailing ships. When she was finished tell-ing me about the book, Mother pushed the hair out of my eyes and asked, "What's the matter, you? Why so gloomy?" Her smooth, rich-colored skin was lovely in the lamplight. It made me want to cry.

"They called me *nigger* today at school. Agnes told." I didn't look her in the face when I said this, but kept my eyes focused on the lurid cover of her science fiction novel, which featured a muscular warrior brandishing a bloody sword on the deck of a strange sailing ship, while a green moon hung in the purple sky above him. She sat still for a long while, straightening my messy hair and brushing my cheeks with the back of her soft hands. She told me things about herself that I had never heard before, what it was like for her when she was growing up. She told me she wished she could change us, change our blood, but there was nothing we could do about it, we were who we were, what we were, what we are. Her eyes filled with tears, with anger and pity, and she pulled me close to her.

"Don't you listen to them, Damon. Don't you listen to anything they say." She squeezed me so hard it hurt, and the book fell off the bed, losing her place. It didn't matter what other people thought, she said, as long as we were together. She repeated this as she kissed me. As long as we were together.

10

A Boxing
Lesson

For a time, our family went through a period of hope. We decided that we were going to be a better family. We were going to be richer, smarter, better-looking. This was right about the time when my mother got a new job. She'd been out of work for six months, and towards the end of her period of layoff, we had been getting desperate. We had government checks from our father's death, but it wasn't enough. It was never enough. Not with eight kids eating everything they could get their hands on. I had started hitting the barbecue sauce pretty heavy during the last month or two, and at least the strong taste of the barbecue sauce made it seem like you were eating something, something good.

We were always running out of clothes too. At the end of summer we needed new clothes for school, but had no money to buy them. We walked through the air-conditioned aisles of Wonderland Mall near the Loop, intoxicated by the heavy incense and patchouli smell of Pier One, bombarded by back-to-school sales, overwhelmed by the splendor and beauty of all the things we could not have. The crisp, stiff cotton cloth of new blue jeans, a deep blue, a dark blue yet to bleed in the wash. So stiff and new that if you tried them on, it was hard to move your legs. But this year, we could not try them on. I lingered near the folded stacks of Levi's jeans, fingering the paper tags stapled over the back pocket, vainly checking to see if they had my size, the size we could not buy. Even though I'd been told we couldn't afford them, still I whined and begged for them, saying I was going to be too ashamed to go to school wearing my old clothes. "Stop that, Damon," said my mother, grabbing me by the arm and pulling me away from the jeans department. "Maybe for your birthday, but I don't want to hear any more about it."

Even school supplies became emblems of wealth and privilege. The rows of plastic rulers, all colors of the rainbow, the fractions of inches embossed into the rigid plastic blades, stained black, not yet worn away, or cracked and broken like all the plastic rulers that I owned. The spiral notebooks full of pure white pages and their grid of blue horizontal lines and red verticals marking the margins. *The Flintstones, Batman,* and *Green Lantern* lunch boxes I would never own.

One day I came home with a rip in my blue jeans and Melody took me into her bedroom and told me to pull them off.

"You're lucky I saw you first. What do you want to do, give your mother a heart attack? What were you doing? Crawling home from school?"

I had ripped them cutting across the fields behind the schoolyard, where we climbed over the barbed-wire fences to get to Olmos Creek to look for raccoons, but I didn't tell her that. While I cowered on the bed there in my white underwear, she took a needle and thread and sewed up the rip. I watched her serious face as she leaned over the pants, pulling up the needle and thread quickly, giving it a sharp tug, then fitting it back where the next stitch should go.

She looked like Mother. Her hair was thick and black. Already there were care lines on her young face, not wrinkles, more like dimples of sorrow. She was the oldest. She acted it, too. She had been the one to teach me how to read, and you could see that she got an unusual, almost painful kind of pleasure from taking on the responsibilities of helping out our mother, of watching over us, of being the second woman in charge. She finished the sewing quickly. It wasn't a very professional job, but it made the rip less obvious.

Our poverty made us defensive. When Louis heard about Brian roughing me up, he decided to do something about it. He brought home a pair of boxing gloves, carrying them in a cardboard box in the backseat of the Volkswagen. They were heavy and puffy, made of old brown leather, with enormously long laces at the wrists.

"Give me a hand." Louis was stern and authoritarian, the way he acted when he had to force us to do yard work. I followed him to our dusty open-air carport in the backyard. It was so full of junk that we couldn't park the car in it anymore. There were rabbit cages, bags of dog food, a shovel with dirt on the blade, a hoe, a rusty pickax. You had to watch your step. There was a plastic milk crate of Dr Pepper bottles in the middle of everything. When we shifted boxes around, the spindly bodies of daddy longlegs spiders bobbed and scattered, a cluster of hundreds of them falling like flight-less bats from the side of a worn-out mattress we dragged out of the back. We carried it awkwardly by its plastic handles to a patch of sparse grass near the rope swing, then dropped it on its side. Louis slapped his hands together to get the dirt off them.

"You gotta learn not to take any shit from anybody. You understand that, Damie?"

"Okay."

"Okay? Just okay? I don't want people pushing my little brother around. You want to come home with a bloody nose? Is that what you want?"

"Oh sure. That's one of my big ambitions."

"Don't get smart with me. I'm trying to help. When I'm around I won't let anybody mess with you if I can help it. But I'm not always going to be there. You see me walking around your schoolyard, looking for you? What do you do if somebody smacks you in the mouth and I'm not there to take up for you? Huh? What do you do?"

"I don't know."

"Great. You don't know. Maybe you'll run and hide. Is that what you're gonna do, run and hide for the rest of your life?" He got the boxing gloves from the VW and tossed them to me.

"Put these on."

"What for?"

"Why do you always have to know what for? Why don't you just do what I ask you to? You know, if you were in the army you'd have to take orders. What would the sergeant say if you were always asking why are we marching twenty miles today? Why are we bombing that hill? Why are we going out on a search-and-destroy mission tonight? What kind of soldier would you be?" Louis was keen on war movies at the time, the thought of Vietnam. And him in it. Killing VC in rice paddies.

I struggled to put on the huge gloves. They were much too big, but I could fit my hands in them, and Louis laced them tightly.

"Put up your dukes." I'd heard the phrase before and thought it was a corny thing to say. I raised my hands into the air, encased in these mammoth, bulbous gloves, halfheartedly pretending to be the boxer Louis wanted me to be. I couldn't take this seriously. Louis towered over me and started dancing on his feet, showing me footwork, telling me it was important to keep moving, but I sagged at the waist and shoulders, and heard myself whine, "This isn't fair. You're bigger than me, Louie."

Then he knocked me down. I picked myself off of the old mattress as fast as I could. There was Louis again, dancing around, telling me to give him a shot, to *get mad*, goddammit, while my eyes filled with tears and I stumbled about on the mattress as if it were a trampoline.

"Hit me! C'mon, Damie. Hit me! Lead with your left. Follow with your right." He socked me on the shoulder as I wavered there, unsure of what to do. I swung at him and fell down.

"Keep your knees bent. Stay on your feet! If you fall down in a fight, the other guy's gonna kick your guts into your ears. Keep your feet moving so they don't go out from underneath you."

I managed to stand up and lift the huge gloves in the air. I knew Louis was going to hit me now if I gave him a chance, so I flinched and dodged whenever he made to come toward me. "There you go," he called out. "That's it. Now hit me!

94   *The Fire Eaters*

Take a swing!" He stayed in place while I rushed at him, swinging, and managed to slug him in the stomach.

"Good one, Damie! Don't let him get away with that." That was Leland's voice. When I got off the mat again I saw that he had walked out to the back porch with a Coke and sat down to watch. "Don't take that shit from Louie. It ain't fair, is it. He's a lot bigger than you."

"I'm teaching him how to fight. He's getting picked on at school and somebody's got to stop it."

I swung at him while he was talking and hit his hip, but my arms felt weightless and weak. It didn't seem to hurt him at all.

"He's a crybaby. You're a crybaby, aren't you, Damon? What are we gonna do about that? If somebody starts beating you up, what're you gonna do if you start crying? You think they'll feel sorry for you? Forget that shit. They'll hit you even harder. They'll hate your guts for being so weak. The only respect you'll get is if they're scared of you. People only respect strength."

"Hey, Louis. Don't be so hard on him. He's just a kid."

I slugged Louis's stomach as hard as I could and he knocked me down again. I stood up and heard the back door slam, then Lizzie's voice telling Louis to leave me alone.

"Stay out of this, Lizzie. I'm teaching him to box."

"No you're not. You're beating him up to show how tough you are."

"What do you want me to do? Let him be a sissy? Leave it to you and he'll be a crybaby."

As they were talking and arguing, he kept knocking me down and I kept getting back up, crying and swinging weakly and wildly at him. My nose was running. I gulped in sobs of air as I stumbled about and tried to keep fighting. I dimly remember Leland telling Louis to cut it out, that he'd made his point, then Melody heard the shouting, came out, and pushed Louis off the mattress, slapping him on the ear. She had power over even Louis.

"Have you gone crazy or something? He's just a little boy, Louis. You could kill him by accident, you know that? You could give him brain damage."

She took me inside and washed off my face. She blew my nose and made me put on a clean shirt, after combing my hair and hugging me. After I quit crying I wasn't mad at Louis anymore. I wanted to try fighting again. I wanted to try it with someone my size. Someone it would be fair to fight against. Someone I could beat to a pulp.

11

The Driest
Air

My best friend in the neighborhood at Moon-
light and Sunburst was Kit O'Hara. His father returned from
Vietnam not long before my mother lost her job when the
company she was working for went bankrupt, in the first part
of the summer. Again, she had to look for a job. "We've
got the lousiest luck," she said. "Or no luck at all."

She was worried about making ends meet, but Aunt Irene
offered to let the girls spend the summer with her, in Galveston, and Louis and Leland got invited to a summer camp
for the high school football players, so with most of the kids
gone, we were able to survive from the government checks
for my dead father. And she tried to find work. She wasn't
like Mr. O'Hara, who refused to get a job, and sat around
his house all day, watching her. In the middle of the summer
he started hanging around his backyard in the afternoons,

calling to my mother when she was putting clothes on the line. She tried to avoid him.

Then one night he came over to our house. He sat in the living room with us, watching the ten-o'clock news. He was a heavy man with deep wrinkles in his sunburned neck, and thin hair mashed down by the baseball cap he usually wore. "You want some of this?" he asked my mother, holding out his can of beer.

She shook her head. She hadn't looked at him since she opened the back door. This was the first time Mr. O'Hara had been in our house. Kit was lying on the floor in front of the TV, but he was over here all the time. He was here when his father knocked on the back door, and Kit didn't even say hi. Mr. O'Hara took a swig of his beer and looked around, squinting his eyes at the seascape painting that hung above the couch. "I like that," he said, pointing with his beer. We had bought it with green stamps.

Mother smiled, still without looking at him, keeping her eyes on the TV. The weatherman on Channel 5, who lived just down the street from us on Moonlight Lane, pointed to a high-pressure zone over Kansas, a circled H. He drew an angry sun, with three quick sweeps of his marker. In the spring, he had drawn clouds, fat and curly, like cartoon ghosts. But for months, during the dry heat of summer, he drew only suns. There was still no rain in the forecast. Outside, the air was calm, and you could hear crickets over the sound of the television. Mr. O'Hara had asked my mother for a date, in the afternoons. She tried to ignore him. He was just one of our neighbors to her, and she had to live in that house, so she didn't want anything special to do with him. I wished he would just leave.

"Your mom thinks she's too good for me," Mr. O'Hara said.

"No she doesn't," I said. "She's watching the news."

"Is that so."

"She watches the news every night, because she likes to know what's going on in the world."

"Every night, huh."

Kit blinked and looked at his father, then walked outside, slamming the door.

Mr. O'Hara waited a minute, then stood up, stretching, showing his hairy underarms. He looked at my mother before he left, but she wouldn't turn to face him, so he set his Falstaff can on the coffee table and said, "Well, good night, y'all. Sleep tight."

When he was gone, I moved over next to Mother, who was watching a Chevrolet commercial without blinking. I patted her knee. "What a creepo."

"I wish it would rain," she said, closing her eyes and sinking back into the couch, relaxing for the first time since Mr. O'Hara arrived. "I wish it would flood."

Mr. O'Hara had been wounded in Vietnam a year earlier, and had a metal plate in his leg. He showed the scar to Kit and me. He claimed it hurt too badly for him to stand up for more than a short time. Kit's mother said he just didn't want to work. Mrs. O'Hara was a nurse at Santa Rosa Hospital, downtown. She wore white dresses, hose with seams up the backs of her legs, and hair nets.

"I do all the work around here," she yelled once when Kit and I were in his room, playing Life. We heard a slap, a door slam, then crying. Kit's father stood in the hall, pounding on the door.

"Beth," he shouted. "Honey . . ."

Mrs. O'Hara left early every morning for work, stirring the dust on Moonlight Lane into clouds that followed her car till you couldn't see it anymore, until the dust drifted onto the oak trees in our front yard, powdering the leaves.

With all my brothers and sisters gone, Mother let me stay up late. Long after she fell asleep I sat up watching television in the living room, all the lights off except the black-and-white picture tube. The room was filled with the blue-gray glow of the television light, and when my eyes were heavy with sleep and my fiercely pounding heart had finally settled into a rhythm that I could sleep through, my father would swim through the living room and around the china cabinet in the dining room, his heavy fins flashing in the dim blue light, the gashes of his gill slits gaping open as he breathed the strange, foreign air of the house he had never lived in, the family that he had left behind now grown older, harder to recognize, so that sometimes his solid black fish eyes seemed to be straining to find something recognizable in the room, something familiar to latch onto, to steer by. And sometimes I felt like I was that landmark he was searching for, the signpost to give him some direction.

Each Saturday, after buying groceries, Mother dampened a sponge, set it on a white saucer, and pasted new rows of green stamps into the stiff pages of her booklets. I offered to help paste the stamps in, but she shook her head.

"Why don't you go read something, Damon?" she asked. "I bought a new Doc Savage for you."

She didn't want me to do the green stamps because I always put them in crooked, with the scalloped edges of the stamps sticking out of the stiff pages. She liked to keep the books as neat and crisp as possible. When I did the books, when they were messy and sticky, it seemed as if we were poor people—which we were—but when they were done by my mother, and were crisp and neat, it didn't seem desperate, just smart. Something every family should do. It made perfect sense.

While we played football in Kit's backyard, Mr. O'Hara watched my mother. Our backyards faced each other, with no fence or alley between them, and Mr. O'Hara sat on his back porch, unemployed, watching her hang wet clothes on the line to dry. In the middle of our game he made us stop playing so he could walk across the field on his hands. He had tattoos of bulldogs and roses on his arms. The veins in his neck bulged as he walked, upside down, across the stiff, dry grass. But his feet seemed to float, like a cat's tail, feeling the air.

At the end of the yard he tucked his body in, did a forward roll, then sat with his arms locked around his knees. "I bet you kids couldn't get halfway. Want to try?"

"No thanks," said Kit.

"What about you?" he asked loudly, trying to get my mother's attention. She pretended she didn't hear him, tucked a towel underneath her chin, and folded it lengthwise. Mr. O'Hara walked up to the clothesline and peeked between the legs of a pair of pink slacks that were drying on the line. "I'm talking to you."

"I'm sorry," she said. "I wasn't paying attention. What did you say?"

Mr. O'Hara smiled at her, scratching his stomach. He was

leaning his weight on the clothesline. It looked as if it were about to break, then he let go, making it spring up, scaring her.

"Don't mind me," he said. "I'm just crazy from this heat." Mother kept folding the clothes, ignoring him as he mopped the sweat off his tattoos with his bunched-up T-shirt and tried to flex his muscles without making it look like he was flexing them.

"I have to get back to work," she said.

"Maybe you should take a break sometime."

"No." She frowned, looking down at the small toes of her beautiful feet against the dead brown grass. "I don't think so."

Mr. O'Hara went back to his porch to play with his deer rifles. He kept watching as she took the clothes down from the line. The sunlight shone through her dress and you could see the outline of her slim, short body. She held the clothespins in her mouth, and the whole row of clothes shook as she clipped off another pair of pants or a shirt.

"Hey," yelled Mr. O'Hara. "You need any help with that?"

She held one hand over her eyes to block out the sun. "No, thanks. I think I can manage."

"Anytime," he said.

Later, Kit and I were in his living room, drinking lemonade in front of the fan, when Mr. O'Hara came in to put away his guns. They were stored in a special cabinet, the rifles in a row behind the glass doors, a drawer underneath full of ammunition. Mr. O'Hara claimed he had killed dozens of men in Vietnam.

"We used to talk about stuffing their heads like trophies," he said. "Wouldn't that be something?"

Mr. O'Hara was a big deer hunter. Every fall he went west

to the Rocky Mountains somewhere in New Mexico, to hunt mule deer.

"They're bigger than whitetails," he said. "And you wouldn't believe the squirrel hanging around some of those hunting lodges."

I went into the kitchen for a glass of water, to get away from Mr. O'Hara's face. I didn't like the way he looked at me, blank and bold. Their house was filled with deer heads, the eyeballs covered with dust. There was even one in the bathroom, with a soggy towel hanging from its antlers. The year before, during hunting season in the fall, Mr. O'Hara had made Kit and me help him clean one of the deer he had killed at a lease in Bandera County, two hours' drive away. He came home with the whitetail on the roof of their station wagon, its tongue visible between the black lips, covered with leaves and dirt. He hung it from the tree-house rope and pulled the skin off with a pair of pliers. But before he skinned it, he made each of us grab one side of its antlers and twist.

"Let's see how strong you little runts are," he said, and when we twisted as far as we could, so that the deer's head was almost pointing backwards, he yelled at us to twist harder; didn't we have any muscles in those skinny arms? He taunted us till the neck broke, with a wet, crunching sound. I hated that sound and always remembered it when Mr. O'Hara was cleaning his guns and watching my mother. After we broke the deer's neck Mr. O'Hara slit its middle open, and the animal's pink intestines flopped into the dirt.

For several days in a row, in the middle of July, the temperature rose over one hundred degrees. The old couple that lived across the street, the Firpos, watered their yard with sprinklers every morning. The sprinklers slowly turned back and forth, sending arcs of water across the grass, and when the sunlight hit the spray, it caused little rainbows, or pieces of rainbows, to appear, shimmer, and vanish. The Firpos had a cocker spaniel that barked at everyone who walked by, but since it was so hot the spaniel stayed on the cool concrete of their carport, with her head between her paws. Fireflies filled the night air, leaving trails that lingered there, against the sky, after they were gone.

One morning my mother and I were in the living room watching soap operas. She wore a sleeveless dress, and you could see the smoothness where she shaved her underarms. There was no wind. Katydids buzzed in the trees outside, just getting started. It always seemed that as the day grew hotter, the katydids grew louder.

Mother said she hoped Louis and Leland were doing fine. The house seemed vacant and unprotected without their presence. "You're the king of the house this summer, Damon," she said. "You little monster. You little butterball." She tickled me until I was helpless, squirming on the floor.

Kit knocked on the window, looking through the screen. "What's going on in there?"

Mother pulled me by my feet across the floor. "I'm attacking this little butterball. He doesn't deserve to live."

"This would be a good day for the gravel pit," Kit said.

"Good idea. Leggo of my leg, okay?"

Mother dropped my ankles. "So you're going to go off and leave me? Leave me all by my lonesome?"

"Why don't you come with us, Mrs. Bell?"

"Are you kidding?" She shook her head and fished a cigarette out of her purse. "I'd drown, sweetheart."

I changed clothes while my mother wrapped some cold chicken in aluminum foil for us, with two apples and an orange. As we left, she called out, "Watch out for snakes!"

Kit and I walked three miles down the railroad tracks to the gravel pit to swim in the overflow pond. The light brown mud along the bank was peppered with the tracks of raccoons and skunks. Turtles and frogs hopped into the water to get away from us, and we ran after them, naked, smearing our legs with the smooth brown mud that looked dark as creamy peanut butter against Kit's white legs, and almost yellow, like oleo, against my darker skin. We squirmed our feet in the bank, making the mud ooze between our toes. It was Saturday, and the gravel pit was deserted. We climbed the black rubber conveyor belts and leaped off onto the tops of volcano-shaped mounds of sand, sliding down them on our bottoms.

"I wish I was a machine," Kit said. "Then I wouldn't care about anything. I could be the meanest football player in the history of the world, because I wouldn't be able to feel any pain."

"That's true. No one could make you do anything, because they couldn't hurt you."

"It would be neat, not to be able to feel a thing," he said.

When a security guard drove by we hid behind the machinery, and later snuck back to the railroad tracks for the walk home. The crossties were sticky with tar, seeping through in places from the heat, and in between the ties were white rocks that formed a bed to support the tracks. We walked the trestles and listened for trains, scared that we'd get caught in the middle and killed.

When we got home, we crossed the Firpos' yard to pet the spaniel, and as Kit scratched her stomach I noticed Mr.

O'Hara walking away from the back door of my house. Kit saw it too. He started walking fast, keeping his hands at his sides, to catch his father before he got inside their house.

"Hey," he said.

His father stopped and stood there, hands in his pocket, looking down at us. "How was the water?" he asked.

"What were you doing over there?" Kit said, nodding his head towards my house.

Mr. O'Hara cuffed Kit's ear, knocking him back a step. "Who the hell you think you are?" He grabbed Kit by the collar and wrenched him off his feet. "Any more questions, smartass?"

Kit shook his head. I started walking to my house. I didn't want to watch.

"What did you say?" Mr. O'Hara said, louder.

"No, sir."

Everything was quiet in our house. The fan in the living-room window turned slowly, chopping the orange late-afternoon light across the rug. The house smelled stale and musty. The door to the girls' bathroom was closed and I could hear water running. Mother was in there a long time, and I sat in the living room and watched television, waiting for her to get out of the tub, but when she finally did, she went immediately to her room and closed the door. I knocked.

"Momma? Are you in there?"

"Yes."

"I'm hungry."

"I'll fix dinner for you later," she said through the door. I asked her if I could have a bowl of ice cream then, and surprisingly, she said okay. "And could you do me a favor?"

"What?"

It was a long time before she answered. "There's a dress

in the bathroom. Put it in the trash out front. Could you do that for me?"

I stared at the door and told her sure, but why did she want to throw away one of her dresses?

"I don't want it anymore, honey. It's just an old rag that we don't need around anymore." She told me that after her nap, she'd make spaghetti for the two of us.

The dress was wadded up on the floor of the bathroom, half wet, and one of the sleeves was ripped on it. I took it to the trash can at the alley, feeling that something strange was going on, but I wasn't sure what. Tony came home about seven in the evening, and asked what was the deal? Where was Mom? I told him she was sick. We warmed up leftovers to keep from bothering her. She didn't come out of her room all night, and the next day she was still lying on her bed. "Are you sick, Momma? What happened to your neck?" There was a scratch below her ear. The skin was puffy in a thick red line, and looked like it hurt.

"Something bit me," she said.

"Are you sure? That doesn't look like a bite."

"Don't argue with me, Damon. I just don't feel good. I think I'll stay in bed today."

"What are we supposed to do for breakfast?"

"Fix yourselves some cereal, honey. Now don't bother me anymore for a while. And make sure to shut the door when you leave."

Kit and I had lunch in the kitchen, cherry Kool-Aid and sandwiches of Velveeta on white bread. I spread on too much mayonnaise, and when we bit into them, thick hunks of Velveeta squirted out the side.

"Where'd you learn to make a sandwich?" he asked.

"You couldn't do any better."

"Where's your mom? I haven't seen her all day."

"I don't know. There's something wrong with her."

"How come?"

"She won't leave her room. She says she's sick."

Kit chewed his sandwich. "Maybe it was something she ate."

"She's got a scratch right here," I said, drawing my finger down my neck below my ear, right where my mother had the scratch.

Kit stopped chewing. He sat there for a moment, looking at his plate, then he stood up, pushed the chair back behind him. He looked like he was trying to say something, but he couldn't get it out. He nodded, dragging his feet as he went to the door. "Later."

Mother strung up an extension cord in the dining room, from the top of the china closet to the cedar chest, and hung our wet clothes to dry on the cord. She wouldn't go outside anymore. She kept the window shades drawn, and the doors locked whenever Tony and I weren't there, while we never used to lock them. We didn't have any food left in the house. It was late in the afternoon, the katydids buzzed rhythmically, pulsing with the waves of heat rising off the dirt road, and the Firpos' dog barked at Mrs. O'Hara's car as she got home from work. Mother peeked out the side of a curtain, watching Kit's mother get out of her car. The wet towels were dripping on our dining-room table, a large dark stain spreading out on one side of the lace doily in the center, which had a wooden fruit bowl in the middle. Since Mother had not been to the supermarket in over a week, there was no fruit.

"I'm starving, Mom. When are we going to the store?"

"Eat some cereal."

"I ate all the cereal yesterday. And I'm sick of cereal. Can't we get something different to eat?"

"Oh, I guess so." She turned away from the window and sat down on the couch. "I guess we could go to Piggly Wiggly."

"Today is double stamp day."

She smiled as she put on a pair of sandals. "We've got to get that badminton set, don't we?"

We locked all the doors and windows when we left, Mother carrying her purse close to her body, holding it against her middle. She took her time getting settled in the car, adjusting the rearview mirror, the side mirror, and the seat, even though she was the only one who drove the car since Louis and Leland were at camp. The Piggly Wiggly was full, and mother looked happy, pushing the cart down the aisle, filling our basket as if a hurricane were in the Gulf and we might be cut off from the rest of the world.

"It's nice and cool in here," she said.

"I wish we lived at Piggly Wiggly."

"Me too."

We bought apples and a watermelon.

"You and Kit can eat that," she said, as I set the heavy watermelon on the bottom rack of the shopping cart, where people put the ten-pound bags of dog food and cat litter.

"Kit said he wished you were his mother."

She smiled, picking out tomatoes and putting them in the produce bags. "I might as well be. He isn't anything like the rest of his family."

"Maybe we can adopt him."

"I don't think so, sweetheart." She put her hand on the

back of my head as I pushed the cart. "I've got my hands full as it is."

Mr. O'Hara was in their backyard cleaning his guns when we got home. Mother walked around the back of the car, to the front of the house, with the groceries, so she wouldn't have to go through the kitchen door. Halfway through putting the groceries away, she leaned against the refrigerator door, holding the hair off her forehead. "Mercy. I feel so dizzy. Can you finish here?"

"Sure."

When I finished putting the things away I walked outside. The light had turned an eerie grayish blue, and the sky was full of dark clouds. It looked like it might rain, and the broad leaves of the fig tree swayed in the wind. Dust devils chased down Moonlight Lane. Kit stood beneath their peach tree, watering the yard and spraying wasps out of the air, making a tight stream of water by pressing his thumb on the end of the hose. From the way he didn't smile when I walked up, and the way Mr. O'Hara was looking at me, I could tell Kit was still in trouble.

"Don't drown the goddam thing," Mr. O'Hara said.

Kit kept spraying the water.

"When you're finished with that, you can clean up your room. Looks like white trash lives in there."

"Yes sir." Kit made a face at his father, which he couldn't see because Kit had his back to him.

"Looks like you're busy," I said.

He nodded, squirted me with a jet of water from the hose as he dropped it to the ground.

"Hey!"

"Hay is for horses. C'mon." He motioned for me to follow as he walked to the faucet to turn off the water. Mr. O'Hara was watching us. He set his deer rifle on the oilcloth, alongside a can of oil, a polishing rag, and a box of cartridges.

"I thought your mother was sick," he said.

I yanked a leaf off the oak tree by the side of the house. "She's better now."

"Figures."

The sky had turned black in the east, and a gust of cool wind hit my face, full of rain-smell, the coolest air in two months. Mr. O'Hara leaned over, put his hands on the ground, then flipped up, arms shaking, his legs bent at the knees, doubled over backwards, and he started to walk across the yard, upside down. We stopped at the porch to watch him. His face was a deep red, his shoulder muscles bulging. Kit sat on the porch, picked up the deer rifle, and pressed it firmly against his shoulder, aiming at the swaying, inverted figure.

"I wish he was dead."

"I know what you mean," I said. I imagined Kit shooting and the bullet punching a wound in his father's chest, the body hitting headfirst and folding up, but he kept stumbling on, until he reached the end of the yard, where he stopped, wavered, then did a forward roll. The rain started coming down hard, and Kit's father got him to help collect the rifle and the gun-cleaning things and they rushed inside. I wasn't in any hurry to leave the rain, and my hair was filled with the delicious wetness by the time I got back to the house.

Mother stood behind the screen door, watching as I walked up. "What is this stuff falling from the sky? I don't recognize it."

We went to her bedroom to watch from her windows, and left them open as rain spotted the dust on the windowsill. The room was full of the signs of Mother's illness. There was a cobweb in one corner that she would usually have knocked down with a broom. The box of tissues on the nightstand was empty. We sat on the bed, in front of the window, watching the sudden gray sheets of rain.

"You're almost as tall as I am now," she said.

"I bet I'll be as tall as my father." In the few pictures I had seen, my father was a tall man over six feet, and looked gigantic next to my mother, who wasn't much over five feet, and had small and delicate features.

"I ought to change these sheets," she said. I knew that she had already washed them twice that week, but I didn't argue with her. We pulled them off the bed, tugging the fitted sheet off the corners, where it was tight, then lay down on the bare mattress, with its stains and faded pattern of yellow buttercups. She was different since the afternoon Kit and I had gone swimming in the gravel pit. She held me tighter than she used to, didn't like to see me leave the house.

The rain faded after an hour until only stray drops made rings in the new puddles in our yard. It was almost nine o'clock at night before it was completely dark, before the amber light of the sunset had completely faded from our backyard. Out the window, fireflies flashed like falling stars, and the twilight rolled over, turning to night.

Years later, I realized, I imagined, how it happened. I imagined this not of my own free will, but as if I were forced to do it, as she was forced to do it. It became a daydream or waking nightmare I could not wake from, since I was fully conscious as I imagined it, how he must have surprised her. How she went out to the backyard with a basket of wet clothes, a plastic laundry basket of my white underwear, or her dresses, Tony's jeans, how she stepped out barefoot into the splintery stiff grass of the backyard, baked by the heat and no rain, how she carried the basket of wet clothes with both hands, the weight of it resting on her belly, how she waddled with it across the yard, until she reached the clothesline, where she plopped the basket full of clothes beneath the middle of the clothesline. How her dress had a dark spot of wetness on it where her belly had been touching the wet clothes through the lattices of the yellow laundry basket. I imagined how she hung the shirts upside down, clipping them to the clothesline with wooden clothespins, the kind held in tension by a small metal spring, how she clipped on shirts, underwear, towels, pillowcases.

How Mr. O'Hara watched her from his back window, their kitchen window, in their house full of animal heads, horns, antlers, tusks, tongues, and fur.

How he sat on his back porch and smoked a cigarette, blew the smoke into the dry air of his backyard, where any spark or burning ember could have set things ablaze, how he smelled the smoke on his hands as he brought the cigarette to his mouth, how he watched the sun pouring through my mother's dress, how he felt his crotch stiffen as he watched her. How he wondered what a woman like that smelled like with the heat on her skin, working all day for her kids, night and day for those stupid brats, with no man to sleep with or give it to her good like he knew she wanted it, she must be just dying to have someone on top of her, someone to fill her up, and he was the man to do it.

How her kids were gone. How she was half nigger.

How he waited for her to finish putting the clothes on the line as he smoked another cigarette, grinding out the first one with the heel of his boot, the black tip of the butt ground into the gray concrete of his porch, how his heart was beating wildly now, how he had a flat metallic taste of blood in his mouth, how something was telling him not to do it but something blind and dark and vibrating was pushing him on, making him stand up and stretch, a queer heaviness of what? of fear in his limbs, an almost sleepiness, a lassitude that made him walk slowly across his yard and then her yard to her back porch, how when he was close enough to the gray wire mesh of her screen door he saw inside that she was not there, how he stepped slowly onto the porch, wiped his feet on the rubber welcome mat of the back door, and opened the screen door without knocking, without hesitation, the queer taste in his mouth now a bitterness, how the air smelled of a heavy dustiness like the middle of a goddam desert or something.

How he paused inside the back door, to let his eyes adjust to the shadows and dimness of the house, where sunlight was heat and everything shaded to keep out this heat. How his heart was beating as it had when he'd been somewhere in the army at night under fire or when he was in the bush, ahead of the entire platoon, on point in a jungle where he had to see before being seen, how he stepped carefully across the tiled floor of the kitchen and turned the corner of the hallway, how he saw her standing in front of the window unit air conditioner, how her eyes were closed and her dress was unbuttoned, letting the stream of cold air flow across her neck, her white bra, the vanilla hue of her skin, the damp sweat of her underarms, the wrinkles in her neck, the wisps of hair at her nape stirred by the cold air, the wet spot on her dress now pleasantly cool.

How he must have surprised her.

How he said, "It sure is hot, isn't it?"

How she said, "What do you want? This is my house. This is my house," she must have said, stepping towards the telephone, the kitchen, feeling the weight of fear suddenly in her muscles, knowing why he had come, what he wanted, feeling the breath pushed out of her lungs as if a huge cat were lying on her face, the breath pushed out of her lungs like a great pressure applied to her, like an invisible pressure, as if she were trying to breathe at the bottom of the sea, how he looked at her as if he were looking at a deer through the sights of his rifle, how he knew this secret nigger was afraid and what she was going to say before she said it. How his ears seemed to buzz or ring as he moved toward her and must have known to catch her before she reached the kitchen, the telephone, I seen you hanging those clothes, nigger lady, just stop, please, please just leave me alone, how he caught her arm and ripped her dress as she stumbled, stumbling, twisting, tried to break free, but now she was weakened by the weight of fear in her legs, how she could not get her breath, how he pinned her there, at the bottom of the sea, how his rough nails scratched her neck as he swung at her to try to grab her, to hold her, how he ripped her dress down the back as he yanked it off her shoulders, how he pinned her with his weight and heard her crying, heard this white nigger sobbing, felt this white nigger trembling and squirming beneath him as he yanked up her dress and pinned her legs with his knees, forcing them apart, how she wouldn't let go of her dress until he twisted her arm backwards and like to have broken it but she screamed and let go, how he forced her legs apart, forcing her skirt above her waist, forcing this secret nigger to do what she'd wanted to do since she'd first seen him she's not kidding me one bit, how he had to squeeze her throat and slam her face against the arm of the couch to free his other hand so he could yank open his pants, how she sobbed and prayed to God for mercy, how she tasted the blood on her mouth, smelled the cotton stuffing and dusty upholstery of the couch her face was jammed against, how her heart broke with dread and disgust as she felt him come inside her, how his grip eased, his breath loud as a dog's behind her, how she felt herself humiliated now as a dog, like a dog anybody can use whenever they want to, how her face was wet with tears and snot from crying, her mouth bleeding, her legs bruised, how after he left she lay there for a long time thinking about what he had done to her. Who did he think she was? What right did he have? How she thought of who to call or whether to scream and what would happen, how she stared into the light of this familiar room, in the middle of the day, this couch her couch she had sat on thousands of times and would sit on thousands of times after that day, the green breaking waves of the seascape painting above the couch, she had saved and bought that painting with fifty books of green stamps from Piggly Wiggly, what Leland and Louis would do if they found out and how they would feel, how her sons would know would never be proven would kill him would ruin their lives hunting him down in blood like their father, how she saw her reflection in the dark television screen sitting on the couch, her dress torn, how she had to straighten up before Damon got home and asked what happened what's wrong what's the matter Mama? Nothing's the matter just throw out that dress would you? How she sat in that living room where my father swam at night, how his fins must have touched her skin, his huge sawfish bill swaying side to side, but all for nothing for she could not see him and the teeth of his sawfish bill could no longer bite, tear, rip.

I wish I could say that Mr. O'Hara got what he deserved, that the police showed up one afternoon and handcuffed him at his front door. That they led him to the squad car, and pushed his head down so he wouldn't bash it against the roof as they placed him in the backseat. But that's not what happened. He lingered on, cleaning his guns on his back porch, drinking beer and watching TV. After Leland and Louis returned from camp and the girls came back from Galveston, he avoided our house and his backyard. I tried not to think about what had possibly happened. Our home seemed back to normal, except that when Melody got back from Galveston the boyfriend she'd had all through high school had written and asked her to marry him. He'd been drafted two years before and was now a helicopter pilot, but would be on leave long enough for the wedding. Mother landed another job and for weeks we seemed to talk about nothing else but the wedding. With Melody happy, Mother seemed relieved. Melody even quit carrying her frazzled Pooh bear around with her.

In September, Mr. O'Hara got a job at a plastics company. He was finally making some money, and his wife kicked him out of the house. Maybe she'd just been waiting for him to get on his feet. Kit hated him. His mother knew it, too.

We saw Mr. O'Hara leave on the morning of Melody's wedding day. The house was chaotic with all the girls rushing about, their hair in curlers, arguing about who was taking too much time in the bathroom, and Melody in Mother's bedroom, slowly getting dressed and collecting all the things she needed for good luck: the borrowed and the blue. In the middle of everything we heard shouting from the direction of the O'Haras' house and peeked through the curtains of our windows to see what was going on. We heard Mr. O'Hara shouting, "Fuck you! That's what I say to that! Fuck you! You can just go to fucking hell, bitch!"

As the doors slammed shut at the O'Haras', Melody swept into the room, holding up the long swishing skirt of her beautiful white lace wedding dress—which had been Mother's—and rushed to the window to see what all the commotion was about.

"Children. Get away from that window," said Mother, but she didn't force us. We watched as Mr. O'Hara carried an armful of clothes to his Ranchero and threw them in the car. He walked back to the house, went in, and slammed the door. He shouted some more, but we couldn't hear what he was saying, couldn't hear anyone shouting back. He returned to the car in the driveway, carrying an army duffel bag and two rifles in their zippered cases. He drove away, spinning out on Moonlight, throwing rocks behind his wheels and raising a long cloud of dust as he left.

"I hope that wasn't an omen," said Melody.

"Don't think twice about him, baby," said mother. "You get back inside and relax. We still have to finish doing your hair." She knelt down to pick at Melody's wedding dress. "The world's better off without him around anyway."

I later heard from Kit that his father ended up making a lot of money by getting a good job at the Army Corps of Engineers on a dam project. And he refused to pay any child support. Before too long, Mrs. O'Hara remarried. But Kit's new stepfather wasn't a great improvement.

Watching him drive away reminded me of the day that Barry left. What was it about fathers? Why did they always seem angry, brutal? Why weren't they ever there? Why were our lives held together by our mothers? I had no answers to these questions then, and still have no answers. What is it about fathers? What is wrong with us?

12

White Circles

That fall, I started sixth grade. One morning my teacher, Mrs. Chizhek, drew a circle approximately eight inches in diameter on the green slate of the chalkboard. A nice, neat circle. Almost perfect. It resembled a cafeteria plate. She drew a nearly perfect circle as we watched in silence. It was in the morning. A rainy and cold day. We could hear the chalk squeaking against the green slate. I needed to urinate, and felt this pressure in my bladder—a hot, burning sensation, telling me I had to go. I could almost smell the chalk, feel it lightly coating my fingers. The chalk that hovered in clouds from the erasers I pounded with lust for Miss LeClaire every day. Miss LeClaire, my former first-grade teacher, whose body was ashamed of its clothing, and wanted to run naked with me through fields of tall grass, both of us leaping like impalas. Mrs. Chizhek drew a circle on the board. We watched. And then she turned around, pointed, and said, "You will walk to the board, Damon, and place your nose in this circle." At first I had no idea why I was being singled out in the class of twenty-six children, except that I was the only student who had black blood, which as I grew older began to set me apart from everyone more and more, something Louis had warned me about.

"We're not like the rest of them," he told me one day. "And they hate us for it."

It had rained all morning, the classroom warm and stuffy, all of us staring out the window at the gray water and rippling sheets of rain coming in from the coastal plains, off the Gulf of Mexico. "When will the sun ever come out?" I had asked. Only, I had a slight lisp, so my sentence sounded like "When will the thun ever come out?" Mrs. Chizhek paused in her lesson on the state of Idaho. My notebook read, "Potatoes in the south. Rockies in the north." She paused, and did not turn around. She tugged on the U.S. map and raised it. She walked to the right side of the board and drew the circle.

"You will learn to pronounce your esses correctly," she said. She spoke in future tense, and there was not the slightest hint that I might do other than I was told, that I might disobey her. I had to urinate. I tucked my hand between my legs, mashing my penis, trying to hold it back. For a moment I was afraid I would wet my pants; the warm liquid would gush out and flow down my leg and out the shoestring holes of my old and scuffed black shoes. Everyone would laugh and point. I had had only a few years' practice in controlling my bodily functions, and sometimes worried that I would forget the lessons. "You will stand up, Damon. You will walk to the board, and you will place your nose"—here she pointed at my nostrils—"in this circle"—her finger moved back to point at the board. Mrs. Chizhek often spoke this way, as if she were hypnotizing us into submission. It worked.

I walked to the front of the classroom, keeping my legs pinched together, so I would not have an accident and further humiliate myself. Behind me, the class snickered, glad not to have their noses in the circle. I stood at the chalkboard, my hands at my sides, and stared at the green wall just inches in front of my face. I was, in fact, touching the wall. My nose was in the circle, the circle of chalk approximately eight inches in diameter. Mrs. Chizhek was beside me. She faced in the opposite direction, toward the class, but stood so close I smelled the Mentholatum she greased her elbows and knees with every day so they would move freely. She had explained that her joints were so stiff with arthritis she was lucky she could move at all. Ben-Gay deep heating rub helped. She asked us to excuse the smell.

Mrs. Chizhek was not a young woman. She still treated us as if we were third-graders, but she didn't realize how fast we were growing. I'd already begun stealing cigarettes from my mother's purse.

I stood with my nose in the white chalk circle and imagined peeing on Mrs. Chizhek. She would have to be on her knees or lying on the ground for me to be able to do this. I would aim at her forehead or eye sockets, rinse her hair with it, tell her, "You will open your mouth, Mrs. Chizhek, so that I may be allowed to urinate in it." I would fill her mouth with my hot yellow urine, splash it into her nose and ears.

"The potato fields of Idaho," she said, "are the result of *irrigation*." She wrote this word on the board, striking it sharply with her chalk. "Irrigation sprinklers spray water into the open mouths of the fields to make potatoes grow." I wondered if I could make potatoes grow in Mrs. Chizhek's fields, if I could cast my seed into her dried and crusty furrows.

Between the strikes of Mrs. Chizhek's chalk, lightning illuminated the room, followed by the roll of thunder. Maybe the lights would go out. Maybe school would close, and free me from this white circle of obedience. Maybe all the other children in the classroom would leave, Mrs. Chizhek would lie down on the floor, and I would urinate into her mouth. Maybe a bolt of lightning would strike her dead. She would fall to the floor, her arms outspread, her eyes and mouth wide open. The children would file by, and, one by one, urinate into her open mouth. The boys would unzip their flies and aim. The girls would pull down their panties and squat.

"You will stand at the board with your nose in this circle, until you correctly pronounce your esses," said Mrs. Chizhek, interrupting her potato narrative. "If you continue to lisp, the world will think you are a homosexual. I will not have homosexuals in my classroom."

Now branded a queer, I stood there and wondered at the chalk circle. It was only an idea that imprisoned me. The concept of roundness. The circle could have been floating in space or could have been a ring of light around the moon, but it wasn't. It was here on the board, imprisoning my nose. I was learning obedience and humiliation because I could not pronounce my esses correctly. There were no chains upon my feet or master at my back. The punishment of the white circle was humiliation. The lesson of the white circle was obedience. Within this white circle, I could not move.

A blast of lightning killed the lights, and several students cried out. On Mrs. Chizhek's orders, we crawled under our desks for safety, in case any bolts of lightning shot across the room about desktop level and cut off our heads, or burned a path through our ears, leaving us physically intact but incurably stupid, like Phillip Colcott, who rubbed himself in Mrs. Schiller's class and ate his No. 2 pencils. According to the teachers, Phillip was just "slow."

Mrs. Chizhek had me crawl beneath her desk. She stood beside it, telling us to keep calm. I stared at the worn heels of her shoes, and the bottom of the desk above my head, curiously free of the thick gobs of chewing gum that dominated the inverted skies of most of the children's desks. When the storm passed, we climbed out from beneath our desks and walked in single file, like Indians, to the cold stone building of our cafeteria to eat red squares of cherry Jell-O and yellow squares of corn bread.

At the end of the day, Mrs. Chizhek kept me after class. "Repeat after me. Suzy sells seashells by the seashore." I did so, carefully lisping each ess. "Thuzie thellth theathellth . . ." This continued for two weeks. Finally she announced, "You are beyond hope and stubbornly refuse to learn. If you continue to lisp, you will be branded a homosexual throughout your life. You will be an outcast and shunned by decent people. What will you do in a job interview? Think of that." She placed a No. 2 pencil in the sharpener mounted on the wall and ground it slowly to a fine point. "When your future employer interviews you and hears you lisp, he will think you are a homosexual. Do you think he will hire a homosexual?" She shook her head.

I was twelve years old. I wondered what kind of job I could apply for. Lion tamer? Movie star? Astronaut? She had a point. I somehow doubted many astronauts would be hired at NASA and sent up in space to orbit the earth if they spoke with a lisp. We did not want homosexuals orbiting our planet.

I told Mrs. Chizhek that I was sorry, and would try harder. I stared at her hand full of sharpened pencils and sincerely hoped she would not plunge them into one or both of my blue eyes.

"Sorry is not good enough," she said. "However, I have spoken with Mr. Bryceland and we are going to try a new tactic. Tomorrow morning at ten-thirty, during recess, please report to the annex room. In that room, three days a week, you will be given speech therapy to cure your lisp. Mr. Bryceland has done this on my suggestion, and I approve of it."

I told her thanks a million.

"You're welcome, Damon." She seemed relieved. "And please behave politely and cooperate with your speech therapist."

I asked who the new teacher was.

"Miss LeClaire has volunteered to spend her free time teaching you correct pronunciation. Please do not disappoint her efforts."

13

Speech
Lessons

For three and a half months, I had to stare at Miss LeClaire's mouth, three days a week, to see how and where to put my tongue. The first day, she leaned across my desk, her lipstick-touched lips just inches from my beating eyelashes and heart, and commanded me to watch her mouth. "When you make the sound of an ess, as in *sweetness* or *succor*, touch the tip of your tongue to the back of your top front teeth, like this." Her lips formed a slight pucker and whispered *scissor*, *salt*, and *soothing* to me. There was more lipstick on her plump, almost swollen lower lip than on the more arched upper lip, which had a small V of a groove in the center and radiated out in two pink sweeps of tender heartbreak to the wicks of her mouth. Her two front teeth had a small gap between them, through which I saw the pink and bumpy tip of her tongue.

"Repeat after me," she said. "Sorrow. Success. Sadness."

"Thorrow. Thucktheth. Thadneth."

"No no no," said Miss LeClaire. "Can you feel your tongue? Feel it. Know where it's going. You're putting it too far forward, until it reaches between your teeth and makes a *th* sound. Now watch my mouth. Sadsack. Softball."

Speech therapy was held in a small portable building that was set off from the main campus of the elementary school. It was a building that the school district moved around to wherever it was needed. We had watched from the windows of Mrs. Chizhek's class as a flatbed truck drove down the side road of the school, the road that led to the baseball field, which formed the border of the playground. This flatbed truck had my speech therapy classroom on it, the portable building called the annex. Dust rose into the air behind the truck as it drove slowly down the road, and we laughed and pointed at it. The funny sight! A classroom driving down the road!

"That," said Mrs. Chizhek, "is our new special education annex. It is for the slow students." We laughed some more at that. "Don't concern yourselves with that building, children. Don't even look at it. Most of the slow students are in Mrs. Schiller's class, and only they will be required to attend classes in the annex." We giggled some more and looked around at each other. "Most of" the slow students? Who was slow in our class? Several of the boys hung their tongues from their mouths and made honking retard sounds.

As the year progressed, as far as I knew, I was the only student attending class in the annex who was not slow.

There were six desks in the annex. One globe. Four small windows, a flat roof, and a small chalkboard. The flooring was tan linoleum. The walls were covered with cheap imitation oak paneling, which covered a flimsy frame of two-by-fours and fiberglass insulation. If you pressed the walls between the two-by-four studs, the paneling would buckle and give, and you would not have faith in the structure. The building itself was perched atop four strategic stacks of cinder blocks. Cinder blocks also served as steps up into this perched and portable structure, and no grass grew around it. The building often sat in a sea of mud, the cinder-block steps covered with black scrape marks from our shoes.

Nothing in the annex gave you the impression that it would be there, in the same spot, after you left. I was always afraid I was going to forget something important there. I had the impression that when I came back to get it, the entire building would be gone, like an unreliable bookmobile. I sometimes imagined the flatbed truck would take it away when I was not looking, and I would never see it again. I had the nagging doubt that nothing of lasting importance or permanence could be learned in that building.

"Watch my mouth," said Miss LeClaire. "Southpaw. Sorrow. Slippery snakes." She explained to me that my tongue must not extend to my teeth, as it was doing, but lightly touch the back of my incisors, so it could allow a warm rush of air to flow around it, like this, she said, and hissed her sweet breath into my face, the redness of her open lips inches from my own. With only six small desks in the annex and no teacher's broad desktop, we scooted two of the desks together, facing each other, our desktops touching. We sat like that every class period, three days a week, facing each other. I was required to watch the red tip of Miss LeClaire's tongue, her glossy lips, her white, slightly gapped teeth. I saw the ridges and ripples of the roof of her mouth, a darker color than her tongue, a purple. I saw the dangle of her uvula. Sometimes we sat so close together that our knees touched. I was twelve years old, and each day in speech therapy for my persistent lisp, I was swollen with lust.

Brian Tunch said, "You're lucky, Sambo. I'd cut off my right foot to be alone with LeTush every day." We were at the baseball field, for practice. I pretended to be absorbed in picking the right bat, lifting several of them and testing my grip.

I often thought of Brian Tunch's stupid face as I was pounding the chalk out of Miss LeClaire's erasers. I did this almost every day for her, collecting all her dusty white erasers, carrying them out to the playground, pounding them clean. To do this I used a wooden box that was constructed for just that purpose, with four square sides but no top or bottom, only a heavy-duty screen stretched across the top. I pounded the erasers against the screen, sending clouds of white chalk into the air, surrounding myself in a miasma of white chalk, as if the white circle on the board had been vaporized, its power over me evaporating into nothing, as I thought with lust of Miss LeClaire, her lips, her tongue, her teeth. When guilt overcame me and it became too painful to think of Miss LeClaire, whom I loved, I alternately thought of the people I hated, such as Brian Tunch or Mrs. Chizhek.

I imagined that the wire screen I pounded was their faces.

I was not a good athlete, and my elaborate maneuvers in bat selection didn't help my performance in the softball games. My not being a good athlete didn't bother me at first. No one seemed to care. My family didn't care. They assumed it was a phase, and that soon I would grow to be tall, lean, and fast as my brother Louis. The other kids didn't seem to care. They were probably glad I was a lousy athlete, since most of them were very competitive, and would do anything to beat anyone else. Coach Henderson seemed the most concerned. "What's wrong with you, Bell? Are you lazy or what?"

Although I feigned team spirit during our baseball games, and actually experienced an odd form of pleasure when the team I happened to be playing on scored more runs than our opponents, for the most part I hated baseball and often felt sick when it came time to play. The glands in my neck would swell and my stomach would feel as if it were floating above third base.

This happened because I was physically afraid of the ball. When I was in the fourth grade, Louis and Leland taught me the principles of the game. They threw the ball at my face and told me to catch it in the leather webs of the outfielder's glove. They taught me to pitch. I pitched to Louis, he swung and hit a ball that struck the ground several feet in front of my face, bounced, and struck me directly in the nose before I got my glove up to catch it. Blood gushed out. My ears rang. Louis had me lie with my head tilted back.

"Look at that," said Leland. "He's bleeding like a stuck pig." A white towel was jammed against my nose, and quickly was soaked in blood.

"You're going to be okay, Damon," said Louis. "Don't you worry."

Leland complained that he was going to be sick if my nose didn't stop gushing. "I never seen so much blood," he said. "He's going to need a transfusion." When I seemed to stop bleeding, I was afraid the blood was still gushing out, only now it was flowing back into my sinuses and would eventually flood the circuits of my brain. I had a headache the rest of the day and could not see or hear very well.

"I bet he's got a concussion from that stupid ball," said Melody. Since we didn't want to get in trouble about it, we decided not to tell our mother. Melody soaked the towel in cold water to get out the blood.

I never liked baseball after that, and decided that it wasn't worth the potential damage to my brain if I got beaned by a fastball. I didn't want to end up being slow. My friend Ramsey was slow. He lived at the intersection of Moonlight and Nightingale. He was slow and white and his mother wandered around their house in her bra and pedal pushers, talking on their black telephone night and day. He had a sister who seemed just a little faster than he was and headed down the same dirty back road his mother traveled, and a brother who wore a big brown plastic hearing aid and was Louis's best friend.

Whatever I did, I didn't want to end up being slow, like Ramsey. Every kid in the neighborhood stole his toys and he never seemed to notice they were gone, until he had no toys left and he sat in his backyard, on the end of his rickety metal slide, with nothing to do. Even I stole his toys. You could order him to make a sandwich and minutes later he'd be back with two pieces of white bread filled with a thick coating of peanut butter and grape jelly. From the hole in his closet, you could watch his mother talk on the telephone and drink vodka stark naked, resting the glass on her white belly. Ramsey didn't care. His house smelled of Phisoderm liquid soap. The trash can in his mother's bathroom always seemed filled with huge used Kotexes, and I associated her excessive bleeding with Ramsey's slowness.

We played baseball throughout most of the year, and lots of the kids were on Little League teams, but in the spring we started track, concentrating on the events listed on the President's Physical Fitness Test. The softball throw, fifty-yard dash, sit-ups, chin-ups, push-ups, and shot put. If you scored high enough on each event and accumulated enough points for a given total, you received a President's Physical Fitness Badge to sew on your shirt sleeve.

I wanted one of those badges. Brian Tunch was already talking about what shirt he was going to put the badge on. Michael Shapiro and even Wallace Conroy were planning on it. At top speed, I slowly ran the fifty-yard dash. I heaved the softball and the markers had to come forward for it, since they had backed up for the kid before me. Even cheating a little, I only got eighty-six sit-ups, instead of the required one hundred, and four pull-ups instead of ten. While the other kids were being timed, Coach Henderson told me to try out the hurdles, that maybe they were going to be my forte. They weren't on the President's Physical Fitness Test, but were an event in track.

They were set up at the other side of the playing field, beyond the annex. There weren't any kids back there. I liked that. No one would be watching me. I ran the hurdles a few times, realizing I wasn't going very fast, because it was hard to work up to each jump between the hurdles. I decided to give it my everything. I raced through the first four hurdles at top speed, barely getting my feet beneath me each time, but on the fifth I was too close to the hurdle when I started to jump, caught my leg, fell, and twisted my ankle.

I lay on my side, twisting in the dirt and grabbing my leg. It felt as if my ankle were filled with napalm. I had landed in a red ant bed and they started to sting me, so I had to get up quickly, with no one to lean on, and limp back to the main playing field on my own.

"What happened to you?" asked Coach Henderson when I walked up, dirt still covering my leg and an ugly, bloody scrape on my right knee. I told him I'd been doing pretty good on the hurdles, but had caught my leg on the last one and twisted my foot when I landed.

He dusted the dirt off my leg and shook his head. He was a heavy, middle-aged man with an Acme Thunderer whistle on a cord around his neck and a baseball cap on his head. He didn't look like he could run fifty yards or leap over any hurdles, but implied that he had done these things in the past. "Well, damn," he said. "It's starting to swell up. You better go see the nurse about it."

He patted me on the back as I started to limp towards the school. He was trying to cheer me up. "You know, I think I figured out what your problem is, Damon." He kept his big hand on my shoulder. "You're just slow. No two ways about it. No getting around it. You're slow. So I guess you'll just have to live with it."

Later the same day, Mrs. Chizhek also pronounced me slow. Brian Tunch asked why we couldn't use the annex for our Easter party, to hide eggs in or to fill with refreshments, since it was the closest building to the field where we were going to hide our eggs. "The annex is not for the use of regular students," said Mrs. Chizhek. "The annex is for slow students, students who need extra help, such as Damon's speech lessons." Some of the children looked at me, but I did not meet their eyes. I stared at Mrs. Chizhek and blinked, not registering any emotion, pretending that she had not actually meant me when she said *slow*. I imagined she wasn't there. I imagined I was filling her mouth with urine.

Throughout the day, I was obsessed with being slow. I realized Miss LeClaire had switched from teaching first grade to special education classes. My friend Ramsey was in her class. Once, when I had to meet him to get a ride home after school in his mother's car, I walked to the annex classroom and found him there, drawing stick figures on the chalkboard with arrows through their heads.

"That's very good, Ramsey," said Miss LeClaire. "I think you're getting much better. Now let's try to use those drawing skills in writing your alphabet more clearly, okay?"

The next day was the last of my speech lessons on how not to lisp and be considered a homosexual for the rest of my life. It was Friday, fish sticks and ice cream sandwiches. At ten-thirty I limped to the annex and sat down. I had not said a word all morning and refused to smile at any of Miss LeClaire's jokes or endearments in the lesson plan. I stared at my unopened books and slouched in my desk. Finally she asked, "What's wrong, Damon?"

"Nothin'."

"Yes there is. I can tell by the way you're acting. Now tell me what it is."

"There's nothing wrong."

"Quit lying. Do you want to be a liar?"

"I don't want to come to speech therapy anymore."

Miss LeClaire stood silently for a moment, then shrugged. "Do what you want."

"Well then, that's what I want."

She reached up and adjusted the polka-dotted band that kept her hair pulled away from her beautiful white face and out of her beautiful brown eyes. "Is it because you don't like me anymore?"

I blinked and stared at the books on my desk. My chin began to tremble. "No."

When she spoke, her voice was softer now, closer to me. "Well, what is it then?"

"Mrs. Chizhek said I was slow. I don't want to be slow. I'm not slow."

"Oh, Damon. Don't be silly." She pulled me out of my desk and brought my body next to hers. I didn't want her to see me like this, my face twisted, breathing out of my mouth because my nose was running. I wasn't slow at all, I told her. I was faster than lots of people. I could prove it, too! What did Mrs. Chizhek know, anyway? I couldn't help it if I talked funny. I wasn't queer!

"Don't worry about what Mrs. Chizhek says, Damon. She's a stupid old dried-up hag who hates the world. She doesn't know what she's saying half the time, and the other half she's full of it."

Miss LeClaire pressed me into her bosom, mashing my face into the lace and rose curlicues of her bra. With her hands on the back of my head, she crushed me against the buttons of her blouse, smothering me in her womanly smell, which seemed somehow like citrus, a mixture of tangerines and salt. It was as if she had drawn a circle in the center of her chest, in the Vitamin D, milky-white hollow of her breasts. Instead of the chalk circle of humiliation in which I had been forced to place my nose, now I was allowed a glorious circle of desire and mystery and fulfillment to wallow in. It was as if she had unbuttoned her blouse and had said, "You will place your nose into the white circles of my breasts and you will breathe in the smell of my skin. You will not be able to feel the toes at the ends of your feet, nor will you be able to feel the tips of your fingers. But your penis will glow like a baking oven in the center of a dark house with neither furniture nor windows."

When Miss LeClaire let me go, I could feel the small circles from the buttons of her blouse on my face, as if I had been tattooed by an African tribe. She fished a small package of pink Kleenex from her purse and made me blow my nose and wipe my eyes. The rest of the day I had a headache and my mouth was filled with the flat metallic taste of blood.

In remembering this, I half imagine that I lifted her skirt and she wrapped her beautiful legs around me, that I pinned her to the wall of that small classroom annex building, the cheap paneling buckling against our passion. But this is, of course, foolishness. I was less than half her age. We did no such thing. Yet I'm less sure about the incantatory voice I still hear, and it is similar to an event that occurred so long ago that you cannot know whether it was in a dream or daylight. In a few cases such as this, I cannot distinguish between imagination and reality. I remember that warm morning in my grade school annex building, the portable building that stood on gray cinder blocks and had tan linoleum flooring, with exactly six desks in it, a globe, and a small chalk board. I remember that was my last speech lesson, and that though I continued to lisp slightly, no one seemed to care. The teacher I loved hugged me close to her, and told me not to worry.

"You will be dizzy and secure," she told me. "You will feel the warmth of my fingers on the back of your head. You will feel them on the hairs at the nape of your neck. The talons of my fingernails will be sharp and deliciously painful, digging into your skin. You will bury your face in the white circles of my breasts and sob, filling my cups with tears. Then you will rise up, like a buccaneer at sea, hacking off arms and legs with single strokes, laying waste to all who dare defy you. You will stand at the helm of your sloop and brandish your saber. And you will conquer the world."

14

Moon Shots
and
a Thief

We were at the football field, taking a break, talking about the moon shots as we picked burrs out of our socks and shoestrings. Dressed in our matching dark blue gym shorts and white T-shirts, we looked skinny and bony. It was the spring of 1969, during the Apollo space program, on the race to the moon. I was obsessed with launchpads, Titan and Saturn rockets, ICBMs, elliptical orbits, and Cape Canaveral. I watched *I Dream of Jeannie* every week, a TV show in which an astronaut blasted into space and returned from orbit to land on a deserted island, where he found a woman in an ancient bottle. She was voluptuous, with a navel big enough to fit your finger into. She always wore Turkish lingerie and was dying to satisfy the astronaut's every desire.

I wanted to be that astronaut. I wanted to zoom through space, to brave meteor showers and encounter alien civilizations vastly superior to our own. I wanted to meet people who, when you went to pay for something, said things like "I do not understand. What is this thing you call money?" I wanted to live with iguana people in jumpsuits and mirror-plated belt buckles, date alien sex goddesses with four gigantic breasts and webbed fingers. I memorized the solar system so I would know where I was going. The smallest planet, Pluto. Io, the largest moon of Jupiter. The rings of Saturn. Venus, the planet of love, whose surface was obscured by dense and swirling clouds. But Brian Tunch insisted my studies were a waste of time. He told me I shouldn't get my hopes up, because I would only be disappointed. "It's a proven fact," he said. "Negroes can't fly. It's scientific."

In the distance we heard Mr. Hernandez mowing the grass in front of the administration building and cafeteria, where they put the sprinklers in the afternoons. We were sweating and hot. Brian tried to set me straight about flying Negroes.

"Negroes can't go to the moon because some chemical in the spacesuit reacts with their bodies. Or maybe it's some kind of cosmic flu or something they get. I can't remember exactly, but I read it somewhere."

"Does it make them sick?" asked Wallace Conroy.

"Sick? It kills them. One hundred percent fatal. They sent a shitload of them into orbit one time, and every one of them spear chuckers came back deader than hell. Space capsule full of dead, bloated black bodies. They'd torn each other's eyes out, too, trying to get free. And one of them—probably the first one to die—was half-eaten, big hunks of meat ripped out of his arms and legs. And from the photos

I seen in this magazine—maybe it was *Time* or *Newsweek*—it looked like they'd been gnawing on his head, too."

"You saw photos?"

"Uh huh. And the funny thing is, they tried monkeys, remember? The guys at NASA figured, hey, the monkeys can take it, so can the spear chuckers. So they loaded up a rocket with 'em and let 'er go."

"That was their first mistake," said Wallace.

"See, they figured they'd test dogs, like the Russians did, then monkeys, then niggers, before they'd put a white man up there. John Glenn didn't go shooting his ass up to Mercury without some dry runs."

"How come the rest of us never heard about this?" I asked.

"It was top-secret," said Brian. "Classified. It leaked out to a few papers and magazines, but for the most part it was all hush-hush."

I focused all my energy on my sneakers, and meticulously picked the sharp sticker burrs out of the shoestrings of my old Keds. They were too tight and gave me blisters. My mother had told me we'd get some new ones soon, but we didn't have the money to afford new shoes, and couldn't I make do with these a little while longer? I could. I could also ignore the stupidity of Brian Tunch. His white limbs were pathetically skinny, except for his oversized left arm and hand, scaly and red as a claw, and his face was wide and fleshy, as if the doctor had hated to pull him into this world and had given his head one good squeeze in the wrong direction to get him out. Maybe he wondered for a moment whether he could refuse to pull the ugly thing out, but no, he's got a job and worries of his own, he's got no choice but to pull it out by both ugly ears, only no harm in giving it a little extra squeeze, a little smash with both palms on his cheekbones and temples, out of spite, you know, but the nurses and the mother can't see, so who's the wiser? A little squeeze, a little birthmark to let the world know this person's a little shit and he didn't want to have a hand in delivering him, but he had no choice, the doctor thought. Maybe that deformed Brian. Maybe that's why his face was so wide, his nose a fleshy knob. Russell Jensen nicknamed him "the Fireplug."

Russell was also obsessed with flying. He invited me over to his house one afternoon to see his birds. "You have to be gentle around them," he said. "Don't go waving your arms or anything when I take them out of the cage. You'll scare them." Russell lived in Shavano Park, a rich neighborhood beyond Lockhill-Selma Road, about five miles from our neighborhood. His father was the president of something, his mother had been a fashion model, and they never worried about money. Their backyard was cool and green, shaded by oak trees, carpeted with dark green grass. A sprinkler system buried in the ground watered it automatically every night when it got dark. They had a beautiful swimming pool, and next to it a small bungalow used as a pool house.

Russell kept his homing pigeons in a network of cages by the side of the pool house. The cages were large wooden frames with chicken-wire walls and slanted roofs. They had sticks running through the chicken wire from one side to the other for roosts. The short curly underfeathers of the pigeons floated about in the cage and clumped up against the chicken wire. The cages smelled of seed and droppings.

Russell opened one of them and stroked some of the birds gently. "Hey Buzz, how ya doing? Hey Chuck. Hey Rita."

The birds fluttered about in the cage, some of them pecking at his hand timidly, some of them stepping sideways across the roosts to evade him, looking huffy, as if they didn't want to be bothered. There were plastic trays of birdseed and water hooked into the chicken-wire walls. Russell filled up one of the yellow plastic trays with seed and told me to go ahead and pet them, but they seemed scared by my hand and rushed to the ends of the roost and the back of the cage, so I told him it was okay, I'd pet them later. The male pigeons strutted about and had huge puffy chests, with iridescent purple-and-green feathers on them. Some of the females were dusky and plain, but one of them had beautiful mottled white-and-cinnamon-brown feathers, like a palomino.

"Watch this," said Russell. He clucked his tongue and tapped the roof of the cage with a sharp staccato beat, and one by one the pigeons waddled down the roost to the open door of the cage, leapt out, and began beating their wings heavily and flying in circles above us in the yard. They seemed to struggle against their heavy bodies with the grace of their beautiful wings, and when a dozen or so of them had filled the sky above us, they took off together, grouped in a vigorous flock, and flew off above the oak trees and out beyond the alley, cutting through the sky, for a moment superimposed against the power lines and telephone poles that ran down his alley. "Isn't that cool?" said Russell. "Don't you wish you could fly like that?"

"Aren't you afraid they won't come back?"

"They're homing pigeons. I could let these loose fifty miles from here and they'd come right back to me."

"What if you put them in a car and drove someplace, like my house, and then let them go?"

"They'd fly right back. No problem."

Russell was also obsessed with the Apollo program. He knew the history of the Russian dog Laika, the first dog in space, Yuri Gagarin, the first man in space, and the first woman in space, Valentina Tereshkova. "Isn't that a cool name, Valentina? I wish we had someone named Valentina in Mrs. Chizhek's class." Russell liked the early Russian successes, but now felt that they were second-rate. "We're kicking their ass now. We're going to land on the moon, and there's not a damn thing they can do about it."

Even the sky above Russell's bed was full of planes. He had model planes of jet fighters, bombers, fighting Tigers, and B-52s perfectly done and hanging by wires from the ceiling, some of them at angles, at different heights, some pointing towards the others, so that there seemed to be dogfights frozen in the air above us when I spent the night over at his house. He had a tiny lamp spotlighting some of the planes, so that the fighter jets were visible even when everything else was dark, and B-52s and biplanes cast shadows against the walls and ceiling of his room.

Russell belonged to the same Cub Scout troop that I did, and he even subscribed to the Boy Scout magazine, *Boy's Life*, which I liked to read, although it always seemed as if it were meant for cleaner, less troubled boys than me. Boys whose parents were rich and could afford to buy their uniform without worrying about it, boys whose parents took them camping in Yellowstone National Park for vacations, and hiked down to the bottom of the Grand Canyon with them. Our den mother lived on a ranch with horses, cows, and a pond in the back where we fished for bass and catfish. To me, Russell's life seemed perfect. He had everything. A maid cooked his meals. His mother was gorgeous, and never seemed to yell at him. Whenever he wanted to go swimming,

Moon Shots and a Thief   143

all he had to do was walk outside and jump in his pool. After his twelfth birthday, it seemed to take him an hour to show me all the presents he got. One of them was a banana-yellow folding fishing knife, with a small silver fish on the handle, that seemed slim and beautiful. He let me handle it, and when I went home that night, all I could think of was how much I wanted that knife. I imagined myself with the knife in my hand, slashing this way and that, its steel blade flashing in the sunlight. If anyone ever bothered me, I'd stick it in his stomach and rip out his guts.

One afternoon we went fishing with our Scout troop, on our den mother's ranch, and Russell left the knife sitting at the base of an oak tree. He completely forgot it. He didn't seem to think the knife was anything special, and had several other kinds of fishing knives in his tackle box. To him, it was just another gift. I saw it sitting there as I was casting one of the den mother's rod-and-reel sets into the pond, with a kind of doughy bread ball on a hook at the end of the line to catch catfish. The rest of the troop were on the other side of the pond or by the small pier that reached out into the water.

No one saw me pick up the yellow-handled knife and put it in my pocket.

At first I planned to give it back to Russell, because I thought he would notice it was gone. He didn't. After fishing, our den mother led us on a hike down one of the dry creek beds on her ranch. We looked for fossils and Indian arrowheads. The knife felt heavy and enormous in my pocket. It was a warm day in April, and we spread out in a line to look for the fossils and keep space between each other. We wan-

The Fire Eaters

dered through groves of pungent juniper trees. The sky above was blue, and black buzzards wheeled in the clear air, catching drafts of warmth, never flapping their ragged wings.

We found a few fossilized snails and clams. The clams looked like white heart-shaped rocks. Mrs. Greune, our den mother, explained that millions of years ago this ranchland had been covered by a deep blue sea. In the sea lived gigantic fish and dinosaurs. Ancient alligators the size of elephants. Armadillos as big as buffalo. She said her ranch was full of their skeletons that had now turned into rocks. That was what you called fossilization. And if we looked really hard, we might be able to find some petrified trees, too. In fact, for all we knew, we had a very good chance of someday stumbling onto an entire petrified forest.

"My uncle found a fossilized eagle once," said Brian. "You could see every one of his feathers, and there was even a fossilized fish in his claws."

"Liar," whispered Russell.

"It's the Lord's truth," he said. "Swear on a stack of Bibles."

"That enough, Brian," said Mrs. Greune. We walked back to her ranch house. Russell's mother picked the two of us up and gave me a ride home. The whole time I was aware of the knife in the pocket of my blue Cub Scout uniform pants. I had to turn the knife sideways so I could sit down. I thought about giving it back to him as we drove to my house. His mother pulled into our driveway. I got out of the car. "Thanks for the ride, Mrs. Jensen," I said. She said I was welcome.

"Call me later," said Russell.

When I got in, Louis and Leland were gone somewhere, but Tony was watching TV. I hid the knife in a pair of my old socks, in the back of my drawer. My heart was pounding. I was even too scared to look at it.

A few days later, Russell asked me if I remembered seeing him with his knife when we were hunting for fossils, or when we were fishing at the catfish pond. I said I didn't. "You didn't lose that knife, did you? Wow. That was really cool."

Russell admitted he had no idea where it was, but he thought it would turn up. "Don't tell my mom, okay?"

"Sure."

At our next Scout meeting, he told Mrs. Greune that he'd lost his knife. "Did anyone see Russell's knife by the pond?" she asked. We were eating cupcakes, and I peeled the paper wrapper from beneath the dark chocolate icing and sucked off the icing that was stuck to the edges of the pleated paper.

"You lost that good knife?" asked Wallace.

Brian said, "I bet someone stole it. I saw you had it when we were out fishing by the pier. Somebody snatched that mother."

"Maybe *you* took it," said Wallace.

"I did not! I don't need no knife from Russell. I got my own."

"It probably fell out of your pocket while we were looking for fossils," said Mrs. Greune. "Maybe we can go look for it after our next meeting."

That afternoon, when I got home, I moved the knife out of my sock drawer and hid it in an old coffee can behind the fire pit where we burned our trash. I hardly even looked at it or touched it, but now and then, when I was sure no one was around, and sometimes at night, I'd go open up the coffee can and look at the knife in the moonlight. I wanted to give it back to Russell, but I couldn't force myself to do it. I knew he'd forget about it after a while. I needed it more than he did. I imagined cutting out Brian's tongue with it.

15
At Bat

We were alone at the baseball diamond, Coach Henderson having sent us out first to carry the equipment. Brian carried a cardboard box of gloves and balls, while I had a load of bats in my arms stacked like firewood. Brian dropped the box by the backstop and sat down behind home plate, one leg bent, one straight, his baseball cap on backwards. "Did you go over to Jensen's the other night? I heard Rachel Amarillo's got a crush on him."

It was a cool day, and when the sun went behind the clouds, goose bumps stood out on my skin. I picked up one of the heavy bats and swung it in the air, trying to warm and loosen up my body. As always before a baseball game, my stomach felt queasy and disconnected. I told Brian that Russell's party was really cool because we played Marco Polo in his swimming pool.

"He's a spoiled little rich kid," said Brian. He sat there shredding oak leaves that had blown up against the backstop. He tore them slowly, folding and breaking the brown, brittle leaves at the dried-up veins. "Why do you hang around with him, anyway? I've been over to his house. I've seen all that stuff he's got."

"What about it?"

"Don't you want to just, like, take some of it? Sometimes? I bet you do, don't you?"

"Rachel Amarillo doesn't have a crush on Russell. She's going steady with Benjamin Fondaminski, who goes to St. Luke's. I heard they make out every afternoon in her mom's car, after he gets home from school." I picked up a ball, tossed it in the air, and swung at it, only clipping it and sending it bouncing towards the pitcher's mound.

"You stole Jensen's knife, didn't you?"

I kept tossing balls up in the air and swinging at them, but I only connected on about every other ball. The sun went back behind the clouds. I wondered where all the other kids were, why none of them had followed us yet. Brian told me what would happen when everyone realized I'd stolen Russell's knife. Rachel Amarillo? She'd hate my guts. She was a little prig as it was. I'd probably get kicked out of school, since no one would be able to trust me in the cloak-room again. They'd all be afraid that while they were at recess or lunch or something I'd be there rifling through their coats, stealing every nickel and dime I could get my grubby hands on. I'd probably have to go to reform school.

"I didn't steal his fishing knife, okay? So just shut up." I rubbed some dirt into my hands, then slapped the extra off and gave Brian a look. He was chewing gum and staring at me, grinning, his hat on backwards.

"Look, I suppose you're right," he said. "Sure. I believe you didn't steal that knife, and I won't say anything about it to Russell or anyone else." He stood up and stepped towards me. "Friends?"

He reached out his hand to shake. I didn't know what to do. I hated him and didn't trust him, but for half a moment I thought maybe this would work out, maybe he wasn't such a jerk after all. I shook hands with him and his grin widened. He said, "I'm Lincoln. You're free."

He laughed to himself as he stepped by me, then leaned down to the equipment box to pick out a glove for the game. I put both hands back on the grip of the bat and stepped forward, and when Brian started to stand up with a glove in his hand, I swung hard and slammed the side of his head. He stumbled to the ground and clutched at his face, falling into the dirt of home plate.

I dropped the bat and tried to help him, tried to get him to stop writhing and grabbing his head, but he twisted free from me. After a few minutes Wallace Conroy and Edward Villanova came running up. "What happened?"

"I didn't know he was right behind me. All the sudden I swung and hit a ball and there he was. I saw the ball fall to the ground and felt my bat hit something. I think I was pulling back to swing, really. I didn't know he was so close to me. Honest."

Edward ran to get Coach Henderson. Brian was on his back, his knees bent. He kept lifting one leg at a time, and moaning. His face was red and tears were coming out of his eyes. He was getting dirt all over his T-shirt and his hair. Some of it was sticking to blood on the side of his face. He screamed between his clenched teeth that it hurt, oh God it hurt so bad, and kept repeating that over and over again. His legs worked as if he were trying to run but couldn't get up, and he was crawling on his back across the red sand of the batter's box.

We had to hold his legs to keep him from moving away from us. Wallace and I sat beside him and told him just to hold on, Coach would be there in a minute. The other kids showed up, and we stood in a circle around Brian. When someone said I was the one who beaned him, everybody stared at me. I couldn't look at their faces. All I could see was a bunch of legs standing around me, and I could hear someone telling how I didn't know he was standing there, right behind me, and had swung backwards and hit him in the head. But why was I swinging backwards? That didn't make any sense. Why'd Brian get so close to the bat? Man, you gotta be careful. He looks bad. Really bad.

They got Brian on his feet and helped him walk towards the parking lot. Coach Henderson came trotting up, his huge key ring jangling, and stopped to look in Brian's eyes. They went toward the administration building, and I followed, a few steps behind.

Coach asked me a few questions, and I swore to God it was an accident, really. He said, okay, don't worry about it, that didn't matter now. It all happened so fast, I told him. One minute he was talking to me, standing by the backstop as I was hitting singles out into left field. They should go look! The balls must still be out there! And the next minute, bam, there was Brian on the ground. Was he going to be okay? I hadn't meant to hurt him, honest.

Coach patted me on the back after the ambulance arrived, and we stood in the asphalt gravel of the parking lot, watching the lights pulsing as the siren faded and it headed down the feeder road to the freeway. "Don't worry about it, Damon. I'm sure you didn't mean to hurt anybody."

Wallace, Edward, and I walked to the administration building together, with Coach Henderson right behind us. "But we've got to be more careful out there. This just shows you how someone can get hurt. You can break a leg sliding or put an eye out if you get beaned by a ball when you're not looking, and we shouldn't let that kind of stuff happen. You got to watch that ball and always pay attention to what's going on around you. Damon should have known Brian was stepping up behind him, and Brian shouldn't have gotten in the way in the first place. You should never get near the path of a swinging bat, because it can knock the bejesus out of you."

I told Coach I didn't feel very good. He sent me to the nurse, who made me lie down on the bed in her office, which was a green Naugahyde platform, with a paper wrapper over one end. It was hard and uncomfortable; lying there, all I could do was stare at the ceiling. Nurse Edwards asked about Brian's injury. "I hope his skull isn't cracked," she said. "Or worse."

I told her I had a headache. She put the back of her hand against my forehead and touched my cheeks. "You do feel kind of warm," she said. She put a glass thermometer in my mouth, placing it under my tongue and telling me not to bite it or open my mouth till she told me to. She looked at her watch to time me. "The skull is a very delicate thing," she said. "It's like your brain is a raw egg, with your skull the shell that protects it. You break that shell and all the yolk comes oozing out."

The thermometer was hard under my tongue, and I felt

even worse than I had before, lying in that room that smelled of antiseptic. I turned my head to watch Nurse Edwards, who was a wizened old woman with a turkey wattle of a neck. She had lightning bolts of purple-and-blue varicose veins shooting down her legs, and her ankles seemed swollen, her shoes too tight. After checking her wristwatch again, she took the thermometer out of my mouth and held it up to the light. "Did he hear ringing in his ears?"

"I don't know. I forgot to ask. But he seemed like he was hurting real bad."

She removed her glasses, which had a silver chain that fastened around her neck, and stared intently at the thermometer. She thought my temperature seemed normal. "I think I'm going blind," she said, as she wiped the thermometer with alcohol. "I suppose before long I won't be able to see a thing."

She fussed in the drawers and cabinets of her office, putting away the thermometer and the bottle of alcohol. "I can't drive anymore," she added. "My husband has to drop me off and pick me up every day. They just keep me on here because they feel sorry for me. You want some aspirin for that headache?"

"Yes, ma'am."

"I remember you," she said. "You were the one who always used to eat his sack lunch before he came to school. You never seemed to get enough food." She nodded, and fumbled in the medicine cabinet, picking up several white plastic bottles to read the labels, before she was satisfied she had what she wanted. "We used to talk about you. You were quite a problem for a time there. But it blew over, didn't it?"

"I think so. I just have a big appetite, is all."

She placed two aspirin in my pink palm and handed me a cone-shaped white paper drinking cup.

"Chew those up first," she said.

The aspirin was bitter and chalky in my mouth, but I chewed as she had told me, and drained the paper cone of water to wash the taste from my mouth. Nurse Edwards stepped on the stainless-steel foot of her white enamel trash can, that made the lid pop up, then tossed my empty paper cone inside.

"That boy was always spiteful and mean, wasn't he? Maybe it was the Lord's work, punishing his soul for its ugliness. If he dies right now, he'll end up in hell. You want to bet on that?"

"No, ma'am."

"I bet you don't. You'll burn too, for sending him there. But I suppose his mother loves him. If they don't get me some more gauze I don't know what I'm going to do. We have some serious accident and some little boy or girl comes in bleeding all over themselves, those school board people are going to see themselves on TV, and they won't like it. . . . Well, what are you looking at? Why don't you call your mother and get her to pick you up? That's the thing to do."

16

Morning Sickness

I didn't call my mother.

After school was out, I took the bus home. No one spoke to me as I walked to the back and took a seat. Everyone was quiet. The clacking of the windows seemed unnaturally loud; so did the engine's straining sound as we left the parking lot. I stared at the back of the cafeteria, where Brian had pushed my face in the dirt, as we rounded a curve in the driveway. How does it feel, Brian? How does it feel? I watched the trees and houses pass by as the bus lumbered through its rounds, full of the familiar noises—the shouts to the driver, the thump of kids running down the aisle, the grind of the gears.

When it neared my stop I shouted, "Next!" and left my seat, holding on to the sides of the seats, stepping carefully on the black rubber mat down the middle, no one speaking to me, not looking at anyone, until I reached the front and held on to the stainless-steel pole. The driver jerked open the folding doors of the bus. I stepped down quickly and was off, out of their sight, waiting for the bus to pass in front of me.

Someone threw a half-eaten apple out the window and hit me in the head, splattering one side of my face. In the windows at the back of the bus, I saw the faces of the other kids, some who had been my friends, staring at me with curiosity and distrust.

I wiped the apple juice off with my sleeve and walked home. Fritz and Hercules ran up, wagging their tails, and licked my hands. Hercules rolled over on his back for me to scratch his stomach. Fritz barked at me for giving Hercules too much attention. It was as if nothing had changed, as if it had simply been another day at school.

Early in the evening, Mother called. She said she wasn't coming home for dinner, that we could have whatever was in the refrigerator. "I'll make something special for you to-morrow night. I'm just out with some friends, and I think we're going somewhere for a bite."

She was probably calling from the pay phone of a bar. I could hear laughter and voices in the background. When Louis asked me what she said, I told him. "She isn't coming home right now. She's going somewhere for a bite." Louis made a face. For the past few months, Mother had been going out at nights, calling from the pay phones of bars, of restaurants, and once, another time that I had answered the phone, a bowling alley—the sound of the pins crashing in the background. We all knew that she was dating again.

"I think Mama's going to catch a man," Lizzie had said,

then she'd lifted her hair off the back of her neck and struck a sultry pose, pooching her lips out.

The next morning I stayed in bed, and when Mother came looking for me, I told her I was sick. "Where does it hurt?" she asked. She wore a dark skirt with black high-heeled shoes, hose, and a white blouse with ruffles at her throat. I could see the outline of the heavy cups of her bra and her bra straps through the gauzy material of her blouse. "Is it your stomach? It seems like everybody's sick. Lizzie threw up this morning."

"I feel kind of queasy."

She sat down beside me and put the warm back of her hand on my forehead. "You're not feverish or anything. It could be a stomach bug. Maybe you and Lizzie have the same thing."

She leaned over and kissed my forehead, where the warm weight of her hand had been. She told me to try some chicken noodle soup if I felt better, and she'd call later to see how I was. As she walked away, I could feel the coolness of her lip print on my skin.

After everyone but Lizzie had left for school, I lay in bed and listened to the silence of the house. It felt good beneath the covers, warm, full of the familiar smell of the sheets and the pillow. I heard the tapping of Fritz's claws on the hardwood floors as he came to check on me. He climbed onto my bed and curled up to sleep, his weight pinning me beneath the covers.

Later, I walked into the kitchen in my pajamas to get some cereal. But instead of opening the cupboard and taking out the box of cornflakes, I opened the doors beneath the sink. I had to move bottles and cans of cleanser and bug spray until I found, in the back, the old shoe box. Inside the box was the mason jar with my father's ear in it. I shook the ear in the salt, and it pinged against the glass.

I unscrewed the lid and for a moment, when I opened the jar, I held my breath, as if I expected my father to materialize, like a genie released from his bottle. I breathed in the queer smell. I remembered what my mother had told me about my father.

He had some bad habits.

Some things he could not forget.

I put the jar back and went to the living room to watch soap operas, but I heard Lizzie's radio in her room. She was sitting on her bed in her nightgown. Her eyes were red from crying, and she had a box of Kleenex beside her. On the floor, near the bed, was a plastic bucket, and I could smell the sour odor of vomit. "Are you okay, Lizzie?"

She nodded and blew her nose. "I'm okay. I'm not feeling so good, is all. My stomach's upset."

"Mom said maybe we have the same thing."

Lizzie smiled at me and shook her head, her eyes welling with tears. "I don't think so, Damon. I think what I have is different."

I was thinking about Brian, about slamming his head with the bat. He shouldn't have pushed me. He just pushed me too far. He needed someone to teach him a lesson. "Yeah, probably not."

Lizzie blew her nose again. "Can I tell you a secret, Damon?"

"Shoot."

"You have to promise not to tell anybody."

"Cross my heart and hope to die."

"I'm going to have a baby."

Lizzie waited for my reaction. She was five years older than me and her life seemed mysterious and foreign. She was always talking about men, about who was *cute* and who was *gross*. She had a crush on the guy who played the older brother on *Flipper*. She wrote him fan mail. She bought *Teen Beat* magazine and read about the pop stars. Melody said she was "boy-crazy," but looking back, I think it was more than just men.

"You're going to be an uncle. Don't you like that?"

"I don't know." I frowned. "You can't have a baby. You're not even married."

"I know that, stupid. We've got plenty of time for that."

She explained how she and David, her boyfriend, were going to get married. "I'm sure everybody will love him once they get to know him. I haven't broken the news to Mom yet. And you better not open your big mouth, or I'll kill you. He plans to go to college. His parents said they'll pay for that. So I asked him why don't his parents pay for the honeymoon? And he said it doesn't work that way."

"I guess it's okay, then," I said. "As long as you get married pretty soon."

"Well thanks a lot! Who died and made you God?"

She told me to bug off, that I didn't know anything anyway, so what was the use of talking to me? I watched TV the rest of the morning. I didn't have the guts to tell Lizzie about the accident at school. What was the truth, anyway? That I was a thief? That I bashed Brian in the head because he knew, because he called me a nigger?

About noon Lizzie came out of her bedroom. "You want something to eat, Damie?" She was trying to be nice. She said she was sick of her room and needed to get out and move around.

We placed folding metal TV trays in front of the sofa and ate lunch while we watched soap operas. I ground up saltine crackers and put a thick layer of crumbs in my Campbell's tomato soup. The sofa was warm, with blankets wrapped around both of us. I felt safe. Tomorrow, we would have to face the truth, but for today, we could pretend it didn't exist.

Late in the afternoon my principal, Mr. Bryceland, called and asked to speak with my mother. Lizzie told him Mom wasn't home and wouldn't be back till later. Could she take a message? She could. There'd been a little problem at school with Damon and another student.

"I'll leave the message," Lizzie said. "But Mom won't be home till late. She's working the late shift. It might not be till tomorrow till she gets back to you."

That would be fine. Just as long as she called the first chance she got.

That night, we had cheese enchiladas for dinner, usually one of my favorite foods. When mother gave me a plate she said, "Now Damon, I don't want you taking seconds until everyone has had their first, okay? There should be plenty, but you need to wait your turn."

I kept my eyes on my plate and didn't look at anyone. The telephone rang. I sipped my iced tea while Leland answered.

"Just a minute," he said. He cupped the mouthpiece and made a face at Lizzie. "Guess who."

She smiled and got up from the table. "I'll take it in my bedroom. Hang up when I tell you."

As she disappeared into the hallway, Mother said, "I don't see why you can't tell him you'll call back later."

Leland smiled and held the phone to his ear, clowning for us, listening in. Mother shook her head. "Leland. Now go on and hang up."

Lizzie shouted from her bedroom, "Mom! Tell Leland to get off the phone!"

"Okay, okay," he said. "Just trying to have a little fun."

After Lizzie finished her call, I waited for the phone to ring again, for Mr. Bryceland to call. But he never did. I went to bed before ten o'clock that night, saying I still didn't feel well.

In the middle of the night I heard Mother and Lizzie shouting at each other in the kitchen. I lay there in the darkness, staring up at the crisscrossed metal X's of the bunk bed frame above me. From the squeaking of the bed, from the tossing and turning, I could tell Louis was awake.

Tony sat up and said, "What's going on?"

We heard Mother shout, "Did I teach you to be a tramp?"

"You're the tramp!" yelled Lizzie.

Leland climbed down from the upper bunk bed above Tony and opened a window, then sat there, smoking a cigarette.

"I can't believe how stupid Lizzie is," said Louis.

"Why's she stupid?" asked Tony. He was the only one who didn't know.

"She got herself knocked up."

"What?"

"You heard me."

Tony shook his head, then whistled through his teeth.

Mother and Lizzie continued shouting. I wrapped the pillow around my ears to squeeze out the sound.

The call came in the morning, while Mother was getting dressed. Her eyes were bloodshot and had bags beneath them. As she sat by the phone, speaking in undertones, she lit a cigarette. From the dining room, where I was waiting to eat breakfast, I could hear the snap of her silver Zippo lighter. The sharpness and volume of this sound were often a signal of something. That morning, the snap of the Zippo meant trouble. She was on the phone for over half an hour. Tony, Leland, and Louis ate in a hurry and weren't paying any attention to me. Lizzie and Agnes argued about a dress that Agnes wanted to wear but Lizzie said was hers.

I tried to ignore them and keep eating my oatmeal, but I couldn't keep chewing. My eyes filled with tears and my lips trembled, but I tried to keep pushing spoonfuls of the oatmeal into my mouth.

"I knew it. Damon's in trouble at school." Agnes laughed. "Little smarty pants must be failing one of his classes."

We heard the sound of Mother hanging up the phone. Lizzie rolled her eyes and hurried out of the kitchen, making a glad-it's-not-me face. Agnes gave me a smug look and followed her.

"Damon." It was my mother, standing at the door with a cigarette in her hand. "Hurry up and get dressed. I'm taking you to school." She came over to stand beside me, her smile wrinkled and tired. She rubbed my cheek with the backs of her fingers. "It's going to be okay, baby. But you can't stay home again today. You have to face the music."

Mother's hand was warm on the back of my neck as she

steered me towards the bedroom. Behind me, as I walked away, I heard Louis ask, "What happened to Damie? What's the scoop?"

Mother drove me to school, because we were supposed to meet the principal before classes started. As we left the house, Mother gave directions about what to fix for dinner that night if she came home late. I stared at the ground and avoided the stares of my brothers and sisters. Louis called out, "Good luck!"

Leland said, "I'd tell him to knock 'em dead, but he might take me seriously."

"Leland. That isn't funny," said Mother.

We drove the few miles to the school in silence. As we neared the turn-in, with the yellow school buses pulling out of the driveway, mother glanced at me and spoke for the first time.

"Did you mean to hit that boy?"

"No ma'am. I didn't know he was so close behind me."

She nodded. "They're saying you did it on purpose. That's what he told his mother. She's going to be there too, Damon. Try not to let her scare you."

"It wasn't on purpose. I just took a swing and I felt the bat hit something. That was Brian. He was supposed to be behind me. It was his fault for being so close."

It felt spooky at the school that early, without kids shouting out on the playground or sitting on the front steps. Mother walked in front of me, dressed smartly in a gray skirt, white blouse, and dark cardigan. Her high heels made a crisp sound as she walked through the hallway. The secretaries looked up as we came in. They didn't smile or say hello as they usually did when parents came to visit.

The principal and Brian's mother were in his office. They

quit talking as we entered. He introduced my mother to Brian's, but Mrs. Tunch just nodded and didn't offer to shake hands.

"I'm sorry we have to bring you down here to deal with this, Mrs. Bell. I hope it's all a misunderstanding."

"Thank you."

"It's not any misunderstanding," said Mrs. Tunch. "That boy tried to kill Brian. He's trouble. Brian says everybody knows that, and that he told this boy he knew about him stealing a knife from one of his friends, and that's why he hit him. He was trying to shut him up, to keep him from telling everybody."

"Damon said it was an accident."

Mr. Bryceland asked, "Damon? Did you hit Brian on purpose?"

"No sir. It was an accident. Like I told the coach, I was tossing up balls to practice my swing, and somehow Brian stepped in behind me when I wasn't looking, and I knocked him on the head."

"Bull," said Mrs. Tunch. "That doesn't make sense at all. How did you accidentally hit him if he was behind you? Brian said he had his back turned when he got hit. You must have turned around to do that."

"Damon's never done anything like that before," said Mr. Bryceland.

"I was looking at where the balls were going. Is he going to be okay? I didn't mean to hurt him."

"Liar," said Mrs. Tunch. She asked what I'd done with that knife. Did I have it on me? The school wasn't safe with me in it. "How do we know he won't stab someone?"

Mother defended me, and when she and Mrs. Tunch started arguing fiercely, Mr. Bryceland waved his hands for both of them to stop. He asked me and Mother to step out of the office for a moment and wait in the lobby. We sat outside the secretaries' area, Mother smoking a cigarette, dropping her ashes on the tile floor. She patted my knee, and the secretaries gave us dirty looks.

Mrs. Tunch left Mr. Bryceland's office and ignored us as she walked by. The principal waved for us to come in, and once we were alone, he explained that it looked as though Brian was going to be okay, thank God. He had a bruise on his forehead and his ears were still ringing, but the doctor thought he would have no complications from the injury, just a mild concussion. But we probably hadn't heard the last of Mrs. Tunch. She was threatening to sue us and the school district, and wanted me to be expelled for the year, although Mr. Bryceland believed I was telling the truth. It was simply an accident, he said. No use complicating matters. I would not be punished. It was probably best forgotten. But in the meantime he was going to assign me to another sixth-grade teacher; he put me in Mrs. Moore's class.

Mother kissed me before she left for work. "Don't you worry about anything that woman said, Damon." She smiled and straightened my hair. "She's a pig. And you know what pigs do, don't you?"

I shook my head.

"They go oink-oink."

17
The Lies About Love

On Saturday morning the house was empty and quiet. Sonia and I were the only ones home, watching cartoons on TV. Mother woke up late, then came in and sat down on the sofa, yawning. Her hair was pushed out of shape and the skin beneath her eyes was puffy from sleep. She wore an old pink nightgown with a robe over it. I went to the kitchen to get her cigarettes, and she walked up behind me, smiling sleepily, and opened the pantry. "How would you like to be a good boy and help me make pancakes this morning? Doesn't that sound good? Pancakes with bacon, syrup, and scrambled eggs for everyone? You think we have enough of everything or do we need to go to the store first?"

"I don't know, Mom. Everybody's gone except for us."

"Gone?" She was shocked that it was eleven o'clock already. Where did the time go? "Well, why don't we plan a big dinner for everybody."

"But, Mom. I was going over to Kit's."

"Mom nothing. You're going to stay home and help me out here. I never get to see you anymore, sweetie."

She put her arms around me and hugged, squeezing my neck so tightly that she almost choked me. I felt her heavy body, stared at her freckled arms, and smelled her strong morning breath. I was stiff and awkward in her arms. I thought I was too old to be this close to my mother. I thought I was too old to be touched anymore.

"What's wrong with this family?" she asked me. "It's like everything's changed all the sudden." She released her hold of me and stepped into the kitchen. Her smile was gone, and she made a racket as she pulled a saucepan out of the kitchen cabinets, filled it full of water, then put it on the stove to boil. "I wake up late one morning and everybody's gone. Couldn't they just wait to see if I wanted to see them for something? Is that too much to ask?"

"Well you come home late all the time now, Mom. We never know when you're going to be around."

"So it's my fault now, is it? Well thank you very much. I go out now and then to see some friends of mine, and suddenly I'm deserting you. What about my life? What about me?"

When I started to answer, Mother told me to forget it, do whatever you want. "Go on, go to Kit's. See if I care."

I went back to watching cartoons with Sonia, and not

long afterwards Mother told us to get cleaned up because we were going to the supermarket with her. She stayed in her room for a long time, and when she came out, her hair was brushed and she had darkened her eyes with mascara and eyeliner. On her lips was a glossy stripe of red. She smelled of a heavy, sweet perfume, even though she wore slacks and a cardigan. In the Piggly Wiggly, she had me push the shopping cart down the aisles. "We're going to have a special dinner tonight," she said, putting five-pound bags of sugar and flour in the cart. "We're going to start putting this family back together again."

Sonia said, "Everything's going to be okay, Mama. Don't you worry."

"I know. I just need to start counting my chickens. I need to rally the troops. Circle the wagons."

"I'll help cook," said Sonia. "I'm a good cook. I've been learning a lot lately."

We filled the shopping basket with Honey-made graham crackers, Kraft macaroni and cheese, Nabisco vanilla wafers, instant banana and chocolate pudding, cans of Del Monte fruit cocktail, Campbell's soup—bean with bacon, cream of mushroom, tomato, chicken noodle. We stocked up on Nabisco saltines, Ritz crackers, oatmeal cookies, ginger snaps, chocolate chips, Oreos. We bought two gallons of milk, sticks of margarine, tubs of sour cream, cheddar cheese, apple juice, Tang, jugs of cola and root beer. We got a twenty-five-pound sack of dog food and a box of dog biscuits, hamburger meat, a pot roast, whole chickens, three dozen eggs, pancake mix, syrup, boxes of frozen waffles. We bought so much food it was hard for me to push the cart straight, and it took the checker a long time to ring up everything. The checker was a friendly fat woman with wobbly arms. "You sure have a lot of food here," she said.

"I have a lot of mouths to feed," said Mother. She smiled as she flipped through a magazine.

"We've got a huge family," said Sonia.

Mother even let us buy a candy bar to eat on the drive home. I chose a Hershey's chocolate bar with almonds. I unwrapped it in the car, as Simon and Garfunkel played on the radio.

The paper of the Hershey's wrapper was crisp, black with silver letters, and I split the seam down the back with my thumb instead of ripping it. The inner wrapper was white and waxy, like a present, a gift, folded on the ends, tucked into the outer wrapper. It was the white color of birthday wrapping paper or wedding invitations, and smelled of the chocolate bar inside. I unfolded the white wrapper on one end and broke off a piece of the bar, with a good chunk of almond in it, and let that melt on my tongue, against the roof of my mouth. The name HERSHEY'S was stamped into the chocolate in beautiful capital letters, as if the Hershey family cared about your happiness.

After we got back Lizzie called from her boyfriend's house and Mother told her to get home as soon as possible, that she had to help fix supper. Agnes would have to give a hand as well. Sonia and I, the two youngest, hung around the kitchen and did what we could. Lizzie came home and beat the eggs and poured in milk to make batter for the fried chicken. Mother cut up the fryers, putting the wax paper bags of liver, kidneys, and heart in the sink, seasoning the chicken before putting it in the batter. After dunking it in the batter she dropped it in a paper sack full of flour. Sonia shook it to bread the chicken. Lizzie and Mother weren't speaking to each other. Sonia said softly, "Think we need more eggs in this, Mama?"

"That'd be a good idea."

At first the bowls of batter and wooden cutting board were clean and neat, but soon the whole kitchen was a mess. On the stove, a black cast-iron skillet full of Crisco sizzled and crackled each time Mother put the white breaded pieces inside. Mother rubbed her arm where the splatters of popping grease burned her. After each piece of the chicken was fried on both sides, she picked them up, held them above the skillet for a moment to drip off the oil, then set the fried chicken on a plate covered with two squares of paper towels. Lizzie put another towel over the plate, when it was full, to keep the flies off.

When everything was done, Lizzie and Sonia set the table, while Agnes made a pitcher of iced tea.

Before dinner, Mother took off her apron and changed into a pretty yellow dress. We were sitting there quietly by the time she came back. No one spoke, and Lizzie slapped Tony's hand when he tried to snatch a drumstick.

Mother sat down and looked around at all of us. "My family," she said.

We bowed our heads as she said grace. I stared down at the loops in the white brocade tablecloth as I listened to her soft voice asking God for his help, for his blessing, thanking him for this food. Then it was over, and we relaxed. Louis passed the bowl of mashed potatoes. Agnes put a piece of corn on the cob on her plate. We ate.

Tony kept pushing his long bangs out of his face with the back of his hand, the hand that held his fork, and Mother told him to stop that. It wasn't hygienic. Louis and Leland were talking about the moon launch coming up in the summer, and how they were supposed to land this time. Wouldn't that be neat?

Lizzie said, "This is nice, isn't it? We never have dinner all together like this anymore. I miss it." She said that we should make a rule that we'd have a sit-down dinner every night from now on, like we used to. "We can take turns cooking. I need to learn how to cook, now that I'm going to be a mother."

Mother paused in her eating, then put her silverware down and closed her eyes. Everyone stared at Lizzie.

"What? What'd I say wrong?" No one answered her. "It's the truth!"

Mother took her hands from her face and her eyes were filled with tears. Sonia touched her forearm, but she was looking only at Lizzie.

"I've never told you what happened to my mother, have I?" she asked Lizzie. Lizzie shook her head.

"I never wanted to, because I figured it would only hurt you. But maybe I should have. There's no use hiding the truth. It comes out, no matter what you do. I guess that was my mistake. Trying to shelter you." She stopped speaking and we waited for her to continue, breathless, silent.

Sonia asked, "What happened to her, Mama?"

"My mother . . ." she began, and, breathing in, her voice shuddered. "My mother never married my father." She bit her lip, closed her eyes, tears welling through her matted eyelashes. "She was humiliated. And heartbroken."

"But wasn't she happy that she had you? Didn't she love you?"

Mother shook her head. "She was ashamed of me. She was ashamed of who I was, of what I was." Her voice quavered. "Sometimes I wish I'd never been born."

"Don't say that, Mama."

"It's the truth." She looked around at all of us. "I'm sick of lies, but that's our life. We can't tell the truth or people will hate us, hate us for nothing, hate us for being who we are."

"Maybe not everybody. Maybe the people who hate us aren't important anyway."

Mother shook her head. "I think my mother hated me, just a little bit. And she was ashamed of me for the rest of her life. She was lucky, though. She died young."

Lizzie said, "That's not going to happen to me, Mama."

"How do you know?"

"Because we're in love!"

My mother said, "Love? What do you know about that? Believe me, Lizzie, you don't have the foggiest."

"Yes I do."

"What do you know about pain and heartache and loneliness? That's what love is, Lizzie. Not you and your stupid boyfriend in the backseat of a car."

"You just wait." She took us all in. "You just wait and see! I'm going to be happier than any of you could ever imagine!" She pushed back her chair and ran out of the dining room.

The rest of us sat there, wanting the world to be different, wanting our lives to be different, to be easier and carefree. We wanted our house to be new and modern, our clothes to be clean and crisp, our cars to start when they were supposed to and never break down. We wanted to put photos of all our family on the mantel, we wanted not to have to change the subject whenever our grandfather was mentioned, not to invent stories that none of us believed anymore. And what bothered us about Lizzie's baby more than anything was seeing it happen before our eyes, seeing the deceptions beginning, seeing ourselves laying the traps we would later fall into knowingly. Perhaps Lizzie was fooling herself when she said she and her boyfriend would get married, but none of us believed her. Leland and Louis knew David, and they'd heard his parents didn't want him to get married so young. They wanted him to go to college, and Lizzie's baby would only get in the way of that.

Sitting there at the dinner table, slowly chewing our dinner of fried chicken and mashed potatoes, food that our mother struggled to earn enough money to put on the table, we realized it would be one more thing we would have to lie about.

As I was trying to fall asleep that night, I gazed out the window beside my bed. In the side of our yard was a large silver-painted butane tank. It was the size and shape of a mini-submarine, and sat atop a cement base. It had a turret on top, where the gas man hooked up a nozzle to fill it from the huge truck. The butane tank was hollow and metal, so that if you tapped it with something like a rock or a hammer, it would resound with a sharp ping. Sometimes we sat on the tank, straddling it like a horse, but it would go nowhere. Fritz slept in its shadow. We rarely tapped it with a hammer, because we feared it would explode. Our neighbors also had butane tanks, and with the frequent talk about the chain-reaction theories of nuclear war—say, if one were launched at New York, it would cause us to launch one at Moscow, that there would be no other way, and so on—I came to be obsessed with the possible chain reactions of a butane tank explosion. If the Westmorelands' tank exploded, it would set off the O'Haras' and the Firpos' and finally ours. I pictured the entire neighborhood engulfed in towering spouts of orange flames from the infernos of raging butane tanks.

Once one of the tanks exploded, there would be no stopping the others from joining in.

18
Broken Windows

The concussion I had given Brian Tunch was minor. He was thick-headed and hard to damage. I later learned that Brian told everyone I had stolen Russell's knife and had stolen other kids' things from the cloakroom, which wasn't true. He seemed scared of me after that blow to the head. It had taken some of the fire out of his walk. And his mother never bothered with the suit. She must have figured you can't get blood from a stone. But I was branded a thief. Ruining my reputation was Brian's revenge on me, and it worked. Twice that year I was accused of stealing other kids' lunch money, even though I had had nothing to do with it.

Sometimes I felt guilty about bashing Brian's head. Sometimes I was disappointed that I hadn't done more—that the injury had left no permanent scars, or at least made him an idiot. He'd gotten what he deserved. He'd know not to make fun of people anymore. I'd taught him a lesson. If I'd had a spear, maybe I could have chucked it right through his shoulder blades. And I could still see him writhing around in the red sand of the batter's box, his feet kicking against home plate.

Most of my friends quit talking to me. Sometimes I saw Russell Jensen's flock of homing pigeons flying over my house. It seemed as if they wanted me to come out to play. Or did they fly over to remind me of the stolen knife, now rusting in a hole in our backyard? Their wings were gray and heavy-beating, beautiful, but the pigeons never stopped to roost. By this time, I was starting to get faster, taller, and stronger than average. I had even become good at bat. Every time I swung I pictured the ball as Brian's head. Hardly any team captains would choose me at first, just after the accident, but by the end of the school year, when I was hitting homers consistently, everyone was eager to use me. But even if I was on their team, some of them acted afraid.

No one used the words "spear chucker" or "jungle bunny" around me anymore.

Kit stopped me when I was getting off the bus one day. "Way to go," he said, giving me a thumb's-up sign. "Tunch deserved it." We started hanging out together again. Since Kit's mother had divorced his father and remarried, he had become quiet. He didn't laugh and joke around as much as he used to.

In the early summer, Kit's stepfather got a job at a vending machine company, as a delivery man. He drove a large white van, big enough to walk inside, stocked with cardboard boxes of chewing gum, potato chips, cinnamon candies, chewy red cherries—every kind of candy you can imagine. "I know exactly how much of everything I have in that truck," he told Kit, while I was there one day throwing the football in his backyard. "If I ever see that even one box is missing, you'll be in big trouble."

"Who wants your stupid candy anyway," said Kit, tossing a pass. "It's all a bunch of junk."

The van had a lock on the back door and a wire gate behind the cab, which had another key lock you had to unlock to get to the candy, even if you were sitting in the cab. Kit made a copy of the key to his stepfather's truck, and one Saturday morning, while he was asleep, we snuck inside, snagged as many bags of snacks as we could in a few minutes, and took off on our bicycles.

During the summer of 1969 it seemed as if there was nothing to do but watch soap operas on television or wander through the fields and woods around our deserted neighborhood. If we rode our bicycles a couple of miles we could reach the edge of civilization, where the newest subdivisions were being built. The newest subdivision, Shenandoah, had Revolutionary War names for all the streets: Concord Lane, Patrick Henry Road, Valley Forge Avenue.

The asphalt of these new, deserted subdivisions was fresh and soft, as black as lava. They reminded me of the story of Pompeii. Only this eruption was spreading a cloud of pavement, chain-link fences, and fire hydrants across the country, across fields of oaks and junipers, fields of meteors and cactus. Every month the housing subdivisions seemed to grow closer, devouring fields and meadows and woods and old farms in their way. Shenandoah had been built on the land owned by the Gables, who had sold out and moved. They had run the dairy farm there, and besides the milk cows, they had grazed horses in their fields: palominos and Appaloosas.

We were angry that these horses were gone, and as we

passed through the subdivision, we picked up rocks and pieces of brick and lobbed them through the new windows of the houses. We liked the sound of breaking glass. I felt kind of guilty about it, but Kit seemed to love breaking the windows. No one had moved into this part of the neighborhood yet. The streets were empty. We had to keep our eye out for salesmen showing the houses. While we were throwing rocks at the windows, no cars passed. "For sale" signs stood in the black earth plots of the front yards. Straight white sidewalks paralleled the blacktop. There weren't any trees in the yards.

"Look at that one," said Kit, pointing to the front window of a Colonial-style house. He had thrown a rock through it the week before, and now it had a large X of masking tape across the new pane of glass.

"They work fast, don't they?"

There was a pile of two-by-fours, white PVC pipe, and trash in the front yard. Kit squatted down on his haunches and poked through the mound. "You know, there's some really good stuff here." He carefully selected a brick. "Cover me," he said.

I stood watch on the sidewalk as he walked nonchalantly across the muddy yard. When he was halfway across, he stopped and looked back at me. "Jesus," he said, lifting one foot, showing me the thick coat of mud on the bottom of his sneakers. Slogging the last few feet to the window, Kit looked at his reflection for a moment, then bashed in the window with his brick. Triangles of glass tinkled onto the windowsill.

Kit smiled and dusted off his hands as he walked back to me. "That was loud, wasn't it?"

I laughed and shook my head. I pointed to an intact window right next to the jagged hole. "You missed one."

Kit shrugged. "Nobody's perfect."

We cut across the fields of sunflowers and cactus, and down the railroad tracks to the castle. This was an abandoned country club around three miles from our neighborhood. It was a four-story building of limestone rock, with two swimming pools, a fish pond, a huge cactus garden, and an old wide driveway. The size of a large hotel, it had forty-four rooms, a restaurant and bar, and was surrounded by a golf course; since the castle had been abandoned, the grass on the golf course was overgrown. The fields were full of bluebonnets. A golf cart still sat on one of the old greens, its canvas awning now tattered and faded from the sun and wind. Someone had stolen the batteries that powered it, and the grass had grown up high around the rusted wheels. "Look at this stupid thing," said Kit. He took a rock and smashed in the small headlights. The sound of breaking glass seemed odd in that field. "Why'd they just leave it here?" He looked at the cart as if it were a personal insult to him.

We hiked the rest of the way to the castle. Weeds grew everywhere. Islands of weeds grew in the gray pebbles of the asphalt driveway, and lines of weeds grew along the curbs. Kit pushed the faded lawn furniture into the bottom of the empty swimming pool. The aluminum frames clattered on the white concrete bottom. There was a pool of stagnant water near the drain, and on the curving sides of the pool, frogs were trying to hop out. Teenagers had tossed brown beer bottles in the grass by the driveway, and Kit threw those against the sides of the pool to watch them shatter.

Kit liked to smash things. He liked to break things. And he liked to steal.

He taught me how to be a better thief. He taught me not to steal from your friends, for one thing, but steal from businesses—convenience stores, department stores, Walgreen's—because they had lots of money, and no one would ever miss what you took. Besides, they charged too much for that crap anyway, didn't they? He taught me how to steal Nehi Reds from Stop-n-Gos by buying a candy bar or a Hostess cupcake, then waiting till there was a line of customers at the counter, and walking out with the cupcake in one hand, the sixteen-ounce Nehi Red in the other. He taught me how to steal bags of peanut M&M's by slipping them into the sleeves of our hooded pullover sweatshirts, how to scope out the surveillance camera angles or surveillance mirrors and have one person stand as a blocker while the other made the move to take the goods off the shelf quickly. We were random and hedonistic about our thefts. Once we stole a watermelon off the back of a fruit truck parked at a gas station on Vance Jackson, then escaped into the vacant lot behind the station. We hid in a circle of oak trees, bashed the watermelon open on a rock, and scooped out the wet red fruit with our hands.

Now and then someone—a clerk usually, who was too busy to chase us—would nab us taking something, but our biggest mistake was becoming dime-store junkies, hooked on sniffing glue and paint.

It was Kit's idea. I was over at his house, with his mother away working at the hospital and his stepfather delivering candy and potato chips somewhere in San Gabriel. We were putting together a plastic model replica of *Star Trek*'s USS *Enterprise*, when Kit started sniffing the airplane glue. He squeezed a glob of it into a plastic bag, as a cousin of his had told him to do, then put the bag over his face and inhaled deeply, over and over again, until he dropped the bag and fell back against his bed.

"Oh, Jesus." He laughed and put his hands on the side of his bed as if he had to hold on to keep from falling. "That's something else. Try it, Damon. It's cool."

I fitted the top of the clear plastic produce bag over my mouth and nose, then breathed deeply. It was a sweet, almost delicious chemical taste that filled my lungs. I'd always liked the smell of airplane glue. After a few deep breaths my head suddenly felt light. I became dizzy, and got that queer disassociated feeling I'd get before a baseball game, when fear of getting beaned by a fastball or the taunts of the opposing team would make me feel as if I'd stepped outside myself.

The sensation lasted only a moment, but was weirdly enjoyable. We were high and we liked it. Kit took the bag back from me and inhaled some more. When the smell got fainter, we squeezed in more glue.

After that, we started sniffing glue whenever we got the chance, whenever we felt like it. But they'd taken the airplane glue off the shelves at Walgreen's because of the sniffing craze, and you had to beg the clerk to sell some to you, or bring in your parents. So we started stealing cans of spray paint, which smelled different but had a similar effect. This was the riskiest crime we committed. The Walgreen's was a large, crowded store with lots of clerks and their own security people, along with mirrors and cameras. It was harder to know where to look and in which direction to watch, how to set up your blocker.

One night we were at the Walgreen's at Wonderland Mall. Kit grabbed a can of spray paint, stuffed it under his jacket, and started walking quickly toward the exit. There were scads of people in the store, and a clerk had been just one row away, talking to someone in the school supplies. I followed Kit, but he was already thirty yards away, outside the store, sprinting down the sidewalk, by the time I stepped out. It was nighttime then, and the parking lot of the mall was shining and bright. I ran after him. We didn't stop until we'd reached the back of the mall, where the loading docks and the delivery doors were. Kit turned around and waved the can in the air, as he skipped backwards. "Yahoo! They never saw a thing!"

His mother was supposed to pick us up in an hour in front of the mall, so we sniffed the paint back there by the delivery entrances, hiding behind a dumpster full of cardboard boxes. It was a can of Ferrari red. We squatted against the concrete wall, and Kit smiled as he shook it up, making the pinging sound as the ball bearing careened inside the can. "Now we're gonna have some *fun.*" He'd brought some small plastic bags, and he sprayed the paint inside one, breathed from it, then, waving his hands as if he'd had enough, handed it to me.

The paint seemed stronger than the glue we usually sniffed. I was high and goofy, leaning against the loading dock, dimly aware that I felt something wet on my face after I'd taken the bag for the third time. Kit had sprayed some fresh paint inside. I didn't realize what I was seeing for a moment when a white local squad car pulled up beside the dumpster, about twenty feet away from us.

We stared at the car and sat there, both of us with spots and smears of the red spray paint on our cheeks and fingers. The policeman got out of the car and shone his flashlight on us.

"Well look what we got here. A couple of juvenile delinquents." He walked over and picked up the can of paint. "You two have a receipt for this paint?"

Kit stood up and made a big show of looking in his pockets

for the receipt. "I had it here someplace, but I can't find it. Maybe I threw it away. You got it, Damon?"

I shook my head and put my hands in my pockets, looking for the nonexistent receipt.

The officer shook the can in the air, pinging. "Manager at the Walgreen's said some kids stole some paint and went behind the store." He picked up the plastic baggie delicately, with two fingers, as if he didn't want to damage the evidence, and walked to his car, put that and the can of paint in the front seat, then unlocked the back door. "Get in. Looks like I've apprehended the suspects."

He sounded as if he were joking, but I had to struggle to keep from crying. We got in the car.

"Sure you can't just let us go, officer?" asked Kit. He was speaking to the policeman through the metal grate that divided the backseat from the front. "We'll promise to never do it again."

"No chance." The police radio was crackling with voices and hiss.

Kit rolled his eyes. "We're in for it now."

Our mothers came to get us from the police station. The officers joked about the young criminals, how we were starting our life of crime a little early, don't you think? I cried, and Kit told them to leave us alone. They didn't file any charges or make any records of it. One of them told us sniffing paint would stunt our growth and ruin our brains. My mother was disgusted with me as she drove home.

"First the trouble at school, and now this. When's it going to stop, Damon?"

"I'm sorry, Mama. I'll never do it again."

"Sorry isn't good enough. You better learn your lesson, mister. You keep this up and you'll be in big trouble. My

God. The police station. What? You want to go to reform school? Is that what you want?"

"No ma'am."

"Well then, you better straighten up and fly right. 'Cause that's where you're headed."

If this keeps up we're all going to hell in a handbasket, she said.

19
The Invisible Woman

By July the ground had become as cracked as the floor of Death Valley, and our driveway seethed with red ant mounds. We poured gasoline down the holes and set fire to the colonies, but it never seemed to work. We also made torches out of old mop heads soaked in motor oil and burned the wasp nests under the carport and in the junipers. It never rained. We kept our yard green with sprinklers, but the grass in the fields became brown and sharp, and in vacant lots the scratchy sunflower plants grew higher than our heads. It was Kit's habit to walk through the empty fields lighting matches and tossing them out randomly when the boredom of August set in, and I followed along behind him, stamping out the flames, saying, "C'mon, man, cut it out."

At night, we watched horror movies full of werewolves,

vampires, or animals deformed by nuclear radiation. In one of my recurrent nightmares a werewolf chased my family through our house, and since I was in the rear—the slowest, the youngest—his ragged claws would always be grabbing my throat as I awoke. When everyone else slept, any chance object like a shirt thrown over the back of a chair or a catcher's mitt on a desk became something sinister and frightening.

One night, when I couldn't sleep, I crept down the hallway barefoot, in my pajamas, past my mother's closed bedroom door. She slept soundly, and even wore a black sleeping mask to block out any light that came through the window. Besides, with school being out, staying up late wasn't much of a sin. As I lay down on the throw rug in the living room, Hercules lifted his head and watched. His long black tail thumped the floor, muffled by the rug, as he wagged it happily for being scratched. Then we heard the lisping sound of slippers. Hercules perked up his ears and turned toward the dining room, letting out a deep woof. I grabbed his muzzle, pinching his black lips together, but his tail kept wagging, thumping against the floor.

"Damon." A whisper. "Damon. What are you doing there?"

I sat up and smiled at Lizzie. "I couldn't sleep."

I turned on the TV, and Lizzie sat in the chair closest to it. She was five months pregnant by this time. She had become quieter and less defiant in the last few months. There was no longer any talk of her getting married to her boyfriend. David had gone away for the summer to work at Glacier National Park. In the fall, he was supposed to start college at UCLA. His parents didn't want him to get married.

Hercules got up and tried to nuzzle his nose between Lizzie's legs, but she pushed him away. I patted the rug beside me and got him to lie back down, then scratched his belly. His leg jerked spasmodically as he scratched the air.

"You better watch out, Damie. You lie down with dogs, you get up with fleas." She squeezed into the seat sideways and wrapped her arms around her knees. "Believe me. I know."

Lizzie's figure had filled out, but she still didn't have a huge belly. Her face seemed wider and more womanly. But sitting sideways in the chair, with the TV light reflected on her face, she didn't look to be pregnant. We watched TV in silence for a while, then she said, "Damon? Why don't you ever talk to me? Nobody around here seems to ever have anything to say to me."

"I'm watching TV. What do you want me to say?"

"It's like I've become the invisible woman. Mom acts like she hates my guts."

"No she doesn't. I don't even think she's mad at you anymore."

"That's what you think. She treats me like a leper. She doesn't want to come near me."

"Well, what do you expect?"

"Mom's not the only one, either. You know what happened yesterday? I called David's house and tried to get the phone number of the place where he's working. He told me he was going to write, but he never has. The jerk."

"Maybe he just hasn't gotten around to it yet."

"He's been gone almost a month."

"Well, I don't know. You know him better than I do."

"Unfortunately." She shook her head. "I can't believe I was so stupid. I could kick myself."

"You just made a mistake."

"I'll say. So anyway. I called and asked Mrs. Kiley for David's address. You know what she told me? She said, 'I don't want you calling this house anymore. David doesn't want to have anything to do with you.' You know what she had the nerve to tell me? 'He's not the father of that nigger baby. If you don't stop calling this house we'll call the police and have you arrested for harassment.' She said, 'I know people in the police department.' "

"You shouldn't even be talking to people like that."

"I told her you just try it. You just try it, bitch, and see what happens." Lizzie leaned back and smiled. "'Course, I didn't add the *bitch* part, even though I was thinking it. I have to be careful, you know. She might become my mother-in-law."

Fat chance, I thought, but didn't say it.

"What am I going to do, Damon? I'm going to have this baby and David doesn't want to have anything to do with it. I'm going to have a baby. And I'm going to be all alone."

"You'll be okay. You can live with us."

"But I don't want to live at home."

Lizzie said that maybe she'd get a part-time job after she had the baby. But how would she have time for that? She didn't know what to do. I stared at the TV, watching a band of Indians chasing a wagon train through the desert. I had no idea of what to say to Lizzie. I didn't really even understand why she was having the baby, what that meant. But I remember feeling the growing bitterness and resentment towards other people that has continued throughout my life when Lizzie told me what Mrs. Kiley said about her baby. Why did she have to say that? What had Lizzie ever done to deserve it? And why did she call it a nigger baby? I was sick of people calling us niggers. They acted like once they had learned this secret, they had some kind of power over us, and could treat us however they wanted to. I've come to realize that we made the mistake of hiding our grandfather's identity and played their game of hatred by their rules. We acted ashamed of him, and by doing that we *were* ashamed, and had to struggle against this shame throughout our life.

During the rest of the summer Lizzie continued to grow heavier, and quieter. The family became used to the idea of her having a baby, and I remember the sound of her laughing at the dinner table one particular evening, at a joke Louis had made, and the two of them talking and smiling as if, for that moment at least, there was no tragedy on her horizon. Apparently there was never any talk or even consideration of an abortion. When she was in the last months of her pregnancy we were embarrassed each Sunday when we attended mass at St. Gregory's.

When it came time for Lizzie to have the baby, we didn't even know how we were going to afford the hospital stay. Mother worried about this. Many nights I would creep into the living room to fall asleep, only to find Mother there, wide awake, smoking and thinking. Sometimes she sat in the dark, and the only way I would know she was in the room was from the smell of burning tobacco, the glow of her cigarette tip, or the snap and click of her Zippo lighter. During mass, I watched as she closed her eyes more passionately than ever, her lips moving in urgent prayer. And it worked. In September, the priests told my mother they would help, and offered to protect and care for Lizzie at a Catholic hospital in New Orleans, free of charge. She left in the fall. By then, Leland had started college at New Mexico State, and all the others were talking about leaving home. It scared me. I didn't want to be the last to go.

20
The Comet

Louis kept insisting he was going to get a place of his own, since he was two years out of high school by then, but autumn came, then winter, and he was still sleeping above me in his top bunk. This wouldn't last forever, although sometimes I wish it had. In January of 1970, I woke at three o'clock in the morning with him standing over me, holding my foot in his hand, shaking it in the air. "I'm Khrushchev," he said, "storming out of the UN."

I squinted and blinked, the hallway light shining in my eyes. "Ich bin ein Berliner," I answered on cue.

Louis dropped my foot, and as I dressed quietly to keep from waking Tony, who didn't have to get up, Louis brushed his teeth with the fat electric toothbrush he'd gotten for Christmas that year. I heard it buzzing faintly through the bathroom door.

We pulled on our heavy coats and walked outside to the backyard, where the gravel driveway crunched loudly beneath our feet. The sky was winter black and cloudless.

We climbed into our '67 Volkswagen Beetle, which smelled of vinyl, as our Volkswagen—or "folkwagon," as Louis called it—always did. "It means 'people car,' auf Deutsch." Louis had started school at San Gabriel College in the fall, studying German and chemistry. And the Beatles had broken up, so the airwaves were full of "Let It Be."

In the darkness before dawn we drove to deliver the *San Gabriel Express-News* to the wealthy suburb of Oak Hills. While driving past the fields of oaks and junipers and prickly pear cactus, we counted the animals we pinned in our headlights.

For a while I kept a spiral notebook, with entries for the totals and types of animals we had spotted that morning: two deer, one skunk, dead possum; alongside totals for the months, which would seem impressive: twenty-six deer, twelve skunks, nine raccoons, eleven possums, sixty-seven rabbits. We saw cottontails, whitetails, ringtails, two different types of skunks, raccoons, and once, a red fox.

But that morning in early January was the first time we saw the Kosaka Comet, short for Comet Tago-Sato-Kosaka, discovered by three amateur Japanese astronomers in October 1969. For more than a week in the first month of the 1970s it shone in the Southwestern skies. It was huge and brilliant, and arced across the sky with a beautiful shimmering tail of ice, in a halo of hydrogen, seemingly frozen in place, although every night we could tell it had moved. We knew it was an enormous object in space, hurtling through the galaxy, and that what we saw of it was just a puny and distant reflection of light. Although there was a piece in the paper about it, the Kosaka Comet seemed largely unheralded. It rose in the middle of the night and few people seemed to pay it any mind. But since we woke at three o'clock every morning to deliver the news, for over a week it stretched magnificently over our heads.

Louis and I didn't tell the others about it. At first it started out as a lark, not telling anyone, but then, as the days went by and we saw it moving across the sky, it developed into something significant and oddly special, until we would have been heartbroken if anyone else in our family had seen it.

And the Kosaka Comet was only one of the many things that Louis and I shared with no one else. Rising at three o'clock every morning created a bond that linked us in ways none of my other brothers and sisters could have realized. We shared the eerie quiet of the predawn highways; we shared the animals in our headlights; we shared the arcane equipment of the paper route, the strange routine we kept.

We could mention to the others, after a bad day, that the newspapers had been late and that screwed up the whole morning, but they wouldn't realize what that meant. These bundles of newspapers were absolutely crucial for our job, since they were the raw material, the basic product. They came bound in baling wire. And they were supposed to be thrown off the delivery trucks promptly at four o'clock every morning. When they were late, because of production problems or the slowness of the delivery trucks, the early-morning air of the darkened Mobil station that served as the drop site filled with tension. We knew we would have to hurry to get our routes done before dawn. And we delivered so many papers every morning, over five hundred, that we seldom had any time to spare.

We would wait in the Volkswagen, facing the red Pegasus

that was the station's emblem, listening to the AM radio and nervously clicking the wire cutters we used to cut the baling wire that tied the bundles. These were an essential piece of equipment. If we showed up at the paper drop without the wire cutters, we would be unable to break the bundles and would have to borrow a cutter from someone else, which meant another crucial delay.

It seemed as if we were always in a race with time. We woke at three o'clock and had to get dressed immediately, use the bathroom, brush our teeth, and leave the house. On cold mornings like this one, Louis would let the VW warm up for a couple minutes, but that was the most he ever waited. We were always still about half asleep as we drove into the city. Sometimes Louis would be so tired he'd be falling asleep at the wheel, swerving and running off into the grass, and when this happened, he told me to keep talking to him to keep him awake.

Louis had removed the front passenger seat of the VW to make room for the mounds of rolled newspapers, and I sat behind him with a stack of loose newspapers in my lap, a cone of white string by my side. To tie the newspapers I rolled them into a tube, wrapped three quick loops of string around one end, then smoothed the string into the middle of the paper, which made the loops tangle in a knot and hold—theoretically. Louis drove with his right hand and threw the papers out the window with his left.

Sometimes the string wouldn't hold, and the newspaper would burst like a shotgunned bird in flight, with the sports, classified, national, and metropolitan sections fluttering to the ground separately. Louis cussed and slammed on the brakes if this happened, because he had to return to the yard and stack the sections neatly on the person's front porch. If too many exploded, Louis cussed me out, shouting and flinging newspapers back at me, making me dodge. If I didn't react fast enough, he'd connect on a direct hit to my head, striking my forehead or ear with the hard rolled-up newspaper.

Sundays were the worst. These papers were much bigger than the dailies, because of the Sunday inserts, magazines, extras, and funnies. The huge papers were too big to roll very tightly, too big for my hands, and we often had a high percentage of exploders. For the first few months of my time working on the paper route with Louis, before I mastered the art of rolling Sunday newspapers—or before my hands grew big enough to fit around them easily—I dreaded Sunday mornings. It wasn't unusual for me to throw up from fear and nausea as we swerved back and forth, back and forth, through neighborhoods that had been built only a few years before, on land that had been woods and fields of cactus, where cattle or dairy cows used to graze, through housing subdivisions with names like Whispering Oaks and Forest Glen. When I felt the looseness of the papers and knew they would explode in midair, I broke out in a sweat. "You need to pull over?" Louis would ask, angry, because it would mean that I was getting carsick again and he didn't want me vomiting in the VW. But if we pulled over for me to be sick, we lost time, and if the papers were late, on a Sunday when many of them were exploding, it became crucial that I not get sick and make him pull over. And the swinging, swerving motion of the car moving from one side of the street to the other to throw the papers from the closest position to the yards made me nauseated. If it was raining, we put the newspapers in clear plastic bags, which were neater to use than the string, but slower.

On a good day, on a dry day, when few of the papers exploded, Louis treated me to a soft drink at a local Texaco station on the way home. Gas was twenty-nine cents a gallon. The keys for the rest rooms were on wooden plaques that said Setters (female) and Pointers (male). I drank a green bottle of Sprite, my face and hands smudged black and blue with newspaper ink.

During the school year, after I finished the paper route I would wash up, change clothes, and catch the bus, only to fall asleep in class after lunch. In summertime, I often wandered around the fields of our old neighborhood, fields full of the rusty red lumps of meteors that looked like rifle shot from outer space. With the meteors in the fields and the comet in the sky, for a time it seemed as if the entire universe were in flux. And it seemed to me, for a time, that my family was an integral part of this flux.

One morning, as we were rolling the newspapers at the Mobil station, with the freeways blazing with light and empty of cars, I told Louis the truth about Brian Tunch. How he had called me names. How he wouldn't let up. How he went too far.

"I couldn't take it anymore," I said. "He had it coming."

"So you bashed him with that bat on purpose?"

"Uh huh."

Louis whistled. He had always told me if someone bigger than you is picking on you, don't be afraid to pick up a bat and use it. He had taught me to box. To stand up for myself.

"No one's going to mess with you anymore, eh?"

I nodded and kept rolling the papers, but couldn't speak because I had the string in my mouth, how I held it while folding the next paper. When I had looped it around the rolled paper and snapped it off, before putting the string back in my mouth, I said, "I taught him a lesson."

Louis kept rolling, staring at me in the mercury vapor light that filled the car from the overhead streetlight. "You just keep your mouth shut about it, okay? Don't go bragging around school about it, ever."

I made a face. "What do you think I am, stupid?"

The March 1970 issue of *Sky and Telescope* magazine said the Kosaka Comet was huge, one and one-quarter times the size of the sun. But like my childhood and the fragile bonds that held my large, fatherless family together, the secret comet was something that would not last forever, that only shone for a particular collection of moments in time. It continued to move away from the sun and the earth, away from our light. One morning Louis and I drove into the city, counting the armadillos, the raccoons, and the deer, until we reached the paper drop, settled into work, looked into the vertical depth of the sky, and it was gone.

21
A New Dad

A white Chrysler Impala pulled into our driveway. I was yanking weeds out of our overgrown rose garden—a failed attempt at beautifying our yard—and since the garden was near the driveway and in front of the house, it was as if the sedan drove right past my head. Tony and I looked up from the weeds we were pulling. So did Sonia, who was watering the grass. We thought the driver was a salesman. He turned off his engine, then got out of the car and hitched up his slacks. The engine ticked from the heat. "Hi," he said, smiling at us. "Doing some garden work, eh?"

"No shit, Sherlock," said Tony, under his breath.

The man was thin. His clothes hung awkwardly on his meatless body, the slacks too long and baggy, his arms lost in the shirt sleeves. His face looked hopeful and intelligent. He wore brown, square-framed glasses and had a high forehead, with a ripple of horizontal wrinkles on it, that gave him the appearance of someone whose eyes are open un-naturally for effect. His wispy hair was swept back from his forehead, parted on the side.

"Is your mother home?"

It was Saturday, and we told him she was. "But if you're selling anything," said Tony, "we don't want any."

"No." The man shook his head and cleared his throat. "No. I'm not selling anything."

He knocked on the screen door, rattling it against the doorjamb. We pretended to work, but listened to see what reaction he'd get. Mother came to the door. "There you are," she said. "Did you have any trouble with my direc-tions?"

"Hi, Clara." He stepped inside and kissed her on the cheek. We could see their hazy faces through the gray mesh of the screen door. "No trouble at all. I was just working on that project I told you about yesterday and couldn't get away till now."

"Better late than never," she said.

His name was Glen and he worked as an engineer at one of the companies in the same office building where Mother worked. They had met in the elevator. One day, on its way down the elevator stopped on his floor and he stepped into our life. He carried a briefcase, his tie was knotted loosely, the back of his suit was rumpled. He watched the elevator lights change and hummed to himself. He rubbed his nose. He must have wondered who that woman was, with the lipstick, the pantyhose, the face shaped like a fat heart ready to burst from unused love. After that they smiled at each other when they happened to meet in the building. He asked her out to dinner.

They'd been seeing each other for two months before she invited him over.

During dinner, Louis sat at the opposite end of the table from Glen and ate quietly. Lizzie and Sonia asked Glen questions and nodded their heads, as if everything he said made the utmost sense. Mother smiled brightly and pointed out Glen's accomplishments as if he were one of her children who had done well in school. She seemed to be holding him up as an example. A star to steer by. "Glen graduated high in his class at Baylor. He helped design the sewage disposal system for that new housing development out on Wheeler Road."

"Oh, it was nothing," Glen said, smiling. "Just a bunch of figures." He dabbed his mouth with his napkin. "Just a mess of equations."

We had no idea what he was talking about.

Glen asked if any of us would like to go to the zoo tomorrow. We were getting a little old for the zoo, but still, there were zebras, the monkey island, the snake house. Sonia and I said we'd go. Louis watched Glen carefully. He'd been fooled by our father and the It Monster, and was not going to make that same mistake again.

Glen started coming to dinner often, and, suddenly, as if it had happened when no one was looking, we realized that Mother was sleeping over at his house some nights after they went on dates. She came home drunk one evening, and when I told her I was hungry, she said, "Well, fix yourself something to eat, sweetheart. I can't fix your dinner every night."

Louis had told me that he didn't like Glen; he thought Mother shouldn't stay over at his house. That night her hair was puffy from a recent beauty shop bouffant and she had on a tight green dress, stockings, lipstick. She smelled of sweet perfume and beer. She took out a cigarette and sat down with the checkbook, trying to balance it. We could see she was having a hard time.

"How are you doing in classes, Louie?" she asked.

He shrugged, and didn't answer for a time. "What do you care?"

"What do you mean, what do I care?" She looked at him, still holding her cigarette. "How can you ask me that?"

"You're never around anymore."

"I don't have a right to my own life, is that it? You don't want me to enjoy myself?"

"That's not what I'm saying," said Louis. "What I'm saying is, I don't think you have a right to abandon Damon and Sonia, that's all. And they're not the only ones."

"Abandon?"

Louis glared at her, not backing down, as if *abandon* was exactly the right word. She stood up and slapped him.

"Momma!" I said.

"Do it again!" shouted Louis. "Is that what you want?"

She slapped him again. "Don't you dare talk that way to me!"

"I'll talk any way I feel like."

"Get out! Just get out of my house!"

He slammed the back door and, in the silence that followed, we could hear his heavy footsteps as he stamped through the gravel of the back driveway to the Volkswagen, started the car, and drove away. Mother told everyone to go to bed.

A month later, she called all of us together for a family talk. Louis had been working on the VW, changing the oil, and he wiped his hands with an oily rag as he walked into the living room. They had been ignoring each other since the drunk-evening fight. Mother told us then that she and Glen had gotten married, and he was probably going to move in with us. Mother said she knew it was hard on the family when she wasn't there as much at night. She hoped Glen's moving in would solve the problem. She hoped we would all come to love him as she loved him—he was a good man. Louis shook his head in disgust.

"Why weren't we invited to the wedding?" asked Sonia.

"We didn't want to make a fuss."

In our room that night, we talked about Glen. "He looks like a scarecrow," said Louis.

"Notice how he hardly looks at any of us?" said Tony. "He's afraid."

"I don't think he's so bad," I said. I liked the idea of having a new father. Maybe I would get an allowance. Glen supposedly made good money at his job. Good money! That's what we needed more of. And he was an engineer. It sounded respectable.

After a while Louis said we had better can it and get some sleep—we had to sling papers in the morning. I thought how I wanted to stay near my mother. I didn't want Glen to take her away. She was there in her bedroom that night, with her cat's-eye reading glasses on, racing through another science fiction novel, smelling of ripe, cloying perfume and Noxzema, her lips bright red, her beehive hair puffed out like a space queen. Tony's mother was dead, but at least mine was there, alive, living on this planet. That was something.

Between us, at least there was blood.

A few weeks later, mother announced that Glen was taking all of us to the coast for a fishing trip. She said this at dinner with an exultant smile on her face, as if we had finally found the life we had always been searching for, as if we would fulfill an *Ozzie and Harriet* or *My Three Sons* version of existence that had always eluded us. Glen sat at the table with us, eating new potatoes with white gravy. His face was pale, his hair thin, and for a moment Glen seemed like a man made of boiled new potatoes—pale, mushy, bland.

"Are we going to Galveston?" asked Sonia.

"No. Not Galveston. Beachport. It's south of Galveston, closer to Corpus Christi."

She was disappointed. "I always liked Galveston, except for the mosquitoes."

"I've got a little place in Beachport I've been going to for fifteen years," said Glen. "You'll like it. You can go fishing or swimming right out your front door. It's right there, next to the bay. Damn pretty."

"Does it have a swimming pool?"

"Nope. No swimming pool. But it doesn't need one. You got all the water in the ocean. What would you want with a pool?"

"The ocean's too salty," said Sonia.

During dinner Tony and Agnes said nothing about the fishing trip. They seemed acutely aware of how the family was shrinking. Louis was rarely home except to sleep. With Leland at school in New Mexico, Tony and Agnes seemed abandoned. More than ever, we realized that our mother wasn't the mother of Tony, Agnes, or Leland. She was just a woman the It Monster had married and divorced, and now she had his children. There was no blood between them. Their mother had died before the It Monster had married our mother. And the It Monster had died. We heard about that two years before, through one of their aunts they kept in touch with. Barry. That was his name. He was dead, and their mother was dead, so they were orphans. This had never seemed important before, when our mother was unmarried. Now that she had remarried, they had both a stepfather and a stepmother. Tony and I didn't seem as close as we'd been before, even if we'd never been close. No one had ever really liked Agnes. And Leland seemed done, finished with this family, nothing to hold him back.

By Friday, when it came time to pack Glen's car for the coast, Tony and Agnes had bowed out. Leland was driving in for the weekend and had promised to take them somewhere.

"You sure about this?" Mother asked them. "You're not going to get another chance."

"We're sure," said Tony. "We've already made up our minds."

Mother shrugged. "I don't know what's got into you two." For a moment she seemed about to say something else, but Glen asked if there was anything she wanted kept out of the trunk, and she walked away, leaving Tony and Agnes to themselves.

"Looks like it's just the four of us, kids," said Glen. We loaded our old suitcases, which had been Na-Na's, in his trunk. It was crowded with fishing rods, a large green tackle box, Glen's zipped leather suitcase, beach towels, air mattresses. We climbed into the car, he and Mother in front, Sonia and I in the back. Before he started the car he took off his brown frame glasses and blinked at us, smiling hopefully. "This is going to be a blast. You kids are going to have the best time of your life." It almost made me like him.

"I love you," said my mother, and they kissed loudly.

We drove across two hundred miles of coastal plains to the Gulf of Mexico. Sonia and I hung our feet out the window and counted hawks on the fenceposts. Glen bought us cheeseburgers, fries, and chocolate malts in the small towns we passed through. At the coast, we checked into a weatherbeaten cottage on the water.

"Don't you just love this air?" said Glen, breathing in, patting his chest with both hands. It smelled like a beach covered with washed-up fish, buzzed by flies. The breeze was soft and humid, the sea green. Sonia and I walked to the end of the fishing pier that belonged to the cottage and put our feet in the cool water. We couldn't see the bottom, and since we had not been to the Gulf in over a year, were shocked by it.

"Hope there aren't any sharks in this water," said Sonia.

We ate dinner at a seafood restaurant that served cups of gumbo and saltine crackers in plastic baskets. Blue glass balls hung from the ceiling in an old net, and the salad bar had a ship's wheel on it. There were paintings of seagulls and sunsets on the wall. Mother relaxed. She drank two bottles of beer and raved about the food.

"You really know how to pick them, don't you," she said to Glen.

He smiled back. "Picked you, didn't I?"

He ordered cheesecake and coffee for all of us. "This place is famous for its cheesecake. Martha Ann, the old black woman who runs the kitchen, knows how to do it just right. People drive for hundreds of miles just to eat her cheesecake."

"Well, we certainly did," said mother.

"She's got the touch. It's in her blood." As I ate the cheesecake, I felt our secret blood coursing through my veins, my heart, my mouth. Glen winked at us as he dug his fork into the cheesecake. "The others don't know what they're missing."

And neither did he.

We returned from the coast with sunburns that made us sleepy, with dull, egg-colored seashells that had looked much brighter when they were wet. The smell of coconut suntan lotion lingered on our clothes. Our swimming trunks were still wet, the pockets heavy with sand. Glen called Sonia "Sonny" and me "Sport." We didn't mind.

As we pulled into the driveway of the house at Moonlight and Sunburst, the eyes of the feeding rabbits in our front yard glowed red. That night reminded me of the night after one of the moon walks, when Louis and I had gone down Moonlight in the dark. We had taken huge steps, doing our best to pantomime the slow-motion movement of the astronauts on the moon, bouncing, even though the gravity of our planet kept us firmly in place. We pantomimed our moon walk in the blue light from above, and if we had had a telescope strong enough, we could have looked up and seen the astronauts bouncing above us. The thick dust of Moonlight Lane was cool and deep between our toes, and fireflies flashed through the trees.

But this night our headlights shone on the eyes of rabbits in the front yard, and Louis was not home. All the windows were dark. The porch light was out. Mother had to dig in her purse for the front-door key, and complained that at least they could have left the light on—any burglar passing by could simply break in and help himself. Hercules came around from the back of the house, his tail thumping against Glen's car. We carried our suitcases inside the house, and after a while, Louis called from his restaurant job. Mother listened intently on the phone, Glen sitting beside her, patting her back. They talked in low voices in the living room for an hour, and wouldn't let us watch TV. "Go to bed," said Mother, distracted. "You have school in the morning."

The next morning, as Louis and I drove around the city throwing the paper route, he told me Leland had taken Tony and Agnes to live with their aunt and uncle, Barry's sister and her husband, in Los Angeles. They were gone. There was no talk of flying out to get them. "It's all that bastard's fault," said Louis.

"You mean Glen?"

"Damn right I mean Glen. Look at it, Damon. He's ripping us apart. He never wanted them anyway."

"I don't know. It never seemed to me he had anything against them. He wanted Tony and Agnes to go with us," I said, though I didn't believe it.

"That's just for show. He's fooling you, can't you see? God, he's even got you believing he's Mr. Perfect."

"He's better than nothing, isn't he?"

Since the time that Na-Na died, when we had gone looking for a new house, our family often fantasized about moving. We criticized our old house; we never thought it was good enough. Its roof leaked during thunderstorms, and we had to scatter pots and pans around the living and dining room to catch the drips. And when the pots were empty, at the beginning of the rain or storm, the many drips and pings sounded like music, and Mother said it was a pretty sound, if you ignored the water marks that looked like coffee stains on the ceilings above us.

We used to play a game called When We Move, in which we would try to outdo each other in our fantasy places to move to. Most of these were either in the mountains or at the sea.

"When we move," said Sonia, "we'll be able to go swimming every day, and I'll have a sailboat, snorkel, and flippers. When we move I'll have a collection of seashells, and go surfing every day. And I'll have a tan and a ponytail, like Gidget."

"When we move," I said, "we'll have a waterfall at the end of Main Street, and in the distance, we'll see snow-capped mountains. We'll only have to go to school two days a week, when we move."

"When we move we'll never have to worry about money."

Although he must have been only in his forties, Glen seemed old to me, sober and reliable—settled. We never imagined that he would want to leave San Gabriel, that he had his own fantasies. Every Saturday he took me and Sonia to the Knights of Columbus swimming pool, where I had first learned to swim, and dropped us off, then came back to pick us up hours later. On a Saturday such as this we first realized we were actually going to move.

It was late spring and already so hot that heat waves shimmered off the black asphalt of the parking lot, and we ran barefoot from one car's shadow to the next, carrying our towels and blue rubber flippers. The grass had recently been mowed around the pool, and the grass and chlorine smell together was a rich mixture of all the summers we had spent at these pools. At the concession stand, we bought Giant Sweet-Tarts, chunks of powdery candy as big and round as bars of soap, which stained our tongues pastel red and made them feel chalky.

While we were swimming that day a storm came up. The sky became dark as an eclipse, the wind gusty, sharp with the smell of rain. We shivered and got goose bumps, waiting in the breezeway near the turnstiles. The rain fell in a blurred grayness to the south of us, and for a moment we saw it was raining in the fields on the other side of the swimming pool, and that soon it would be upon us.

Glen arrived early, knowing they would close the pool. On the ride home, wrapped in towels, we were still shivering.

"You know," Glen said, almost casually, "when we move to Beachport, you'll probably be able to go swimming every day."

For a minute we thought he was playing the game of When We Move with us, but he had never done that before, and we didn't even know if he knew about our game. He seemed oddly matter-of-fact.

"We're not really moving, are we?"

"Would I lie to you?"

Sonia smiled. "Maybe. So when's the big move supposed to happen?"

Glen reached out and rubbed the fogged-up windshield with the back of his hand. "You'll find out soon enough."

It turned out that Glen had gotten into an argument with his boss, so he decided to quit his job, move to the coast, and open a restaurant in one of the resort and fishing villages on the Gulf Coast that he visited each summer.

It happened suddenly. After all these years of living at the intersection of Moonlight and Sunburst, we were going to move. Some of us were, anyway. Louis said, "I don't like this one bit. I'm not moving. I'm not selling the house either. I'm going to stay right here."

"I'm not asking you to move, sweetheart," Mother said. "You're in college now. You don't have to go chasing after the family whenever we decide to take off someplace."

Louis didn't say anything. "He's splitting up the family," he told me later. "They shouldn't just go off and leave like that."

"Well, Mom said that you could keep the house. At least you'll have a free place to live."

"That doesn't matter. We're never going to be a family again after this."

So only Sonia and I were going to move with my mother and Glen to the Gulf Coast. It was near the end of the seventh grade for me, and the eighth grade for Sonia, but Glen could hardly wait for summer to move, because he wanted to get started on the new business before the tourist season. He started going down to Beachport on the weekends as we finished the school year. We didn't realize what was happening. We didn't realize that once we left, we would never see our old neighborhood again, or at least see it in the same light.

And Louis was right. Our family would never be the same again.

22

Dream
Come
True

With our family now down to four—Glen and mother, Sonia and I—we lived in an old motel, the kind called motor courts that sprang up during the Great Depression. It looked like the Bates Motel in *Psycho*, only it didn't have a scary mansion behind it. And in front of it was Tornado Bay, with short, gentle waves, row after row of faded fishing piers, their posts covered with barnacles and oyster shells visible in the low tides, many of the planks missing and most of the entire piers crooked and twisting from the effects of hurricanes and storms. We lived so close to the bay that we constantly heard the slow waves slapping at the shore and the piers through our open windows.

Beachport, the fishing village we moved to, seemed not so much to have been built as to have been washed up by the sea. All the buildings were weather-beaten, warped and gray. The streets and parking lots were filled with oyster shells and fish skeletons. Seagulls swooped in the sky above. At low tide, egrets and herons picked through the mud flats. Coots wobbled between the creosote posts of fishing piers and boat docks. In the convenience stores the clerks sold live shrimp for bait.

We fished at first, on the pier in front of our new home, but caught nothing but slimy catfish we called hardheads. They were considered trash fish, and catching them was worse than not catching anything at all, because you somehow had to get them off the end of your line without getting snagged. They had poisonous barbs behind their gills, which would hurt like hell if they jabbed into you, and to get them off our lines we had to pound them against the sides of the pier, or cut the line and leave the hook in their mouths.

Glen quickly began work on the restaurant. He had bought a hamburger hut and the land it was on for a bargain price, and decided we would build out from there, using the old hamburger hut as a kitchen area. But when we first arrived it was just a crummy, tiny little hamburger hut, built for selling tourists fast food. This was before everything was either a McDonald's, Wendy's, or Burger King. The hut was a square building made from cinder blocks, painted white, with a window in the middle and a sign that said ORDER HERE above it. The white front wall of the hut had hamburgers painted on it, with their prices, and slogans like ICE COLD SOFT DRINKS! THICK, CREAMY MILK SHAKES! FROSTY FLOATS! There were crudely painted replicas of banana splits on the walls, and hot dogs with dull red ketchup, dull yellow mustard. It looked like a concession stand at a football stadium. Glen sank his life savings into it.

"Someday this is going to be a top-notch family restaurant," he said, standing in the oyster-shell parking lot, gazing at the low building.

"Sure, Glen," we said, sipping our chocolate shakes. But secretly it worried us that the man who had owned it before us had died bankrupt. Glen had bought the land and hamburger hut at an estate sale.

Sonia and I waited on customers at the drive-through window, while Glen built the restaurant and our mother cooked the food. We ate as many french fries and strawberry malts as our bellies could hold. The strawberry malts were made from half-gallon jugs of strawberry and malt syrup mixed with soft ice cream. I drank so many glasses of lemonade that I got the hives—huge welts breaking out on my arms and belly and face, welts that itched so urgently I would almost go insane trying not to scratch, and the only way to get rid of them was to take warm showers.

Glen was an engineer, but he had never built a restaurant before. He drew the plans on white butcher paper laid out on the floor of our kitchenette at the motor court. There was no place to step when he had his plans laid out. Mother looked down at the butcher paper and smiled hesitantly. "Are you sure you know how to do this, darling?"

He nodded, drawing a slanting line with his T-square. "I had two semesters of architecture in my sophomore year."

"You did?"

"Uh huh. At one time I was going to be an architect. But I was never very good at drafting."

He was right. The plans on the butcher paper were a mess.

But there was no stopping him. Around the hamburger hut, we poured a concrete slab, a foundation for the other dining rooms of the restaurant. The cement was a thick gray mud the team of foundation men smoothed out with crusty two-by-fours and trowels. They described arcs and circles in the darkening mud, smoothing it out, making a gravelly, scraping sound, working out the flaws. The air above the wet foundation filled with a wet mud smell, the smell of something taking shape. Glen let us put our initials and the date in it: D.B. and S.B. 6/15/70.

After the foundation was hard we bought a nail gun to hammer the studs down. Before long the walls were up, the roof beams across them. We spent much of our time going to the Western Auto store and the lumberyard. While my stepfather shopped for threepenny nails and Johns Manville insulation, I walked down the rows of apple-red lawn mowers, the clean and shiny shovels and picks propped against each other like rifles, the wheelbarrows green and empty, their paint still perfect, their small black wheels solid and hard. The Western Auto and the lumberyard were filled with fathers and sons and men who knew each other, and standing among the racks of screwdrivers, pliers, and crescent wrenches made it seem as if you knew how to use them. They all looked so perfect and functional there, above and beyond the rust- and oil-stained mess of broken engines, stripped bolts, and rusted hinges.

The sea was brown that summer, the surf choppy, churned by waves that didn't move forward but just stirred up the sand. They looked like the waves on the inside of a washing machine. The air had the sharp tang of the ocean, a fishy smell. One day a tide brought in thousands of jellyfish, filling the bay as far as the eye could see, pulpy white alien-looking creatures, trailing a wedding veil of stinging threadlike tentacles, pulsing slow, graceful, sinister. For a time, the ocean seemed malignant, filled with poisonous things. Stingrays whose barbs broke off in your foot if they jabbed you, the

The Fire Eaters

pincers of crabs, the teeth of barracudas. A woman's arm was bitten off by a tiger shark at a popular and crowded beach. We watched her husband frantic by the police car on the five-o'clock news. A surfer stood in the background, pointing out to sea. Portuguese men-of-war washed up on the beaches. You had to watch where you stepped to avoid the purple-and-blue air bladders, the powerful venom in their tentacles.

I saw small hammerhead sharks, too—the thin blade of their heads tipped with two black eyes—caught in the murky water off Mustang Island, which was only twenty miles from Beachport. And a few months later, one of our few customers at the restaurant, a deep-sea fisherman, told about seeing hammerheads almost as long as his thirty-foot Chris-Craft in the blue water of the Gulf. While I was body surfing one day on the island, I saw a stingray swim by in a curling wave. I was later stung by jellyfish, pinched by crabs, and I stepped on slimy things that wriggled away immediately, as I did my best to leap out of the water with dignity. I saw photographs of the stumps and severed limbs of shark attack victims, which the deep-sea fisherman had a collection of, and brought in one day to show me.

This wasn't my first experience with the Gulf. Even though, for a long time, I knew the sea was dangerous, and even terrifying in a way, I refused to be frightened by it. This probably began with the summer vacations we spent on the island of Galveston, before Na-Na died. Both my mother and father had been raised on the island, and this familiarity with island life had become a hereditary trait in our family. Or, as my mother put it, we had "sand between our toes." During a vacation on Galveston's West Beach, I remember Louis once reached to the sea floor in water about three feet deep and came up holding a fistful of living sand dollars, whose dark green bodies—the color of kelp—were covered with tiny hairs, like the cilia that line our lungs.

At the beach my mother had once explained how the continental shelf extended far out into the Gulf of Mexico. She told us that somewhere out there in the water was a place where the bottom of the sea drops steeply off and the water becomes very deep. The giant hole I imagined became a metaphor for me, a symbol of the uncertainty and danger of life. A realization that danger is there, all around you, but that you can't let yourself give in to fear or despair. The hole in the continental shelf was where the monsters of the sea lived. Sharks. Stingrays. Giant squid. If I—or Louis, Leland, Sonia, or all the rest of us—slipped into that hole, we were goners. Because of this, I remembered the beach as a place full of claws, teeth, and tentacles, an abyss I could slip into if I didn't watch where I was going.

For a long time I believed that anytime a wave lifted me off my feet, I could never quite tell whether I would be touching bottom when I came back down.

In the fall Sonia and I started school at Beachport, and in all of our dreams and all the times we were playing our When We Move game, we had never anticipated such a change. The new school shook my view of the world. I had always assumed that I would get good grades, that I would enjoy going to college later, and I had assumed that everyone else wanted these same things too. That's what it had seemed like in San Gabriel. Glen had graduated from Baylor, and although I knew very little about the university,

I was proud of him and envious of the Baylor football teams I watched in the fall.

All of these assumptions seemed false at my new high school in Beachport. Many of the students had failed several grades and ridiculed books and knowledge. Some of them were seventeen years old in the ninth grade, bigger and meaner than I was. They sat in the back rows of my algebra class, chewing gum and whipping their forearms with leather thongs. This was a sign of bravery and toughness. They raised huge welts on their arms, and showed them off. They wore dark sunglasses and slept during class. They spit on each other and thumped the better students on the back of the head with their middle fingers, students like me.

And yet the high school looked like any other school, except that it was on the edge of a swamp. Actually, it was between two large marshes. The brackish water of one of the tidal marshes started not far from the football field, and during history class I saw airboats cruise by as I daydreamed, looking out the classroom windows.

Mosquitoes thrived in the stagnant water of the many puddles and swamp grass, and after lunch it was hard to pay attention as everyone scratched their mosquito bites and stared at the algebraic equations written on the board and hoped they wouldn't be called on to solve them. Quadratic equations were popular in that class, things like

$$x^2 + x - 6 = 0$$

Solve for x.

Sometimes the marsh and swamp animals passed through our school, crossing to the marshes on the other side of us. On my first day of classes, while walking to the cafeteria I saw a catfish flopping on the ground. I kept walking, and saw another one flopping there, with a pinkish belly. Soon I noticed there were dozens of them flopping on the ground all around me, most of them small, not even keepers, but some of them larger, ten or twelve inches long, flopping across the path to the cafeteria, which was between two marshes. I stood there, dumbfounded, watching as a school of walking catfish passed by, and my fellow classmates kept going, completely accustomed to the sight.

During the fall semester the restaurant was finished to the point that customers could sit at tables, although in the back of the dining room you could still see sawhorses and, in the daytime, hear the whine of a power saw. We nailed black tar paper on the roof, and, inside, put rolls of fiberglass insulation between the studs, then covered it all with paneling. We bought tables and chairs on credit. We had menus printed, and matches. Mother did most of the cooking, and Sonia and I waited on tables, while Glen managed the business and helped out in the kitchen or dining room whenever he was needed.

But still we had no business. The front wall of the restaurant was filled with windows, and at night we watched the few cars on the Beach Road drive by, hoping one of them would turn in. Glen had us place fliers under the windshield wipers of cars, good for 20 percent off the price of a meal, with a map showing how to get to our restaurant, which was called the Poop Deck. But the fliers didn't seem to work. In history class, one of the other students said, "My mother's friend told me they ate at your restaurant, and that someone found a fly in their salad."

"No they didn't."

"That must have been the Poop Special," said someone else.

Drunken fishermen came in, and drank cup after cup of coffee, talking too loudly and filling the air with cigarette smoke, not ordering dinner. They scared all the other customers off, except the ones who decided that fishermen made the restaurant seem "colorful." We had the closest coffee to the boat basin. The fishermen smelled like the oyster houses and shrimp boats they worked on, and Mother sprayed the air around the cash register and front door with pine scent to mask the fish smell. She wanted ours to be a respectable, clean-smelling restaurant.

Then one evening late in November it rained with the force of a tropical storm, huge gray sheets slanting down, flooding the Beach Road. The only customers in the restaurant were an old couple having dinner. Sonia and I stood by the front window and watched the lightning. The air felt close in the dining room, stuffy and humid. We watched the rain lash puddles in the parking lot. Mother came up behind us and said, "Isn't it pretty?"

As we stood there, watching the slanting rain in the white headlights of the cars driving down the Beach Road, the streaking red of the taillights following and stretching out on the wet black asphalt behind them, we relaxed in the first relief since the dryness of the summer.

Then the roof began to leak.

First we heard the drips. Light, tiny pings caused by drops hitting a fork or spoon somewhere in the dining room. Soon we noticed drops spotting the tablecloths, speckling the stainless-steel tops of the salt and pepper shakers. Then, all around us, rivulets and drips began to appear, until soon we had placed pots and pans throughout the dining room and kitchen, just like at our old house at Moonlight and Sunburst.

Glen was defeated. "Maybe this wasn't such a great idea after all," he said. His shoulders slumped as he mopped the front dining room. With a crash of lightning, the power went out. After we helped our only customers out to their car with flashlights, we sat in the darkened dining room, listening to the drips and pings all around us.

"I bet the power is never coming back on," said Sonia.

"I guess I didn't do such a good job on the roof," said Glen. "Must be rain getting underneath the tar paper somehow."

Mother broke out the candles, and started singing. It was a silly little song she had sung to us sometimes when we were little, back before she had started working as a bookkeeper and never had the energy for singing us to sleep, when she was still married to the It Monster. It was a song called "You're Pretty When You're Blue." Soon the dining room was filled with candlelight, and the drips and leaks from the ceiling flashed through the light surrounding us. Mother hugged Glen and told him not to worry. We could fix the roof with a little more hot tar. Things would be okay.

"I don't like living here, Mama," said Sonia suddenly, almost in tears. "It's so weird and creepy. There are snakes everywhere."

"It's just different, honey. You'll learn it has its good side."

"But no one *believes* in anything here," I said, trying to control my voice, to keep it from trembling. But she knew better than that. In the candlelight, her eyes were clear and steady.

"Yes they do," she said. "You just don't know them well enough yet."

And she was right. We didn't move away after that, and before too long, the restaurant began to make money. We still hated working there, Sonia and I, but we grew to like our crowd of oddball, misfit regulars. I missed Louis, and for several years tried to make my way back to him. When I did, it was too late. But I remember that night, while the lights were off, my mother held me so tightly that my face was smashed against her neck. I felt her human ribs, and as I did, was filled with a definition of faith in the cradle of her bones.

23
Drifting

The morning after the storm, Glen took me with him to the hardware store.

"We're not going to give up," he said. "We're going to lick this sucker with both hands." His grip on the wheel was tense. He seemed a little fanatical to me, but I held my tongue. With Glen, I always held my tongue. He didn't want to hear my opinion of his career move to the restaurant business from being an engineer, his weird obsession with remaking this hamburger hut into a café, his loopy search for the good life in a sleepy, warped-wood town washed up by the sea. "We're going to make this work, goddammit. Pardon my French. But I'm not going to let this roof thing break me."

We drove the rest of the way to the Western Auto in silence. The sky was clear and blue now, the clouds blown over the Gulf, but you could see the storm's destruction. The palm trees along Shoreline Drive were blown askew, some of the fronds torn away. A white county public works pickup was parked on the shoulder of the road, its yellow revolving light flashing, as workers in hard hats tossed storm debris into the bed of the truck. The storm had overturned some of the city litter baskets. Styrofoam cups, beer bottles, and aluminum cans floated in the water-filled ditches off the four-lane road. And over the wreckage the graceful wings of sea gulls steered their lazy course. When we pulled into the parking lot of the Western Auto, Glen killed the engine and set the parking brake with a jerk. He looked at me as if I'd just said something. "Yes sir, we're not going to let it break us. We just need to do a little repairs, is all."

At the Western Auto, Glen joked with the store manager. "Harvey, you old pirate. How the hell are ya?"

"Glen Flanagan." Harvey opened his eyes wide in mock surprise. "Thought we'd finally gotten rid of you. How's it hangin'?"

"Oh, you know me, Harv. I wrap it round my waist three times but it still hangs to my knees."

They both grinned, and Harvey went, "Yeah yeah yeah."

"So what're you in for? Storm mess things up at the café?"

"You know it. Looks like I might as well just hand you my week's profits. That's where all the money's going anyway."

"Ah, don't you worry. Freak storms don't matter much. With that location, you'll be rakin' in the dough come summer."

"What you got in here to fix a leaky roof?"

Harvey said he had just the thing. He pointed to the back of the store. "You two go on back there and Curtis will show you where the roofing tar and felt paper is. I better stay up here in front." He leaned over the counter, to get closer to Glen, and spoke in a lower tone of voice. "Got a couple of jigaboos there by the radios, probably just waiting to grab one and run if I don't keep my eye on them." We glanced over at two young black men near the front of the store.

Glen shook his head. "I hear you talking, Harv. It's a characteristic of the species."

At the Western Auto I was always Glen's good son, Harvey even slapping me on the back if I was within reaching distance. Glen never introduced me as his stepson, but always said, "This is my boy, Damon." And if the person made a remark like "Damon, well, that's an unusual name. How'd he ever get that handle?" Glen would shrug and laugh. "His mother's idea," he'd say, as if he didn't like the choice, but what could he do?

While Glen chose the five-gallon buckets of roofing tar and the roll of felt roofing paper, I drifted away. Almost in a trance, I gazed at the rows of shiny shovel blades, the racks of claw hammers, the candy-apple-red Briggs & Stratton lawn mowers.

After a while Glen found me in the back of the store. "Damon? What are you doing?

"Nothin'."

"Well that's what I thought. So quit moping around and help me carry this junk. It must weigh a ton."

We loaded the pickup bed with the buckets of roofing tar and paper. I dented one of the cans as I was hefting it over the tailgate of the pickup, bashing the truck so that Glen said, "Easy. This thing ain't paid for yet." He'd traded in the Impala for it when we were building the café. I noticed that whenever we went to the Western Auto, Glen's speech took on more of a rural, Southern accent and became much more folksy. He complained about how *dreamy* I was becoming. "You have to focus on what you're doing, son. You're never going to get anywhere in life just moping around like that."

$\Large{T}$he café was only a one-story building, but from the roof you could see a long way. You could see the whitecaps on the waves of Tornado Bay. You could see the entire fleet of the boat basin, the white shrimp boats at dock, their net booms raised in the air like masts on a nineteenth-century schooner. You could see up and down the Beach Road that paralleled the bay, the sea gulls, the white clouds, and if you were lucky, dolphins surfacing in the boat basin. I hated working on the roof but I liked being there. The afternoon when we came back from the Western Auto, Glen leaned the ladder against the back of the roof and took a tar bucket in each hand. "Now I don't want you daydreaming while I'm on this ladder, Damon. You hear me? I could fall and break my neck."

That didn't sound like a bad idea to me. With Glen dead, maybe we'd move back to San Gabriel. He'd been okay at first, but now, like Barry before him, Glen was turning into a different person. He was always lecturing about something. He was always trying to teach me a lesson I wasn't interested in learning. And there was that business in Western Auto. Another secret.

Glen balanced with a bucket in each hand as he stepped slowly up the ladder. I held it firmly, but had to struggle to pay attention. I'd developed an almost pathological ability to drift whenever he lectured me. I felt the tremble of his body through the wood of the ladder. After he placed both buckets on the roof I followed him up, holding on to the ladder with one hand, balancing the roll of roofing felt paper on my shoulders with the other.

On the roof, Glen unrolled the paper near the peak, where he thought the roofing job had been lax, and gave me the task of hammering. I banged away at the short, large-headed nails, the gunshot sounds of the hammer blows echoing back from the boat basin. We wore short nail aprons with the name of a local lumberyard on them, heavy cotton things with large pockets, slung around our hips, with a loop to hold our hammers. I liked wearing a nail apron. I liked the heaviness of the roofing nails, the way it made you feel, holding them below your guts. We developed a laconic and macho attitude whenever we worked on the roof. In a very real sense we were above it all, and could stand upon the top of the roof, in view of everyone for miles around, hammer in hand, not giving a shit about anything. I held a handful of the roofing nails in my mouth while I was hammering, since it only took two quick blows and the nail was in, a third to sink it squarely below the felt paper. Working on the roof was murder on our backs, knees, and stomachs, since we had to crouch on one knee to hammer or to coat the nail holes with a smear of roofing tar, but that element of physical exertion made us feel all the more manly. For this one time in my life I could kid myself that I was good with my hands.

On the roof, Glen and I were the closest to being friends we ever were or ever would become. He taught me how to

The Fire Eaters

nail, and when we were first working on the roof, it made me feel important. "Don't choke the thing to death," he'd say. "Hold it at the end of the handle. Let the weight of the hammer do the work. If you're using it correctly, your arm shouldn't even be doing much work, but the hammer should kick those nails in on its own." This was in the early period of our work on the roof, when we were sliding the four-by-eight-foot sheets of half-inch plywood over the frame of two-by-twelves. We were optimistic then. Even cocky. It was the first part of the job, the yellow pine frame of the café rising up in early summer against the blue sky, white clouds. If the traffic was slow on the Beach Road we could hear the laughing cries of the gulls and terns as they followed a shrimp boat back to the harbor, diving into the green sea behind the boat to feed off the crabs and fish the deck hands tossed out as they culled the catch.

By the time we were doing the repairs the café was more or less in place and a new tone had set in. A tone, an attitude, of thinly veiled disappointment, distrust, and pessimism. The roof leaked. The plumbing in the new bathrooms was screwy. The water pressure was weak. The shrimpers kept stealing the toilet paper for their boats and pissing in the sink. Somehow the concrete had set incorrectly in one section of the dining room and it bulged unevenly, throwing off all the tables so we had to place matchbooks under the table legs carefully to keep them from wobbling.

And I drifted. Privately, even subconsciously, I had decided the repair job wasn't going to work. When I held the nails in my mouth my mind drifted. I daydreamed of going to the beach, of moving back to San Gabriel, of talking to girls. I mulled over the classes I hated at school, the other students to watch out for. When I held the nails in my mouth I remembered the way my mother used to hold the clothespins in her mouth, the way she would stand there in the backyard with Kit's father watching her, the way we hadn't been there—the way *I* hadn't been there—when Kit's father attacked her. Sometimes I found myself drifting back into the past, swinging the bat again at Brian Tunch's head, playing on the sand dunes of the gravel pit while my mother was being raped, and I sank in my own quicksand of gloom that Glen knew nothing about and had nothing to do with, but every comment of his about "jigaboos" pushed me further away from him, knowing he hated me without his knowing it. Maybe he deserved to fail. Maybe the roof deserved to leak.

He lost patience with me. "Damon? What in the goddam world is the matter with you? Why, when I was your age, I was full of piss and vinegar. Are you sick or something?"

"No sir."

"Well then what the hell is it? You've only done half a row, while I've already finished mine, and caulking the holes takes longer. Why are you so slow?"

"I don't know."

He clambered down the ladder to drink a beer while I finished pounding the nails.

Those repairs seemed to work. During the worst storms there were minor leaks, but for the most part the job seemed watertight. I continued to climb onto the roof, though, going up there in the afternoons when business was slow and I wanted to take a break. I could smoke pot up there without getting caught. The wind would blow the smell away. Customers sometimes complained about the sound of footsteps above them, but I kept to one corner, and managed to stay out of trouble. I liked sitting there in the afternoons, watching the seagulls, stoned, watching the cars drive down the Beach Road. And that's where I was, sitting on the roof, drifting back into the past, back into my thoughts, two years later, when I saw Louis's blue VW Beetle driving up, coming home for the holidays.

24

Barmaids
and
Bottle Rockets

Louis had visited when we first moved to
Beachport, but he and Glen had had some words. Glen was
a diehard conservative and Louis had grown his hair long.
He marched against the war and argued politics with anyone
who would listen. Glen said the war protest was a disgrace
to our country, and if the future of our country was in Louis's
hands, we were in big trouble. After an argument over Nixon
and McGovern, Glen told Louis, "Don't bother coming to
visit if you're going to start that stuff. I won't have it in my
house."

Now, when he drove up in the same VW Beetle, I saw
him coming from my perch on the roof, and climbed down
the ladder. By then he was in the kitchen, with Sonia on
his back, Louis piggybacking her, and Mom smiling at both
of them. Glen was gone somewhere. When Louis found this

out he made an elaborate production of swinging around the kitchen, bumping into things with Sonia still on his back, peeking into pots on the stove, as if looking for Glen. "So where is the old bigot? I know he's around somewhere, waiting with a pair of scissors to cut my hair and make me vote for Tricky Dick." He told Sonia she'd better get off before his back broke. "You must be getting fat."

"I am not!" she said, and refused to jump down. "Momma, tell him to take that back."

Mother told her he was just kidding, and now that she was sixteen she was too big for horseplay. After Louis let Sonia down he poked me in the stomach.

"Hey, little brother. Que pasa?" His hair was shoulder-length, tied in a ponytail. He made me give him a hug, because he hadn't seen me in a while and he missed me.

I tried to act as if it were all a joke. I said, "Look what the cat dragged in."

"Man, you're growing up." He was holding me by the shoulders, trying to look me in the face, although I was looking down at the floor, grinning.

"Oh, look at that. He's embarrassed. My little brother is embarrassed. Don't be afraid to show your feelings."

"Louis, what has gotten into you?" asked Sonia. "Would you leave Damie alone?" She slapped him playfully on the shoulder.

His eyes were pink and puffy, and I found out later that he was stoned, and had been smoking pot on the drive up, to relax and get in the mood for seeing the family.

Glen returned from running errands and nodded at Louis when he saw him, but they didn't speak to each other. Mom had to get back to work and didn't have time to talk to Louis, and she seemed careful not to show too much attention to

,

him when Glen was around. After the lunch rush, I tried to interest Louis in a hand of gin rummy, but he just sat there during the game, playing listlessly, staring out the window at a fireworks stand across the street. He asked me if I liked working at the restaurant.

"I guess. I don't have much choice, do I?"

He shrugged. "Sure you do. Just because Glen's your step-father doesn't mean he can use you."

"Mom wants us to work here, too. It's not just Glen."

"It was his idea, right? Without him, you'd probably be back in San Gabe right now. I don't like how he's moved you guys away. Now, even Mom acts weird. It's like she's divorced *us* now."

Louis seemed scruffier with his hair longer, and he was even thinner than he used to be. He'd finished up his two-year degree at San Gabriel College the spring before and didn't know if he wanted to go on and get his bachelor's degree. He was nervous. "Let's go for a walk, Damon. I'm going to go crazy if we stay in here all day."

I had to ask Mother if I could leave the café, because I was supposed to be waiting on tables. She told me to ask Glen. He was in the back of the kitchen checking the inventory.

Glen didn't like the idea. "If you leave, who's going to wait on the customers?"

"I don't know. Sonia might take over if I asked her."

"She's helping your mother cook. And besides, how do you know she doesn't want to go for a walk too? Have you ever thought of that?"

"Does that mean I can't go?"

Glen didn't answer, but gave me a disgusted look. He went on counting bags of frozen french fries in our deep freeze. I walked back to Louis and told him I couldn't leave. "I have to wait on the tables."

"But there's no one here." Louis looked around the dining room. "The place is completely dead."

"Sometimes we get customers in the afternoons. There wouldn't be anyone here to wait on them."

I knew Mom could hear us from the kitchen, so I held up one finger to my lips.

"I don't see how this place makes any money, anyway," he said in a hushed voice. "What's going to happen if the business goes belly up? Who's going to bail you out?"

We heard the bump of the swinging door to the kitchen behind us. Glen had his reading glasses on. "Go on and go, Damon. I'll hold down the fort here, but don't be gone long."

"Thanks, Glen."

Glen and Louis didn't speak to each other as I went to get my jacket. A cool fog blanketed the Beach Road, rolling off Tornado Bay. As soon as we stepped outside we zipped up our jackets and flipped the collars, and Louis headed straight for the fireworks stand. "*Thanks*, Glen," he said, sarcastically.

"Give me a break. I've gotta live here, you know."

"I know. I'm just razzing you. Let's buy a Roman candle to stick up Glen's fat Republican ass."

"Louis."

"What? Relax." We'd walked across to the fireworks stand, but no one was around. "We could probably grab some of these and no one would notice." He made as if he were going to steal some of the fireworks. I rang the bell on the counter.

"Jesus, Damon. You've become such a goody-goody."

"I know these people. Besides, we'd never get away with it."

We stood at the wooden counter for a few minutes, till the guy who worked there came out of the corner store, whose owners sold the fireworks. He stepped through the side door of the fireworks stand and stood there, not even saying hi or anything. He seemed suspicious of us. He'd probably seen Louis act like he was going to steal something.

Louis loaded up on fireworks. He bought six dozen bottle rockets, two long strips of Black Cats, six Roman candles, and some special Star Boosters with metal wings and a thick gray fuse. After we crossed the street back to the café's parking lot, Louis got in his Volkswagen and said that he wanted to drive down to the wharves and see if they were catching any fish off the county pier. I hesitated. I could imagine what Glen would be thinking. *They said they were going for a walk. Why are they getting in the car? Why do you need to drive when you're going for a walk? He's a bad influence, Louis is.*

I climbed in the VW and rolled down the window, then put my arm out. The curtains across the front row of café windows were open but I didn't look inside to see if Glen was watching. I didn't have to look.

"I hope Glen didn't see us buying the fireworks," I said.

"Why?"

"Because I'm not supposed to play with them."

"Who says?"

"Glen. He thinks I'm going to blow my hands off or something."

"Jesus." Louis shook his head as he drove the VW down the back alleys off the Beach Road. "He treats you like a baby."

"I know. I'm sick of it."

At the boat basin we walked along the wharves. The air

The Fire Eaters

was filled with the fish smell. Some of the shrimpers' nets were stretched out on the mounds of oyster shells near the docks. The fog rolled off Tornado Bay, and we couldn't even see the end of the county fishing pier on the bay side of the basin. The pier melted into the mist and fog, and could have been going on forever, leading out into the grainy horizon. Louis leaned against the railing and fished a pack of Marlboros out of his blue-jean jacket.

"Can I have one?"

He tapped out a pair of the filter-tipped cigarettes and offered one to me. "I didn't know you smoked."

I shrugged.

"I think you should move back to San Gabe before you're all broke and on welfare," said Louis. "And if Glen likes it so much here, he can stay. But you, Mom, and Sonia move back."

"Glen'll never go for that."

"Glen this. Glen that. God, a few years ago you'd never even heard of this guy. Now he's running your lives."

Louis tossed his cigarette butt into the waves. For a moment we stood at the railings, watching the butt float on the surface, the waves pushing it forward, then pulling it back.

"You know, I'm really pissed with Mom for selling the house. She didn't have to do that. But I bet it wasn't her idea. No, that smells like another one of Glen's brainchilds."

About a year after we moved to Beachport, Mom and Glen had decided to sell the house on Moonlight, saying they needed the money. Louie had been the only one living there then—he'd been making the mortgage payment for a few months, after Mom had said it was too much for them.

But it had been almost paid off, and they wanted the money for equipment and building materials for the restaurant.

"We needed the money, Louie. Mom told you that. The café has cost a lot more than Glen figured."

"Well that's where he screwed up, right? That was his mistake, but I'm the one who pays for it. Mom swore I could stay there rent-free as long as I liked. She *promised*."

We lingered on the pier for a few more minutes, until the cold seemed to catch up with us. Louie said, "God, I'm freezing out here. Let's get back to the car."

The fishing lights had been turned on early, because of the fog, and were surrounded by blue-white haloes, a row of them leading back to the parking lot. We could see crabs swimming in the waves in the illuminated water. Our jackets and hair were damp, and Louis crossed over from the Beach Road to Highway 36 to warm the engine and get the heater to kick in. He drove south towards Aransas Pass, the next small town on the highway, fifteen miles from Beachport. About halfway there he pulled in at a cocktail bar on stilts built in the swamp flats between the two towns, where the highway crossed close enough to San Rafael Bay to see it from the road. The intracoastal canal cut through at that point, headed for Corpus Christi, and you could watch barges and the big oceangoing ships passing through. Louis wanted a drink. I asked if he thought they'd let me inside.

"Hell, they'll probably serve you if you don't make a fuss. Doesn't look like they have any customers. They'll probably roll out the red carpet for us."

We walked up the wooden stairs to the front door, but Louis stopped me before we entered. "And Damon, this'll be our little secret. No word of this to Glen, okay?"

The Fire Eaters

"Are you kidding? You think I'm stupid or something?"

Louis put one arm around my shoulders and gave me a good shake. "There you go. You're starting to loosen up, Damie."

The bar was called the Canoe Club but the name didn't make any sense. This was not canoe country. Canoes were for clear, polished-stone rivers in the Rockies of Idaho and Montana, or the Smoky Mountains of Virginia. The water here was brackish. The bar itself was surrounded by swamps, marsh grass, cattails, ponds full of blue crabs. It could have been called the Plywood Club. We were in plywood country. Entire towns, houses, signs, bars, restaurants, supermarkets made of plywood here at the edge of the sea, just waiting for a hurricane to come by and blow it all away. Inside the bar was the usual setup—long counter with mirror and rows of liquor bottles, jukebox in the corner, beer signs on the walls. The place was empty. Cheery Christmas decorations hung from the ceiling—cutout snowflakes and reindeer that looked as if they'd been made as a grade-school art project. The barmaid set down her Harlequin romance as we took our seats at the bar. She wished us Merry Christmas and asked what we wanted to drink.

"Scotch on the rocks, water on the side for me," said Louis.

"The same."

She looked at me and arched one eyebrow. "Are you two related?"

"He's my little brother," said Louis, cuffing me lightly on the back of the head.

"I thought so." She took two glasses off the shelf with a twirl of her hands and set them below the counter, clinked in the ice, then poured the Scotch with an elaborate gesture, pulling the bottle up and swinging it in the air. Finished, she set the drinks on the bar, saying, "One for you, and one for you," winking at me. Then she filled up a tall glass with Coke and set it down beside my Scotch. "And so's I don't lose my license, if anyone comes in that door, you're drinking Coke, right?"

"Gotcha."

She smiled. She was a good-looking woman, in her own way—almost six feet of her—and her body had that big-woman look to it: wide hips, long arms, and long legs. She wore a clatter of silver bracelets on her arms and a turquoise necklace. And she was probably ten years older than Louis.

"What are you two roustabouts doing out on a holiday night? Shouldn't you be home wrapping presents?" The next day was Christmas Eve.

"We're just trying to keep from going crazy," said Louis. "I'm visiting my family here in Beachport, and I can only take so much at one time."

The barmaid smiled. "But don't we just love our families?"

"Oh yeah." Louis grinned and tossed off his Scotch. "Love them like the plague." I'd never drunk whiskey before so I had to sip it slowly, fight the impulse to cough every time, struggle to keep my face from scrunching up.

"Every time I go home to see my mom in Beaumont she gives me the third degree," the barmaid said. "I don't even tell her where I'm working. A little white lie, actually. Friend of mine runs a souvenir shop, and I told my mother that's where I work. I don't want her nagging me about working at a bar. She'd probably imagine I was topless or something." At that she opened her eyes wide in mock shock, putting both open hands to her face. We laughed.

"Not that I'm an angel." She smiled and made us two more drinks without us having to ask.

"But that might be a bit much, eh," said Louis.

"Sometimes I wish I had the guts to do that. You know, those girls clean up in tips."

"I bet."

By the third drink Louis and Louise, the barmaid, were old chums. And I was hunkered over the jukebox, playing country-and-western songs like "Why Don't You Love Me Like You Used to Do?" and "Thank God (and Greyhound) She's Gone." They got a lot of mileage out of their names, saying they'd make a great couple. She told how her father had wanted a boy and was going to name him Louis, after the fighter Joe Louis, the Brown Bomber. "Didn't matter one bit that he was blacker than the ace of spades. Daddy still wanted a son named Louis." I didn't look over at Louis when she said that. She told how her father had been disappointed with a girl. "That's me, the disappointment." But how he named her Louise anyway. "He figured I'd be a fighter one way or the other. And I am."

Here she held up her fists. "Don't mess with me 'cause I got a mean left hook."

Louis looked at me and said, "You know, maybe I was named after Joe Louis. You ever think about that, Damie?"

"Could be."

" 'Course my grandfather's name was Louis, but we always thought that referred to Louis Armstrong."

"Why?" asked Louise.

Louis smiled and shook his head. "Long story."

I kept trying to get Louis to leave, but once he got close with Louise, there wasn't a chance. We stayed till closing. Louis and I helped her sweep up and stack all the chairs on top of the tables. When Louise locked up I walked over to the VW while Louis followed her to her car. A northern had come in while we were sitting in the bar, so the sky had cleared and the wind was gusting, coming from the northwest. The sound of the wind filled my ears so I couldn't hear what they were saying. Louis leaned against the side of her car, smiling and talking to her. She nodded and seemed to be giving him directions, pointing south towards Aransas Pass, which was about ten miles from us. I was freezing. The door was locked. I couldn't get in, so I shuffled my legs back and forth. It was after midnight by then. My stomach felt queasy and I was nervous. We should have been heading home, and we weren't.

Louis dashed back to the car and shivered as he was getting his keys out of his pocket. The warmest thing he had on was his blue-jean jacket. After he got in the car he said, "What is this? Antarctica?"

He revved the puny VW engine and rubbed his hands together. "We're going to Louise's for a drink." He looked at me and grinned. "Keep your fingers crossed, Damie. I might get lucky."

"But Louis. Mom and Glen are going to be pissed."

He shrugged, putting the car in gear and following the red taillights of Louise's Pontiac onto Highway 36. "They'll get over it."

*　　*　　*

Louise lived in a subdivision of weekend homes called Playa del Mar, a collection of weather-beaten wooden houses on stilts with oleander bushes in the backyards and palm trees in the front. Beyond the oleanders was a canal that opened out onto the bay. Here and there a ski boat or a fishing boat sat in a trailer by the dock. Louise had an old-style ski boat with an outboard motor docked at her wharf. She let us in through the sliding glass door in the rear of the house.

"Excuse the mess. My mother would have a coronary if she saw this place."

Inside, her house was full of sleeping cats and tropical fish. The cats woke up and stretched as we walked in. There were three aquariums in the living room, big ones full of bright fish slowly pulsing or darting back and forth. Louise named off what they were but I was too far gone to pay attention. She and Louis were holding hands and bumping into each other as they walked around the house. I asked if I could take her boat out for a spin. She said she didn't think that was a good idea. "Why don't you have a drink instead?"

The bar at Louise's house was almost as big as the one at the Canoe Club. She had several kinds of Scotch, vodka, and tequila. "What'll it be, tiger? Courtesy of the house."

She fixed me a vodka gimlet with bottled lime juice and Stolichnaya from her freezer. I said, "Thank you, house."

"Funny boy. Your brother's a funny one, you know that, Louie?"

Louis winked at me. "He's a card. A regular Tommy Smothers."

"I was thinking more of you two as a team. Like Abbott and Costello."

"Abbott and Costello? Well, which is which?"

"He can be the short cute one," she said. "You can be the brains."

I finished my drink and clinked it down on the bar. "The short *fat* one, you mean. Hey. I'm not fat."

"No one said you were, sweetie. It's the cute part that's important."

Halfway through my third drink I found myself petting a huge calico cat, who was purring in my lap, and I realized I was alone in the living room, alone in a strange house. I felt weird and uncertain, as if I'd just left home for a trip on which I'd be gone for months and had forgotten some crucial life-saving and life-protecting item. The room was spinning around me. Cats fish fins fur blurred together. I felt as if I were riding a children's carousel in a pet shop. I stumbled towards the back door, bounced off the white refrigerator, surged ahead to the sofa in the living room, where I plopped down heavily then rose back up, almost fell against one of the fifteen-gallon aquariums, but I caught myself, steadied the wobbling tank, then crossed the carpet to the sliding glass doors, in which a hunk of the curtain was caught. Then I made it through and into the backyard.

The cold air felt great. And for a few moments it made me feel sober. There were some old wrought-iron lawn chairs at a matching wrought-iron table by the canal, grass grown high under them. I decided to sit there in the cold north wind till I stopped spinning. I got a pack of Marlboros from the VW and grabbed the bag of fireworks from the backseat. The tobacco smelled good, my hands cupped around the ember to keep the wind from burning it too fast, the smell soaking into my fingers, mixing with the sea smell, the bay smell, and cleansing my mind. The iron chair was cold and hard. Soon I was chilled to the bone, but the alcohol kept me warm inside, my face burning, my eyes watering in the wind. A piece of the moon was in the sky, dimly illuminating the canal and the backyards of the weekend homes, although the porch lamp cast light around where I was sitting. No one stirred. No one seemed awake or even home. A tattered American flag popped in the wind, strung from the upper porch of one of Louise's neighbors' decks, the metal hooks at the guy lines and grommets clanging rhythmically against the metal pole.

With the glowing tip of my third cigarette—chainsmoking them, thinking that it would keep me warm—I lit the fuse of a bottle rocket, watched as it kicked sparks, then tossed it into the air as the fuse got close to the tip. The rocket streaked horizontally across the canal, ricocheted off a neighbor's garbage can, then popped. The wind muffled the sound, making it more like a weak firecracker than how I remembered bottle rockets to be, a huge pop and shower of golden sparks.

I shot over a dozen that way, holding the cigarette in my left hand, the stalk of the bottle rocket in my right, waiting till the fuse nearly reached the head of the rocket, then tossing it into the air. If I did it correctly the rocket would shoot into the sky, veering south, pushed by the wind, leaving a twisting trail of golden sparks till it exploded above me, a distant pop, a balloon shower of sparks. But they didn't always burst in the sky. Some fizzled, fizzed out, shooting up to a silent end, leaving a trace of smoke but no sound. And only about one in five made it into the sky. The others shot like assault rockets into neighbors' yards, bounced off neighbors' boats, walls, the shutters of an upper-floor window. And some streaked directly into the canal, popping below the surface.

Halfway through the second dozen, one blew up in my hand. I lit the fuse, tried to take a drag on my cigarette with my left hand, and was too spastic in my timing to toss with my right. It exploded, knocking my hand back as if it had been hit with a baseball bat. Suddenly my ears were ringing and I was shaking my fingers. They were numb and stinging at first, but as the shock wore off and tears came to my eyes, I spread my trembling, blackened hand out. Then it felt as if it had been immersed in fire. I closed my eyes and grabbed my wrist, my entire body stiffening up, but the liquid flames that seemed to coat my fingers wouldn't go away. I got up and lay across the boat dock on my belly and stuck my hand in the cold bay water. Soon as I pulled my hand out of the water the pain came back, so I kept it in. I lay still there, resting my head against the wooden planking, feeling the rough splinters on my cheek and temple. The wood smelled like old gumbo.

I must have lain there for some time before I heard Louis calling my name. "Damon! What the hell are you doing here?" He pulled me up by my shoulders. I cringed as I tried to hold my body up with my hand. "What's the matter?"

He stood there in bare feet, his jacket unbuttoned, his shirt tail untucked. I told him about the bottle rocket and that my hand hurt like hell. "Oh Jesus, Damon. Your ass is grass, you know that, don't you? Glen and Mom are going to freak when they see this." He put his arm around me and took me inside. Louise sprayed my blackened fingers with Bactine, and I began vomiting in her bathroom. It kept coming and coming. I could feel Louise's warm hand on my arm, as she tried to make me feel better, but I just wanted both of them to leave. When I had retched all that I could, they cleaned my face and bandaged my hand.

Louis wanted to leave after that, but he couldn't find the keys to the Volkswagen. I fell asleep on the sofa while he and Louise were looking for them. It was after seven o'clock, with the gray light of dawn along the highway, when we drove back to our house. I remember, when we came in, my mother fussing over my hand, her hair still in curlers, wearing the house robe that she always cooked breakfast in, Sonia in the background, looking worried. Glen was talking on the telephone, telling the sheriff to never mind. I heard him say, "It was just a big mistake." They put me to bed. My eyes stung when I closed them. It felt good to hold them shut, and to try to ignore the shouting in the next room.

Louis was gone when I woke. It was Christmas Eve. When the owner of the fireworks stand saw the bandage on my hand later that day, she asked what had happened. I told her the truth. It made me sound stupid, but I told everyone the truth. She shook her head. She was a homely woman with a bouffant hairdo like my mother's, only she was older, and her hair was completely white. That day her beehive hair seemed even more enormous than usual—maybe she'd had a holiday visit to the beauty parlor—and it seemed to radiate out from her head in cotton-candy swirls, starchy and stiff, but her bulldog face was set against my foolishness, against anyone who didn't know the first thing about shooting fireworks, about the right way to handle dangerous explosives. I think she felt a little guilty that we had bought the bottle rockets from her stand. No one in her family had ever hurt themselves with fireworks. She told me so. She pointed out the error of my ways. They sold fireworks. They didn't blow their fingers off with them.

They knew to let go before it was too late.

25

I Have Become
Comfortably
Numb

My fingers healed more or less in the months following the bottle-rocket wound, though the tips of my thumb and index finger never regained any feeling. The nerves were shot. And nerves never heal. That wasn't the first time I found that if you suffer a brief, intense pain your body makes some adjustments. It learns. It learns how not to feel, how to shut down when a sensation might get in the way of living. The beauty of scars is that they never hurt again. But sometimes they itch.

The rest of the years that I lived there, Louis never visited. For a time, I tried to get back to him. I hated living in Beachport and, in my mind, I glorified our lives back in San Gabriel, our old neighborhood at Moonlight and Sunburst. I concocted a plan to move in with Louis in San Gabriel, wrote to ask if he thought it was a good idea, and he called back, said there was plenty of room at his new place. And he added that as long as I did my share of cleaning around the house, I was welcome. He seemed excited by the idea. "It'll be just like the old days."

I thought about it constantly, and finally one day I worked up the courage to ask my mother's permission to move. It was late one afternoon in the summer after my sophomore year in high school. I was working in the restaurant, but it was the slowest time of the day for business. The only customers were a table of wino fishermen with purple noses who had nowhere else to go. Glen was sitting behind the counter, reading a recent *Popular Mechanics*, now and then looking out the front windows of the café at the tourist traffic.

The wino fishermen called for another round of beer. Glen had to serve them, since I wasn't old enough. I carried the fly swatter around for a few minutes, seeing how many I could kill, counting them. Glen didn't like me to do that, so he said I could take a break if I wanted to. I rode my bike back to our cottage. Glen had bought some land on the bay and planned to build a house on it, but he hadn't gotten around to that project yet, so we had stayed at the cottages, which were cheap, anyway. Mother was lying in bed, reading, wearing her cat's-eye glasses. She was resting up for the night shift. I lay on my bed and tried to take a nap, because I also had to work that night and would be up till midnight or one. But I couldn't stop thinking about my plan to move back to San Gabriel and live with Louis.

I had it all worked out. I could lie to the school district about my address so I'd be admitted to Oliver Wendell Holmes High School, where Louis, Lizzie, Leland, and Melody had gone. I'd get back all my old friends, and the people that hadn't liked me very much wouldn't remember me anyway. I could grow my hair out, stay up all night watching horror movies if I wanted to. Louis and I could get the paper route again. That's how we could make money together. We would wake at three-thirty every morning and walk out to the VW half asleep. We would smudge our faces with newspaper ink. I would once again cut my hands with the cones of string we used to tie the papers with. Sitting next to each other, weirdly awake in the early morning light, Louis and I would listen to songs on the AM radio, would be together again.

I walked to my mother's room and stood in the doorway, waiting for her to look up. She had on a floral print dress that she wore nearly every day now. She seemed small and tired and wary, almost afraid of what I was going to say, when she asked if I wanted something.

I told her I hated it there in Beachport, that I wanted to move back, to go back to the way it used to be. I told her that I missed Louis, and he'd promised I could come live with him. I told her it would work out. Really, I knew it would. I could get a job, go back to my old school. We would come visit Beachport, too. Glen wouldn't mind. He seemed busy enough with the restaurant, anyway. He didn't need me hanging around getting in the way, did he?

What she said. What she answered. I knew the answer before I heard it.

"You can't do that, Damon. You wouldn't want to run off and leave me, would you?" She stroked my cheek. I had sat down beside her. "What about Sonia? Who would she have to talk to? Who would she make those special cheeseburgers for? What about Glen? How would he get anyone else to help in the café as good as you are? One day you're going to own that restaurant, you know that?"

I didn't want the restaurant. The book she was reading was *The Martian Chronicles*. She was always reading science fiction, forever cast away on another planet ruled by beings of vastly superior intelligence, who didn't use sound to communicate, but who could read each other's minds, so there was no lying, no secrets, no hatred, nothing hidden.

She hugged me close as I mumbled, "But we'd come see you all the time," a whining, watery voice that I knew would fail and collapse in shame. Shame at the desertion, betrayal, abandonment I had implied. And never did again.

26

Cafeteria Joy

So I didn't live with Louis until many years later, and by then, it was too late to return to what we'd been before. After high school I went to Tulane. I wasn't sure why I'd been accepted there. My entrance exam scores were high, but my high school grades were uneven. I hadn't belonged to any "extracurricular activities" in high school except the Slide Rule Club, and that seemed pretty lame, especially since calculators were becoming popular and making slide rules obsolete. I figured that I might have been accepted because I checked AFRO-AMERICAN under the racial category on my questionnaire. In the essay I had to complete for the application, I described what it had been like, growing up with the stigma of mixed race, how I blamed not only the people who taunted me, but also myself, and my family as well. It was a raw essay. I told them how I actually felt, but after I was accepted into the school, and received a scholarship that covered most of the tuition, I wanted to deny it. I wanted to keep my secret. For all these years my identity had been a liability. I wanted payback.

I knew nothing about my grandfather's life, or even who he really was, except that Louis had been named after him. I'd conjured up a glorious past for him as a talented jazz musician, and created a kind of mythic Louis Armstrong in my mind, even wondering if *Satchmo* had been my grandfather. How did I know he wasn't? During my years at Tulane I learned that Louis Armstrong had been born in 1900. That made him the right age. I didn't try to track him down or find out if it really was true. I think I liked the possibility of it, and if I'd found out that it wasn't true, I would have been disappointed. I pictured my grandmother as a kind of Roaring Twenties emancipated jazz groupie, wooed in a speakeasy, dying young after giving birth to her love child, my mother. But still I felt like an impostor. A fake. I didn't know anything about black culture. I shied away from the black bars and nightclubs in New Orleans.

If anyone ever asked about my unusual coloring, I said I was Italian.

I lived in a dormitory the first year, and did my best to fit in. It was easy to do. No one seemed to think twice about me, except perhaps my roommate. We shared a small room with twin beds on opposite sides of the room, built-in bureaus in the center with a shared mirror, and built-in desks on either side. There was a communal bathroom down the hall, with communal showers. My roommate had already stocked his side of the bureau top with an arsenal of hair and skin care products when I arrived. His bed was covered with a fake-leopard-skin bedspread and matching pillowcases. On his desk was a framed photograph of a plump and sultry girl leaning against a tree, her arms folded behind her. Beside the photo was his clock radio. He had pinned two posters to the walls beside his bed. One was a winter scene of a snowy mountain at night, with skiers carrying flares, fireworks bursting in the sky above, the legend ASPEN, COLORADO at the bottom. The other poster featured what appeared to be an English polo player, with one knee-high boot on the fender of a Rolls-Royce. He was smiling into the camera, holding a glass of champagne. The legend was POVERTY SUCKS.

While I was still unpacking my clothes, my roommate arrived and we introduced ourselves. His name was Alan Bishop Coolidge, but he didn't like Alan, he told me, so everyone called him Bishop. Weird, huh?

"But mine's nothing compared to yours. That's some moniker. Damon. Like 'demon,' eh? I better watch out. You're not going to sacrifice a goat or anything to start the semester, are you?"

I told him I hadn't planned on it, but if I did, I'd let him know, so he could watch.

"Right. And whenever I get ready to jerk off, I'll let *you* know." He made stroking motions in the air with his right hand. Bishop was good-looking, with dark brown hair, thick and tawny eyebrows, and an Abe Lincoln beard. He spent a lot of time standing in front of the mirror, brushing his hair. He even had a special comb for his beard.

He had several goals in life, he told me. He knew what he wanted and he knew how to get it. He'd been raised to believe in hard work and intestinal fortitude. Of course, it didn't hurt to know the right people, and have a little spending money in your pocket. But he wasn't going to sit around waiting for things to happen. No sir. He was going to *make* things happen. He had a list of goals. You have to have goals!

"Once you get to know me, you'll see. I get what I want. I'm not a quitter."

"I never said you were."

"But you *thought* it, didn't you? Come on. I *know*. I know you don't believe me. I can see it in your eyes."

He even had categories for his goals. They were defined chronologically. First he had weekly goals. He called them weeklies. "My current weekly is to score my first Tulane lay. The first, that is, of what I'm sure will be my many Tulane lays. But that's an easy one. Hell, I won't even have to *try* to do that."

"Like stealing candy from a baby," I said. One of his childhood weeklies, I guessed.

"Then I have monthlies, yearlies, and lifetimes. My monthly right now is to pledge Pi Kappa Alpha. It's the fraternity that most senators belong to, the one that I think will help in my big lifetime, and that's to become a member of the Supreme Court.

"There it is again! I can see it in your eyes! You don't believe I'm going to make it."

"Yes, I do. Well, no, I mean I don't know. It's none of my business. Besides, I just met you. How do I know what you'll accomplish?"

Bishop followed me into the communal bathroom, describing his closer long-term goal. He wasn't sure if it qualified as a yearly, but it was less than a lifetime. That was to be a member of the U.S. Olympic ski team. Coming to school here in Tulane was a setback for that one, he knew, but sometimes you have to compromise. He figured a degree from

Tulane would get him into more law schools than one from the University of Colorado in Boulder, where he'd thought about going for the ski slopes.

There were a half-dozen sinks, stalls, and urinals in the communal bathroom. I sat on a wooden bench across from the door to the showers and took off my clothes while Bishop described how he was going to become an Olympic downhill skier. He'd been skiing since he was five years old, and you knew where he was going to be over the Christmas holidays, right? He idolized Spider Sabich and Jean-Claude Killy. He followed me into the shower and kept talking as I shampooed my hair. He soaped up his naked body elaborately and kept on talking.

"Hey, where'd you get that tan, Demon? You're pretty goddam dark, you know that?"

I shrugged. "I spent the summer in a little resort town on the Gulf."

"Well, I guess. But it sure is fucking *even*."

I rinsed the shampoo out of my hair, stepped out of the shower, and started drying myself off. I was trying to ignore him, but Bishop kept talking, asking me another question I didn't want to answer. "Hello! Demon! Earth to Demon! Are you there, Demon?"

I combed my hair in front of the mirror. "Bishop. Did anyone ever tell you you talk too much?"

His face appeared beside mine in the mirror. "Pay attention. You might learn something."

I was glad that Bishop pledged Pi Kappa Alpha, because it kept him out of the room most of the time. The fraternity brothers made life difficult for Bishop by forcing him to do their laundry, transcribe their notes, and run errands for them. I secretly enjoyed watching him sort some fraternity brother's dirty laundry, although I did my best to keep my face neutral when he was around. But he paid me back for my silence. Each night, about eleven-thirty or later, he forced me to overhear his long-distance telephone conversations with his high school girlfriend from Tulsa, who was now living in Dallas, going to SMU. Her name was Kelli, with an i. He liked the sound of their names together. Bishop and Kelli.

"People are going to remember the two of us."

Kelli called so often that we struck up a telephone friendship. She had an Ann-Margret kind of voice, soft and breathy. She was joining the Delta Delta Delta sorority at SMU, but was sick of the life and the people. If she called while Bishop was out of the room, we'd linger on the phone, asking about each other's classes, how we liked New Orleans or Dallas. She was coming to visit after Thanksgiving and said she was really looking forward to meeting me.

"You seem so nice and intelligent, compared to most frat boys, and especially Alan's friends. I swear, most of those guys are animals."

I asked her why she called him Alan, and explained that no one here called him anything other than Bishop.

"I don't know where he got that crazy idea. Do you think he's a little odd? He didn't use to be so . . . obnoxious."

"I don't know. He's certainly full of energy."

She called one night when I was in bed, reading, and Bishop was there. He answered the phone. They spoke for a few minutes, then he said, "Yeah, he's here. Uh huh. Hey Demon. Kell says hi."

I waved. He made a big production out of listening to a long speech at the other end of the phone, flapping his thumb and fingers in the air to mimic a flapping mouth.

"I'll call him whatever I want to call him, Kell. Besides, he doesn't mind." He put his hand over the mouthpiece and asked, "You don't mind being called Demon, do you?"

"It's not my name."

He said into the phone, "He says it's not his name. But that doesn't mean he minds." He listened to Kelli. "She says you're just being polite, that I don't deserve you as a roommate."

"That's true."

As the semester wore on, Kelli called less frequently when Bishop was there late in the evening, although she still called now and then in the afternoon to chat with me. Bishop spent most of his free time with his fraternity friends trying to become a Pike. Whenever he was home, he had to answer the telephone with "Hi! This is Pi Kappa Alpha pledge Alan Bishop Coolidge speaking. Can I help you?" My dorm friends thought he was a weirdo. If he'd been a lieutenant in Vietnam, he would have been the type to be fragged by his platoon soldiers. When he called Kelli late at night, I would double pillows over my head to block out the sound, but I couldn't help overhearing most of the conversations. It sounded like their relationship was on the rocks. He whined and begged, often telling her he'd called earlier and she hadn't been there. Where were you, Kell? You're not going out with someone else, are you? He wanted Kelli to transfer to Tulane, but she wouldn't go for it. After he hung up, he'd say, "I tell ya, these long-distance love affairs suck. If you want my advice, find some nooky in your own backyard and save yourself a lot of trouble. And a lot of dough on stupid phone bills."

Of all the pleasures I experienced during that first year in college, one of the most intense was the total freedom of the cafeteria, the wealth, the abundance, the near-heartbreaking opportunity to eat anything I wanted, however much I wanted, and to be as wasteful or efficient as I chose to be. And no one gave a damn. There was so much food that we threw it at each other, sometimes hurling fruit cocktail Jell-O or chocolate pudding into the air, into some total stranger's face, laughing and ducking, showering the mustard out of our hair later. After we'd moved to Beachport I'd had plenty of restaurant food to eat, but never so much that we threw it at each other. Here at the cafeteria we had deep freezes full of buckets of ice cream. Help yourself! Eat as much as you want! Pots of cheese broccoli soup with a stack of bowls and a basket of melba toast or Waverly Wafer crackers beside them. And the salad bar! Plastic crocks full of potato salad, three-bean salad, cole slaw, pasta salad, chicken salad, tuna salad. Wedged into a layer of ice to keep them cool, crocks full of cherry tomatoes, celery sticks, black olives, carrot sticks, cauliflower, broccoli spears. Huge clear plastic bowls of lettuce. Your choice of salad dressings.

I would make my way through the cafeteria line, passing the stainless-steel steam table full of cheese enchiladas, Hawaiian pork, Salisbury steak, and fish sticks. I was enthralled by the trays of warm rolls, pads of butter on white squares of hard paper, with a tiny wax paper square atop each of them. Milk delivered from a stainless-steel refrigerator that had a spigot you lifted to shoot a stream of white or chocolate into your glass.

After selecting everything, filling my tray with food, each item on its own shiny white china plate or bowl, I would walk into the large dining hall and find a place to sit. My biggest fear in the cafeteria was that I would drop my tray. Whenever anyone did this the entire cafeteria would clap and hoot. At a space on one of the tables, I would remove all the bowls and saucers and plates, the silverware, napkins, and milk or iced-tea glasses, and place the tray on the seat beside me, so that I couldn't see it. I liked all the bowls and saucers. I was wasteful, and would carry things back to my table that I never ate. I'd grab anything that caught my eye.

The cafeteria reminded me of years before, back at our old neighborhood in San Gabriel, back before we moved to Beachport, before Glen, before Lizzie got pregnant and left the house. She'd been living in New Orleans since then, and I'd been meaning to see her, but she never called me, and I'd been at Tulane for almost two months before I got in touch with her. She was now living with her husband in a housing subdivision out in Metairie, a suburb of New Orleans. When I called she said I'd better rush right over if I wanted to catch her before she left. I borrowed a friend's car and drove out there. She lived at the end of a cul-de-sac in a neighborhood that had been built in the sixties, although the houses already looked dilapidated and weather-beaten. Some of the lawns were overgrown and there seemed to be more cars in the driveways and parked beside the curbs than people to drive them. Many of the cars looked like they didn't run. As I drove up to her house, there were two men working under the hood of a Buick in the driveway next to hers.

When I walked up to her front door it was open—the spring on the screen door unlatched—and there were boxes everywhere. I knocked anyway. Lizzie came out from around a corner wearing blue jeans and an old sweatshirt. "Well if it isn't my little brother," she said, and hugged me. "All grown up."

We weaved our way through the living room crowded with boxes—some full and taped up already, others apparently in the process of being packed. Boxes of knickknacks, tablecloths, paperback books. The kitchen still had a Formica kitchenette table set up in it, though the curtains had been taken down, and sunlight streamed in. Outside, the backyard was littered with red and yellow plastic Fisher-Price toys, and there was a baby pool in the back, near the wooden fence.

Lizzie told me I was lucky to call when I did. "We're moving to Alaska. Can you believe it? From bums on Bourbon Street to grizzly bears. Mitch is a mud engineer for Exxon, and he got transferred out there. I'd been meaning to call you but never got around to it. We've been so busy and all. You want something to drink?"

I thought she was prettier than I remembered, her hair black and wavy. Her two kids, Tawnya and Joey, came in from outside while we were talking. Lizzie said, "This is your uncle. You've never even seen these two, have you?" I tousled Joey's hair. He was seven years old and smiled at me. He kept tugging on his mother's dress and whispering things in her ear the whole time I was there. Tawnya, who was three, hid behind the kitchen counter and peeked out at me now and then.

We talked about the old house, how Lizzie's kids were growing up so fast. She was worried about Louis. "I don't know, Damie, but every time I talk with him over the phone lately he seems to be getting weirder and weirder. He needs to settle down and get married, is what he needs to do. And he's into drugs, too. I think he's been hanging out with some pretty scruffy types. I know he was doing a lot of acid for a while there. That's none of my business, but I don't think it's good for him. He needs to get some kind of real job. Or go back to college. Or *something*."

I tried to defend Louis. Maybe he was just a late bloomer. "College isn't for everyone," I said.

"Don't you think I know that? I mean, I had to take my GED just to get my high school diploma. But that's different. I've got kids and everything. I don't have time for anything else. But Louis is on his own, and if he doesn't watch out, he's going to stay on his own."

"I don't know what's going on with him," I said. "I haven't seen him in a while."

"I just hope he doesn't turn out like our father. He looks *exactly* like him, you know. It's spooky. But you were so little when he killed himself, you probably don't remember much, do you?"

"Killed himself? You're putting me on."

"What do you mean?"

"I never heard that."

"Well, what'd you think happened to him?"

"I thought he died in his sleep."

"What?" She made a face at me. "You believed that for all these years? And I thought you're supposed to be smart. People just don't die in their sleep, for nothing."

"Well I don't know. Yeah, I guess I thought that was a cover-up, somehow. But I figured it was probably cancer or something. Hepatitis, maybe."

Lizzie laughed. "You *are* the baby of the family. In more ways than one."

"So how'd he do it?"

"The truth is . . . ." She turned her head and paused. "The truth is, we don't know the truth. We don't know the *reason*. There's got to be a reason, right? That we don't know. But we know he killed himself with a shotgun. Put it in his mouth. And pulled the trigger."

"But why?"

"I don't know. Mom will never talk about it. They were divorced by then, so I think she feels guilty. You knew that, didn't you?"

"No."

"Jesus." She shook her head. "You don't know much of anything, do you?"

"I guess not."

"Well, our father was a big drinker and a gambler. Maybe he owed a lot of money or something. That's what Melody thinks. But I think there's more to it than money. I think it had something to do with us. I think he felt like a failure. It was only a few months after they divorced that he did it."

Lizzie made a spaghetti dinner, and I left before her husband came home from work. I said I had to get back to the dorm to study for a test the next day. I lied. It just felt so odd to be around her, after what she'd told me, and knowing she was leaving New Orleans in a few days. I needed time to think. And it was almost as if I didn't want to know her, since she wouldn't be here anymore. She made a big deal about my being at Tulane.

"Well, you know we're all proud of you. My brother. The brain. Hard to believe, but true. You know, when you were a little kid, I always thought you were kind of slow. And look at you now."

"I still think I *am* a little slow. But I get by."

"Oh, nonsense." She hugged me and I said I'd give her a call and come visit again before they left. But I never did. While I was driving away, she stood on the front porch and held little Tawnya in her arms, holding her wrist and making her wave to me. Before I reached the end of the block I realized that I had left my sunglasses on the kitchen counter. I didn't turn around. Now that I was away from there, I didn't like the idea of going back.

Kelli flew in to spend homecoming weekend with Bishop. Tulane was playing Vanderbilt, and Bishop wanted to show Kelli to his frat friends. "They're going to be drooling when they see her. You know it. And I've got to be careful, too. Some of these guys are real bird dogs. I'm not going to let her alone for one minute with any of them, you can count on that." He told me how a girl had gotten plastered at a recent rum punch party and passed out in a bedroom upstairs. The pledges had all taken turns with her. He said it was a lot of fun. But he wouldn't want that to happen to Kell.

They were sitting on the bed, talking, when I got back from classes on Friday. Bishop said, "This is the moment we've all been waiting for, folks. Demon, Kelli. Kelli, Demon. Roommate, meet girlfriend."

We shook hands. She looked slimmer than in her photograph, but was shorter than I'd imagined. Short, with huge eyes. And she was dressed more casually than most of the sorority girls I met at Tulane, in blue jeans and a white cardigan sweater over a light blue T-shirt, with black cowboy boots. I thought she was pretty. Too much makeup, but beautiful eyes.

Bishop kept his arm around her and acted as if he were showing off a trophy catch. "So what do you think of my main squeeze?"

"Jesus, Alan." Kelli rolled her eyes. "Can't we be a little more mature?"

"I think not," I told her. "I think maturity isn't part of the Pi Kappa Alpha tradition, and we've got to follow tradition."

"He's just jealous," said Bishop.

Kelli made a face. "Of what?"

"Of my obvious superiority." He winked at me.

There was an awkward silence. I shrugged.

"What is it with you two?" asked Bishop. "Can't you take a fucking joke?"

I wanted to get out of there, so I told them I thought I'd head down to the cafeteria to miss the dinner rush. "It was nice meeting you, Kelli."

"Me too," she said. "Maybe we can get together for lunch sometime before I leave on Sunday."

"Lunch?" said Bishop. "With Demon? No chance. I see enough of him as it is."

They went to a homecoming cotillion at the Pi Kappa Alpha house that night, and then were at the football game the next day, so I didn't see them until late Saturday, when I came home from dinner about nine o'clock. Kelli was propped up on pillows on Bishop's bed, reading *The Sound and the Fury*. "It's for a class," she said, holding up the cover.

"I'm about fifty pages into it and have absolutely no idea of what's going on."

"Don't worry. It gets easier by the end."

"I hope so."

I sat in my only chair and propped my feet up on the desk. "Where's Alan?"

She rolled her eyes. "He's at the Pike house. And for all I care, I hope he stays there."

"Aren't you guys going out tonight?"

"We were supposed to. But two of his *brothers* called and told Alan to go wash their cars. And since he's a pledge, he has to do what they tell him to, or he gets kicked out. I don't think he's one of the most popular people in the frat house. In fact, I think they kind of hate him."

"Oh. Sorry."

"But what really gets me is that here I am in New Orleans for the first time in my life and I have to stay cooped up in this room till he gets back. I'm about to go stir-crazy."

We talked for a while, then I suggested going to the French Quarter for a drink and leaving Alan a note. She loved the idea. Over her shoulder I read the note she dashed off. It didn't say when we'd be back. It read, "Got sick of waiting. Call me when you grow up. Kell."

I took her to a place called Napoleon's at Chartres and St. Louis, dark and smoky, and she told me it was exactly what she'd imagined a French Quarter bar would be like. When we got our first drink, she touched my wrist to stop me as I was about to clink her glass and say cheers.

"Can I tell you a secret?"

"Shoot."

"I'm calling it quits with Alan after this weekend. I've had enough." She went on to say what a jerk he'd been that afternoon at the game, that she'd decided never again.

"Good for you. Here's to a brief but convincing Dear John letter in the mail."

"A Dear *Bishop* letter." We toasted. After she set down her glass she put her hands in front of her as if she were reading a letter. "Dear Bishop," she said. "Adios."

I laughed. By the fourth White Russian we were holding hands under the table, drawing up a list of all the things we hated about Alan. She began with self-centered, egotistical, loud, vain, pigheaded, and bad breath. I added racist, fascist, chauvinist, insensitive, stupid, and that excruciatingly squishy sound he made when he stuck his index finger in his ear after he took a shower.

We didn't leave the bar till two. I drove her back to her hotel room. The concierge gave her a sheaf of phone messages from Alan. I walked her through the lobby as she read them, shaking her head. She was still reading them as we reached the elevator.

"Well, thanks for keeping me company," I said. "It was fun."

She wadded up the notes, placed them on top of a large stainless-steel waste bin that was beside the elevators, then pressed the up arrow. I was about to walk away when she said, "Hold on there. You're not going to just leave me, are you?" She reached out and grabbed my belt loop, then pulled me towards her.

"Well. I don't know." I smiled. "Don't you think I'd better go?"

She shook her head. "Uh-uh." She leaned her head against my shoulder and rubbed against me. "What if there's a mugger in my room? What if there's a *rapist?*"

"What if there's a Bishop?"

She pulled me into the elevator and we made out all the way to her room. We paused to catch our breaths for a moment, and it was just long enough for her to say, "Bishop? Bishop who?"

We never admitted where we were that night, and Alan never found out—they had broken up by the end of the next week. I was in love with her for a month or so, but gradually it faded, and I never saw her again. Meantime I had to listen to him swear that she'd come begging on her hands and knees to get him back. You'll see! But no, I didn't want to bet.

By the end of the semester he'd been accepted by the fraternity, and I was overjoyed, since it meant that he was moving into the Pike house at the start of the next semester. The last time I had anything to do with him was the dead week before finals. He got me to give him a ride to pick up his Trans Am at the shop. It was about a twenty-minute drive, through the poor neighborhoods next to campus. We were so sick of each other by that time that we weren't talking much, but he pointed out a trio of young black men sitting on the porch of a run-down house. "You know what they call that in Tulsa?"

I didn't ask. I didn't care. Besides, I knew I'd hear it whether I wanted to or not.

"Porch monkeys." He thought that was funny. It seemed to lift his mood a little. I thought about it as I drove along, turning it over in my mind. Each time I had to slow down and speed up for the stoplights, my hands were shaking as I shifted the gears. It was hard to get my breath to speak, but finally I did.

"You know, Coolidge, you are one stupid motherfucker.

You know what? My grandfather was black. So for the few more hours or days that we have to be around each other, and believe me it can't be soon enough for me, cut with the *nigger* crap. I'm sick of it. And I'm sick of *you*." I didn't—I couldn't—even turn to look at him. We were stopped at a light. I kept my eyes on the intersection in front of me.

"In fact, why don't you get your fucking redneck ass out of my car."

27
Villa
del Sol

Being around Bishop and other people in my dorm, people who called their fathers on the weekend to ask for more spending money and who wore clothes their mothers bought for them, I realized how different my history was. Whenever my first college friends asked about my family, I avoided the subject. Or lied. My brothers and sisters were scattered across the country by then—Melody with her family of five kids in Utah, Lizzie in Alaska, Leland, Tony, and Agnes somewhere on the West Coast, Louis drifting from one job to the next, one city to the next. But my mother and Glen still lived in Beachport.

I still kept in touch with Sonia, who was back in San Gabriel, working as a waitress. She was in love and happy. She and Lionel, her boyfriend, lived together in a small house not far from our old neighborhood. We often talked on the phone, and agreed that our family was a loose collection of weirdos, but what's a body to do? We joked about it. And Sonia helped me out with money whenever I needed it. She was glad I was going to college, and wanted to make sure that I graduated. It looked as though no one else would, except Leland, and since he'd left the family, he didn't count anymore.

At the end of my third year at Tulane I needed a summer job, and Sonia's boyfriend said he had one for me at an apartment complex near our old neighborhood in San Gabriel. He'd become the assistant manager there, and would hire me and give me a vacant apartment to live in for the summer. Sonia called and told me about it.

"A janitor?" I said.

"Well, yeah. That's what it is, basically. But you'll get six fifty an hour. Plus a free place to stay. And Louis called last week. He's moving back here from L.A. Come on. It'll be all of us together again. You *have* to, Damie."

"But a janitor?"

"It's not a janitor. You'll be shampooing carpets. And it'll be easy. You'll see."

I remembered one of Bishop's "jokes."

Q: What do you call an unborn black fetus?

A: Janitor in a drum.

I drove to Sonia's house in San Gabriel at the end of May, following the directions she'd given me over the phone. She lived off Vance Jackson, a couple miles from our old place, and as I was driving down the road, almost there, I passed a man walking down the shoulder on the opposite side. I pulled over and waited for the cars to pass so I could make a U-turn. As I was waiting there, I remembered riding down this road on my bicycle with Kit. I was near the subdivision called Shenandoah. We'd smashed the windows of some of those houses. Back then the yards had been bare black earth, and now, ten years later, many of them had big trees, and the neighborhood had already taken on a homey, lived-in look, with shaded sidewalks, basketball hoops above the garage doors, tricycles in the front yards. When I got a break in the traffic I turned around and headed back in the opposite direction. The man I'd passed had a stiff-legged walk that I'd recognized. He was farther down the road by the time I caught up with him. I pulled over onto the shoulder and honked. He looked at me and seemed frightened for a moment. He scrambled farther away from the road, closer to the ditch beyond the shoulder, and I had to pull my Datsun nearer. Then I opened the door and shouted his name.

Louis turned and squinted at me. I motioned for him to come and finally he smiled and walked over to the car. He was carrying a paper grocery bag and set it down on the floorboards. We shook hands. "Long time no see."

Louis looked a little jumpy.

"Where were you headed?" I asked.

"Oh, the car's broke down so I was just going up here to the Stop-n-Go for a pack of smokes. Thought I'd trade in some of Sonny's bottles while I was at it. She's got a ton of them in her garage."

Louis's clothes were ratty. His hair already had gray in it, and his voice was hoarse and cracked. There were wrinkles in the skin around his mouth and chin. I asked what he was up to now that he was back in San Gabe.

"I'm staying at Sonny's till I can get back on my feet. Things are kind of fucked up right now. I was laid off in

L.A. and ran out of money. Then on the way out here my water pump quit on me near El Paso, so I had to pay to get that fixed, plus the tow and everything."

"Are you going to settle down here?"

"For a while, maybe. Least till something better comes along."

The clerk at the convenience store seemed to know Louis, and treated him impatiently, as if he were a bum. I bought him a couple packs of Viceroys and told him to save the bottle change for later. As we were walking out I told Louie, "You know, I used to steal candy bars and Dr Peppers from that Stop-n-Go."

He nodded and laughed. "The good old days."

Later, Sonia made us a lasagna dinner. I talked to her in the kitchen while Louis was in the living room. She was worried about him. He'd been sleeping on her couch for a couple of weeks and didn't show any signs of trying to get a job. The starter was out on his VW, so he couldn't go anywhere. She told me he'd sit around the house for hours, talking to himself. "I don't think it's good for him to stay home alone all the time. He's getting kind of nutty."

So we decided Louis should move in with me at the free apartment. We bought a new starter for his car and got it running again, then a few days later we loaded what few things—clothes and books mainly—he had and drove over to our new place. It was a one-bedroom apartment, but I agreed to sleep in the living room on a sofa bed Sonia loaned me. We had hardly any furniture, and had to stack our clothes on the floor because there weren't any dressers to put them in.

The first day we were setting things up, Louis opened the

refrigerator and looked inside. "First thing we have to buy is a huge bottle of barbecue sauce, eh?"

I laughed. "I kicked the habit, Louie. I'm on the wagon now." We went to the balcony and looked out at the swimming pool, where there were women tanning themselves.

Louis said, "This is great. Maybe I'll get a tan."

Our apartment reminded me of the open houses we used to visit in the housing subdivisions near our old neighborhood. The walls were freshly painted a flat white latex, with a spackled drywall surface. The carpeting was gold-colored, and had a used look. It still showed a dark path by the front door and in the most worn paths of the hallway and in the doorways.

Louis said he needed to get a job fast. "I'll start looking in the want ads this Sunday."

"Don't worry about it, Lou. At least we're back together again, eh? That's something."

Louis nodded. "But I don't want to mooch off you. You'll get sick of that pretty fast."

"Don't worry about it."

The name of the apartment complex was Villa del Sol. House of the Sun. The people who rented there always seemed to be moving in and out. They didn't seem to stay in one place very long.

When an apartment became vacant, the complex management had a system for readying it for the next renter. The walls were repainted. I did the carpets with the vacuum and the shampooer. Then the maids came in and gave each place a thorough cleaning. Some of the people seemed to have moved out in a hurry. The painter and I went through the things they left behind and took what we wanted. The painter was a husky guy who drove an old station wagon filled with cans of paint, drop cloths, paintbrushes. He had flecks of white latex paint in his curly brown hair.

"Vulture patrol," the painter would say to me when it was time to case an empty apartment, arriving in his station wagon. Villa del Sol was a big complex, with over a thousand units, so it was easiest to drive from one unit to the next. As we walked into the empty apartment, the painter would flap his arms as if they were heavy black wings, and caw. The most glamorous things we ever found were crummy, abandoned appliances, old stereo speakers whose sound was fuzzy and crackly, toasters with crumbs still scattered on the top, maybe an iron.

It was pitiful to go through people's lives like that. You looked into what they had left behind for something good, for something worth keeping, and were always disappointed. Once a family left during the middle of the night, owing three months' rent. They just took their clothes and drove away. Everything else they owned was left in the apartment. Except I never saw so much junk. We spent two days carting it out to the dumpster. Then the painter patched the holes where someone had punched through the walls and painted over everything. We replaced light bulbs, the maids cleaned the bathrooms and kitchen, and I vacuumed and shampooed the carpets. When we were finished it looked almost new.

I quickly settled into the work routine. A monkey could have done the job, and after a few weeks, humiliation began to settle on my life like dust. I would wake at eight-thirty and quickly dress in my brown maintenance man uniform, then check in at the manager's office to pick up the morning's assignments and chat with the other employees while we ate doughnuts and drank coffee. Although the painter could drive from one unit to the next, I had to wheel the huge shampooing machine on its rollers down the sidewalks, heaving it up the steps to upper-floor units, because it wouldn't really fit in my Datsun. I felt achingly conspicuous walking down the sidewalk with the shampooer. I felt like a loser. For lunch I'd either go out with the other employees for a hamburger or Mexican food, or go back to the apartment and eat something with Louis.

Living with him was driving me down. He smoked constantly, and often missed the ashtrays. The apartment smelled like dead cigarettes, and there were burn holes on the carpet in his bedroom and on our balcony. He couldn't get a job. At first he went out and filled in applications for waiter and restaurant jobs, but he looked too scruffy to be a waiter and didn't want to wash dishes. We were optimistic in the beginning, when he'd come back from an interview, but after a couple of weeks and no callbacks, both of us started to change our attitudes, to give up.

What do you do if you can't make a living, if you don't have money to begin with? There's no place for you to go, nowhere for you to fit in. I wondered what would happen to Louis if Sonia and I weren't there to help out. Would he be a street person, ragged and filthy, sleeping in a cardboard box under a freeway overpass? After a few weeks of hanging around the apartment all day with nothing to do, he seemed stunned and spaced out. He quit shaving and taking showers. He hardly moved. He would sit on the balcony, smoking cigarettes, talking to himself, laughing at the private jokes in his mind. He would lie by the pool in an old pair of blue-jean cutoffs. The gardeners complained that he put his cigarette butts out in the soil of the shrubbery, so I had to tell him to cut it out.

One day in particular, I came back to my apartment for lunch. Louis was sitting on the floor, smoking. The curtains were still drawn. It was spooky. First thing I did was open up the curtains and fold back the couch, putting the cushions in place.

"I was just getting ready to do that, yeah," said Louis. "Let's straighten up the room, huh?"

"You want anything special for lunch?" I asked. I looked into the refrigerator for cheese and bread to make sand-wiches. He didn't say anything. He was sitting on the couch now, talking to himself, smoking another cigarette. I was starting to count them. That was his third since I'd gotten home.

"How about an omelet?" I said, louder. He looked over at me, but it was as if he still had not heard.

"Louis?"

"What?" he said. "You talking to me, Damon?"

"You want to share an omelet with me?" I said.

"Sure. That sounds great. Yeah, an omelet would be good."

I chopped up bell pepper and tomatoes, grated some cheese. Sonia had taught me how to cook omelets, and I remembered that Louis had been on an omelet craze, many years ago.

When I was finished I called out, "It's ready." I brought over a plate for him, with half the big omelet on it.

"Hey, Damon, that's some omelet. You really went all out."

He picked up the fork and started eating. His cigarette kept burning in the ashtray, sending a thread of smoke into the room. I started to reach over to put it out, but I waited. I waited for him to do it, and when it was really small, almost burning the filter, he took one last drag, then jammed it into the ashtray, where it smoldered.

"You want to listen to some music?" I asked.

He kept staring out the window. It was as if he had a hearing problem. Or was in space. Somewhere else.

After lunch, I was glad to get back to work.

During this time I was staying in touch with my girlfriend from Tulane, who was home in Kansas, staying with her parents for the summer. We wrote each other and talked on the phone at least once a week, and had plans for me to drive up to Wichita in August and go camping together in the Rockies before returning to New Orleans.

"That's what I need," said Louis. "A woman. That'd help me get my confidence back. I just feel so *down* all the time. Like I'm in a hole below ground somewhere and there's no way to get back up."

I loaned him what little money I had and he called an old girlfriend from high school, who agreed to meet him at a nightclub for drinks. His clothes were all wrong, but at least he showered and shaved. He blow-dried his hair and put on cologne. "Vickie really used to be a fox," he said. "Hope I'll recognize her. It's been a long time."

"Good luck," I told him. "I'm sure she'll be glad to see you." I let him drive the Datsun, since it looked a little better than his VW.

I stayed home reading that night, and when Louis hadn't returned by two in the morning, I felt good. I figured things must have gone well. I'd fallen asleep by the time he got home, but woke up when I heard the door open. I listened as he stumbled around in the dark.

"That you, Louie?"

He sat in the only chair in the living room, next to the sofa I was sleeping on, and said, "Damon? Man, I'm fucked up. You awake?"

"Sure." I sat up in bed. "Go ahead and turn the light on if you want to."

"That's okay. You don't want to see me."

"What's the matter?"

I listened as Louis tapped a cigarette out of his pack and struck a match. When he held the flame and lit the cigarette, it seemed there was something wrong with his face. It looked lumpy and discolored.

"I got the shit beat out of me, Damon. And they bashed in the window of your car."

His date had never shown up, so he sat at the bar drinking for most of the night. After he was drunk he got up and went to a table to ask a woman to dance, but it turned out to be a guy with long hair, who had cussed him out, thought that Louis was making fun of him. Louie said he'd apologized and gone back to his place at the bar, but apparently the guy was with some other friends, and they waited till Louis left, then followed him out to the parking lot. They caught up to him as he was getting in the car. He slammed the door and locked it, but one of them had grabbed a rock and smashed the door window. Then they pulled him out and beat him. They kicked him in the face and side. Louis said he tried to crawl under the car to get away from them, and he had bruises on his back from where they'd kicked him.

I took him to the bathroom to clean him up. Both eyes were black-and-blue, and one of them was swollen shut. There was a deep cut on his forehead and blood streaming down from it on his cheek and shirt. The flesh of his ear was ripped at the top, and when I tried to clean it, it started bleeding again—thick, deep purple blood oozing from the wound. He refused to go to the hospital.

"This isn't the first time I've had the fuck beaten out of me. I'll live." He didn't want to pay any medical bills. "Besides, how can we pay it? I don't have any money and you can't afford it. Let's just buy some gauze at a drugstore. That's all they'd do, anyway."

In the morning I cleaned out the Datsun. The window had shattered into square glass pellets and they were littered over the seat, floorboards, around the emergency brake. There was blood on the steering wheel and the door. I used a sponge and a bucket of water to clean it off, and the water was a dark rust color by the time I was only halfway finished.

After that, Louis didn't like going out, because his face looked so awful. He couldn't hunt for jobs looking like that. The beating happened in early July. I tried to take care of him, and after a couple of weeks he was better. The swelling in his eyes went down but the bruises were still there, although they faded from black-and-blue to a yellow-and-greenish color. I thought that he'd cracked some ribs, but he wouldn't get X-rayed to find out.

One evening, while Louis was recuperating, we went for a walk down the streets of our old neighborhood. I thought it might cheer him up. We'd been planning to do it ever since we first moved in. It was early in the evening. The moon was almost full, and the sky was a deep lavender color. There was a grove of juniper still standing behind Villa del Sol, and we cut through these undeveloped lots to get to Vance Jackson, and once across Vance Jackson, we walked down Moonlight Lane. As we cut through the undeveloped lots, the air was filled with the pungent scent of the juniper trees, and we heard whippoorwills. Louis asked if I remembered when we used to play Blackout. "This is the best time of the night for it."

It was a game of hide-and-seek that we played on summer evenings, like this one. Louis had invented it, and had given it the name of Blackout. We usually played it at dusk, after the sun had gone down but before it was completely dark. The air would be full of fireflies. One of the brothers or sisters was chosen It, and whoever was It had to turn around in a circle fifty times, with eyes closed, while the others ran off and hid anywhere inside or out, but you had to be touching the house. Whoever was It stumbled around in the dark and tried to find people, and when he or she did, the other brothers or sisters helped look for the ones still hiding, until by the end of the game, the last person had a whole crowd searching. The last time we played Blackout had been almost ten years ago.

Moonlight Lane was paved now, smooth and hard. It had orange reflectors in the middle of the road, to separate the lanes at night. There were streetlights where it used to be totally dark. As we reached the intersection of Moonlight and Sunburst, Louis was silent. I said, "You know, we never should have sold this place. We could be living here if we'd kept up the payments."

Our old house still stood there, but the lawn was overgrown with Johnson grass, weeds, and flowers. In the back, near the peach trees, the St. Augustine was thick and lush. The house was for sale again, but the red paint of the "for sale" sign was faded, as if it had been sitting there a long time. Weeds grew in the gravel driveway. Some of the rose bushes were still alive, although grown long and thin without being trimmed.

The air smelled of overgrown honeysuckle vines beneath the dusty windows, the walls of peeling paint. Hundreds of black birds filled the branches of the oak trees in the front yard, and when Louis walked between the trees, the birds rushed out of the leaves and branches, seemed to explode out of the knots, the trunk, the bark itself.

I told Louis this reminded me of years ago, when our family was huge and close. He nodded, and said something under his breath that I couldn't hear. The trees burst open and dissolved into a whirl of black wings around us. Louis watched them and smiled.

I followed him up the driveway to the house. He looked in the windows, wiping dust off in a circle with the cuff of his shirt. The front door was locked. I figured that was that, and stood in the weedy flower beds by the living-room window and looked through the clear window pane where Louis had wiped it off.

As I watched, Louis suddenly walked into the living room. He must have found the back door open. In the gray-blue light of dusk, he looked like my father walking through the deserted house, looking for his lost ear. He was just a shadow, a silhouette. He said something to himself—or maybe to someone else, someone not present—and peered into the dark maw of the fireplace. He reached inside and smeared soot on his face. I banged on the window, telling him to come on outside, he shouldn't be in there. He turned to look at me and frowned, but the face I looked into, the eyes I beheld in the dim light, were not Louis's. It was my father's face. His ear was gone. In its place was a mutilated stump, a flap of flesh. I realized then why Louis could not hear anymore, how he had also lost his ear.

For a moment I saw him clearly, my missing father, tall

and thin and bruised by fate, not a man who dies in his sleep, but one who bleeds to death from a wound too big to heal, to patch, to sew shut. He stared at me through the window as if he didn't recognize me, his own son, as if I had developed into something foreign, unknown. A threat. A fake. A stranger. I tried to speak, but my mouth refused to move.

He vanished down the hallway, while I felt ants biting my ankles, but I couldn't move from the window. The sky turned from lavender to black. The black birds funneled down from above, landing on the telephone wires and flitting through the eaves of the house. As it grew dark, the house filled with a warm yellowish light from the kitchen.

In this yellow light, I watched my father swim by in the shape of the sawfish, lazily swinging his great tail through the living room, his black beady eyes registering nothing, his gash of gills flashing. He swung his head back and forth, then disappeared with a flick of his tail into the dining room. I tried to go in the front door but it was locked. I ran around to the back of the house, and the back door on the concrete porch was open. From there I could see into the kitchen.

The yellow light flickered against the walls of the cabinets, the countertop, the stove where my mother had cooked food for us. I walked inside the kitchen and there was Louis, standing in front of the sink, and beneath the sink, where for years we had kept a salty dried piece of our father's ear, there was a fire burning brightly. The light shone on the broken glass that littered the floor and it was as if I suddenly awoke from a dream that was not a dream, and realized that Louis was standing in front of a fire, the room was filling with smoke, the flames catching on old curtains and flickering up to the ceiling. I shouted for him to get out of there, and when he wouldn't move, I dragged him by his arm out the back door and through our old backyard, crossing the yard of the house where Kit used to live. We stood back in the trees of Kit's yard and watched the house grow brighter and brighter with flames, filling the windows, the peach trees set ablaze, the roof smoldering with dense white smoke until it burst into huge orange-red flames—curving, obeying a kind of reverse gravity, pouring upwards like an inverted waterfall, pouring heat into the sky.

For weeks afterward I waited for us to be arrested for arson. I walked around the apartment complex, wheeling the shampooer from one unit to the next, half expecting a squad car to pull into the driveway any minute. It never happened. Finally I drove by the old house. It had burned virtually to the ground. The fireplace still stood in the center, in what had been the living room. Around it the walls and floor were a jumble of blackened boards. The house itself symbolized our family—a victim, a result of too much heat. I had often felt as if we were a circus act. Like freaks. Maybe we should have been touring the country. A family of freaks, fun for the whole family. The bearded lady. The tattooed man. The sword swallower. The fire eater. It felt as if we'd swallowed too much and that we had held it down, held it in for too long. Sometimes it felt as if the fire we'd eaten was going to burn through our minds. I wondered if this had happened to Louis. And now the fire had come bursting out.

I left for New Orleans in August. Lionel was going to let Louis stay in the free apartment, for now. He didn't have much of a choice. Louis still hadn't been able to find a job.

He lived off food stamps and welfare checks. He wouldn't even talk about the fire. And because I was afraid that both of us could go to jail, I didn't want to bring it up. I had to cancel my camping trip, because Sonia and I put our money together so Louis could get back on his feet. I was supposed to give it to him before I left.

It was about eight o'clock when I packed the car. It didn't take long, since I hardly owned anything. I'd decided to make the drive at night, while it was cooler. We had put the money in an envelope and written a short note about what it was for. I had thought Louis was taking a nap, but when I returned for one of my last loads, I noticed the sliding glass door to the balcony was open, and he was leaning against the railing, staring down at the courtyard. When I finished packing the car I placed the envelope with money on the kitchen counter, then stepped out onto the balcony and stood beside Louis.

All around Villa del Sol, people had their lights on, were playing music or sitting by the swimming pool in lawn chairs. Some people were barbecuing at a grill on the landing next to us.

"Well, looks like it's about that time."

Louis nodded and flicked his butt down into the courtyard below us. "Listen, Damie. I've been meaning to apologize for screwing up your summer. You probably would've been a lot better off if I hadn't been around."

"Oh, knock it off. You didn't screw anything up."

"No, man, I screwed everything up. It seems like everything I touch turns to shit. I don't know what's the deal. I just can't get back on the right track."

"You've just got a run of bad luck, is all. Stay here for a

while. You'll find a job soon. Something's bound to turn up."

"I don't know." Louis shook his head. "But I think I need more than a job, now."

We shook hands before I left, said we'd keep in touch. As I drove away, I wondered what he'd be doing in his threadbare apartment after I left. It scared me. I couldn't face it. I didn't want to *know* anymore. I felt like there was nothing I could do to help. I was glad to be getting away. Once I made it to the interstate, I felt free.

28
Fish
in
the Sea

After leaving Tulane I went to Rutgers for graduate school, and that Christmas I flew to Beachport to spend the holidays with Mom and Glen. They had sold the restaurant by then, had even made money off the deal, and Mother was working as a bookkeeper again; Glen was a night watchman at a mansion, and his new obsession was building a house on Tornado Bay. Now that our family was scattered all across the country, Mom had invited us there for a reunion of sorts. I was the only one from out of state who had flown in, but Sonia had driven down from San Gabriel, bringing Louis with her—all the unmarrieds showed up. Louis was only thirty-three then, but he looked fifteen years older, at least. His hair was so thin you could see his scalp. He had a salt-and-pepper beard with stubble covering his neck.

When he saw me he said, "How our little genius doing, eh?" Then he gave me a hug.

"Louie, I'm no genius."

"Oh come on. You're the brains of the family." His voice was hoarse and cracked. "The rest of us are all dropouts and flunkies, but not you, man, you stuck with it."

Louis sat on the unfinished deck of the new house, smoking cigarettes, because Mom had quit smoking and didn't like the smell. Like most of the summer homes in that housing development, the bay house was perched on stilts—huge creosoted posts like telephone poles—to keep it off the ground in case of storm tides from hurricanes. This could happen, too. The bay was only about twenty yards from the back door. The exterior of the house was finished, with the roof and walls in place, the windows in, but inside, you could still see the two-by-four studs of the walls, the floors of naked plywood, the exposed wiring. Mom had placed an old sofa in the middle of what would be the living room, and we sat there and talked for a while, staring out the sliding glass doors to the deck, where Louis sat at the edge of the balcony. It seemed as if we were watching him through a two-way mirror, studying a patient. He smiled and nodded to himself from time to time, laughed, shook his head. There was no one out there with him, of course. He was talking to himself. His shoulders were stooped and he seemed impossibly old.

"He scares me, sitting so close to the edge like that," said mother. "He could fall off. He could jump!"

"He wouldn't do that, Mama," said Sonia. "He's not that crazy."

Mother shook her head. "I don't know. The other night he started singing that *Wizard of Oz* song, 'Ding Dong the

Witch Is Dead,' in the middle of dinner. It made no sense whatsoever. It scared me."

The entire time I was there, it seemed as if my mother's idea of me and my brothers and sisters had scarcely changed from what it had been when we were young, the family all together, still living at the intersection of Moonlight and Sunburst. She seemed to think of me as about twelve years old, the age I was when I bashed Brian Tunch in the head.

Now I was twenty-six years old and she had bought me a Masters of the Universe toy. I didn't know what to do when I opened it. I didn't want to hurt her feelings. She was my mother. And she was watching me, smiling, so I said, "Hey. It's a Master of the Universe," holding out the package for everyone to see. "I've always wanted one of these."

"His name is Roboto," she said. "Look. You can see the gears inside his heart. And on his arm he has an ax instead of a hand."

My mother was now short and chubby. She only came to my chest, and her arms were wobbly with fat. Besides the toy she gave me a shirt in a size I had not worn since the tenth grade. When I tried it on, the cuffs showed a lot of wrist, the shoulders were ridiculously tight.

"Now that's too tight, isn't it. Well, I saved the receipt, so you can take it back and get one that fits. Are you still growing? It seems like every time you come to visit you need a bigger size."

"But I like the shirt itself, Mom. I'm sure they'll have the right size. Thanks a lot." I kissed her on the cheek. "I never have enough shirts."

Our living room was full of torn, colorful wrapping paper and boxes. Mother collected all the ribbons and bows we had discarded. She kept them in a box and saved them for next year. I saw the same bows every Christmas. The tree was aluminum. Its branches were covered with thin, shiny strips of foil. The leaves glittered, stirred by the window unit's fan. Christmas Eve and it was eighty-three degrees in Beachport. When I left New Jersey it had been snowing, bumper-to-bumper traffic along the turnpike to the Newark airport. In Beachport, cotton-ball clouds floated in the blue sky. Out the second-story window we could see Tornado Bay, and watched as a boat sped past, pulling a water skier.

This wasn't the climate for sickness.

After we opened our presents, I said, "Maybe we should go skiing. Wouldn't that be fun?"

Mother said, "You never liked skiing before. Where'd you get this idea all of a sudden?"

"Yeah, Damon. You always used to hate to ski," said Sonia. She shook her head at me. "You're a weirdo, you know that?"

Sonia had gained a little weight, and she looked like she was poured into her blue jeans. She wore a yellow silk blouse and Reeboks. She was still working as a waitress, but was now taking classes at San Gabriel College. I thought she should get a better job, make more money than waitressing, since I knew she was more talented and intelligent than most of the people she worked with. She didn't seem to have enough self-confidence. "Don't you think you should get a better job?" I told her. "You don't want to be a waitress all your life, do you?"

She sighed at me, and with her fist clenched, shook it in the air. "Don't you think I know that?"

Now she thought I was weird for wanting to go skiing.

"You used to hate to ski," she said. "I never could get you to drive that old boat Glen bought when we were in high school."

"Well maybe I realized what I've been missing all these years. People can change, can't they?"

Sonia and I tried to talk about Louis, but there was really nothing to say. He was supposed to stay with Mom and Glen for a while. He didn't seem to like that idea, but he had nowhere else to go. Mom wanted him to go back to college. "Maybe if he'd just take some classes, get interested in something, he'd get out of this funk that he's in," she said.

I knew that would never happen. Sonia had told me that she and Mom had tried to talk him into seeing a psychiatrist, but he'd refused to go. He said he didn't see any point in it.

Sonia had been there a couple of days before I arrived, and had to leave early the afternoon of Christmas Day because she had to return to work the next day. With her gone, Mother and I were alone with Louis. Glen was out fishing in his inboard-outboard Mercury. While we were sitting there, pretending to watch TV, I remembered another Christmas, years ago, when we were still living at Moonlight and Sunburst, when the family was still together, and Louis had taken me with him to get a Christmas tree for the house. It was back when Louis seemed completely normal, and had his whole life ahead of him, and I couldn't have imagined that it would be anything but the best.

He'd borrowed a pickup truck from one of his high school friends, and we headed into the hills west of San Gabriel, towards Bandera, looking for a deserted place, where we could get away with trespassing and chopping down a tree. We figured we could pick up some fallen branches for the fireplace at the same time. We drove for about two hours down back roads, past gray wintry fields punctuated only by highway signs. We drove past ranchland of prickly pear, limestone bluffs, the Medina River. There was not another car in sight. Here and there a jackrabbit watched us pass, shadowed by hawks perched atop power lines. The telephone poles seemed like black crucifixes.

About the time we were ready to turn around and head back, still without a tree—we were afraid some rancher was going to shoot us for trespassing—we stopped at a country store that doubled as the local post office. The woman behind the counter seemed glad to have some company. "Cold enough for ya?" she asked. As we filled up Styrofoam cups with coffee, Louis turned a wire rack of joke postcards, pointing out the jackalopes—jackrabbits topped with antelope antlers. The country store sold hunks of beef jerky with the price tags attached with twine. Whitetail deer and javelina heads hung from the wall above the cash register. Behind the glass of the white counter were orange wheels of cheddar cheese, beef briskets, platters of hamburger meat, jars of cow tongues. The posts of the store were juniper trunks, some with the bark still attached, and the place smelled of wood-smoke mixed with tobacco and barbecue.

The woman said, "What are you boys up to on a cold day in December? You should be home by the fire." Louis told her what we were doing, and asked if she knew of anybody that wouldn't mind if we chopped down a Christmas tree from their property. She said sure, and told us we could get one from her brother's land—he didn't care squat about an old juniper tree. She drew elaborate directions on a napkin, and even gave us two extra doughnuts for free. We felt lucky then. We lingered longer in the store than we needed to, and drank our coffee there, sitting on tree-trunk stools near the counter. Just before we left we bought two big strips of jerky for lunch.

Following her directions we crossed a barrage of cattle guards, the pickup's front end bucking, and finally reached a corrugated metal gate whose lock consisted of a loop of wire that slipped over one of the fenceposts. It was early afternoon by then, but the sun didn't seem to be putting out much heat. A thin film of white and grayish clouds coated the sky. The fields were stony, full of cactus and parched grass. Our breath puffed out in white clouds of frost. To chop down the tree, Louis had brought a hatchet and a machete that had been Barry's—one of the few things *he* left behind. Louis carried the machete and I the hatchet, befitting my little brother status.

The junipers—we always called them cedars when we were growing up—were less than perfect Christmas trees. Not the classic fir tree models of wide base tapering to a twinkling, star-topped crown. Most of them looked like giant shrubs. Wide at the bottom, wide at the top. The boughs were long and fluffy green. And most of the trees were too big. Maybe only fifteen feet high, but thirty feet in diameter, with thick, gnarly trunks we would never manage to cut. No Scotch pines here. After sizing up a dozen or so, we finally decided on one that would do. "This one's got character," said Louis. "I think he'd be a good addition to our household." The tree was fairly short, just a little over our heads. One side was definitely fuller than the other.

Louis started with the machete, hacking away chips of wood, scoring the trunk with lacerations but making surprisingly little progress. As I waited for my turn, I had to shuffle my feet to keep them from going numb. It was eerily quiet there, no highway sounds or honking. It seemed to get quieter as it grew colder. Louis hacked away at the trunk for almost an hour before stopping. Our shadows lengthened to thin strips stretched out three times our length on the dead grass and cactus of the fields. When I took over with the hatchet, Louis's nose was bright red from the cold. My small blade barely seemed to scar the wood. "C'mon, Damie! Hustle!" said Louis. "You act like you're scared of that tree."

I hacked away, finally digging a substantial nick in the wood and raising a blister on my palm, before Louis took back over. He started talking to the tree as he chopped. "We're gonna get you, tree. So you might as well give in." It seemed to work. Soon we were making progress. I hacked from the other side, and in a final frenzy, with our feet completely numb by this point, we made it, and laid the tree over on its sparse side. The sun was just a vague orange glow on the western horizon. The clouds above were curdled and rippled gray. We headed back for the truck, taking turns dragging the tree by its trunk, the scratchy bark killing the blisters on my hands. I cussed myself for the umpteenth time for forgetting my gloves. Louis offered his, again, but I refused to give in, saying that it was my mistake, and I should be the one to suffer for it. Besides, I told him, I was tough. I could take it.

We were halfway to the pickup when it began to snow. Just a light dusting at first, just enough for us to be amazed. Look at that! Snow! Wouldja believe it? Our cheeks were stinging from the cold, and we weren't even sure we were headed the right way, but we laughed and felt like a million bucks. It felt like we were returning from a battle that we had won. We were together, my big brother and I, out in the fields of snow. By the time we reached the truck, with our bushy, lopsided Christmas tree in tow, the snow was thick and swirling. The flakes were huge and soft. After we loaded the tree into the bed of the pickup, we started the engine and let it warm up, sputtering at first, before we took off. Louis pulled the jerky out of his coat pocket and we ripped into it, gnawing salty chunks of the dried meat like Neanderthals, amazed that it could taste so good. When we got the tree home the whole family was excited. It looked pretty good, actually, especially with lights on it. That was later. But there, on that chilly evening, at the edge of the early winter darkness, I remember how the cab felt unbelievably warm, as my brother and I gnawed delicious hunks of jerky, and the common miracle of snow descended upon us.

But now it seemed as if we had no miracles left, even common ones. As we sat there, watching the football game, Mother talked about Glen's heart condition.

"It was really awful for a while there. I thought we were going to lose him."

"Why?"

"He fell off a ladder and his knee swelled up like this." Mother held her hands about six inches away from her knee. "He couldn't walk and the doctor was giving him this medication that made him dopey. It was scary. In the middle of the night he'd say, 'Mama, tell those people to keep the noise down.' And I'd say, 'What people, honey?' And he'd say, 'Those people in the living room. They're making so much noise I can't get to sleep.' So I finally got the doctor to take him off that medication. It was full of codeine, and you know that's the worst thing for a heart condition. They prescribed something else to make the swelling in the knee go down. It worked much better. He's even gained a little weight now."

Louis was eating the chocolates from a Whitman's Sampler he'd gotten for Christmas. He ate them one by one, methodically, crinkling the delicate little cups in the box when he hunted for a new piece. I couldn't stop myself from watching him. He read the diagram on the inside of the box describing each candy. He didn't offer me or Mother the box. He didn't even seem to realize we were in the room.

I felt as if I couldn't breathe.

"Sometimes I wish Glen didn't like to fish and hunt so much. I'm afraid his heart's going to act up on him when he's out in the boat somewhere, and there'll be no one there to help." Mother shook her head.

Out of the blue, Mother said, "You know what he bought me for my last birthday?"

I had no idea. A gun, maybe.

"A subscription to *Field & Stream*." Mother looked at me, then shrugged. "I don't read them." She turned to the football game on TV, but I could tell she wasn't really watching it.

I stayed in Beachport for a few more days after Christmas, and since it was only me and Louis there with Mom and Glen, I tried to talk to him, tried to connect. But it was like visiting with a grandfather who can't hear anymore, or sitting in the hospital room while someone you care about—someone you love—wastes away, lying in a bed, not able to speak or to move or to resume the image you once had of them. Louis liked to sit on the deck and stare at the bay. He complained of headaches. "Well," I said, "why don't you go to a doctor then? It could be something serious, Louie."

He shook his head. "They're not going to tell me anything I don't know. I've got migraines. I've had them for years now, and there's no cure for it."

When I pressed him on the details of how he felt, how he knew there was nothing that could be done about it, he refused to answer me, acted as if he were deaf. I sometimes wondered if he was only pretending not to hear. He would shut us out, and make it difficult to talk to him, because you had to repeat yourself over and over again, and struggle to get him to pay attention. It was frustrating. I wanted some easy answer, I wanted Louis back the way he'd been years before, I wanted him to be happy and smiling, and he seemed to think this was impossible.

"There's no magic cure for me, Damie. I'm just fucked up, man. That's all it is. And there's no changing that."

"How do you know, Louie? If you don't see a doctor, how do you know what's wrong with you?"

"I know, man. Believe me. I know."

We argued about it whenever he would bother to respond to me, and finally, the day I left, when we said goodbye on the deck, he gave in and agreed to see a psychiatrist in Corpus Christi that someone had recommended to Mom. We shook hands and I told him to keep his word—maybe there was something they could do about the headaches.

"Don't worry about me, Damie. I'll be okay."

I went back in the house and said good-bye to Glen. Mom followed me out to the car to see me off. She knew about my plane reservation, but asked if I had to leave so soon anyway.

"I guess so."

She gave me a paper bag full of fruit and turkey sandwiches for the road. The sandwiches were wrapped in foil and, placed in a plastic produce bag, a paper towel in each. She slipped a twenty-dollar bill into my pocket when I picked up my clothes bag to walk out to the car.

"Mom, you don't have to do that. I'm not a kid anymore."

"It's just a snack," she said. "You know that airport food isn't any good." The sky had clouded up. It was cold, and my mother tightened her cardigan around her shoulders.

"Let me know if there's anything I can do to help Louie, okay?"

"Don't you worry."

We hugged. I kissed her on the lips and told her I loved her. Her lipstick was sweet, but I waited until I was out of sight before I wiped it off my lips. As I was leaving town I stopped at the 7-Eleven.

The walls were glass, and I could see everything inside the store. Across the front a banner proclaimed, FREEDOM IS WAITING FOR YOU AT 7-ELEVEN! I was struck by how bright and alluring the store was, filled with bluish fluorescent light and all your little heart desires. Things to buy. Things to eat. Things that glow in the dark. Things you can throw away. Get something else. Try that for size. New things come in every day. It's beautiful. It's clean. It's disposable. Like a life-size 3D television. And don't just stop at things, you can throw away people, too. Go ahead. It's a free country. Nobody's stopping you. There are a lot of other fish in the sea.

29
Blackout

After that Christmas, true to form, Louis left Beachport without telling anyone where he was going. The last postcard we got from him was postmarked Culver City, California. He'd said that he was still looking for a job and had a new apartment, that everything was okay. We sent letters to that address but never got a reply. For several years then we knew Louis was lost in California, and we came to believe that his life was over. Neither Sonia nor my mother nor any of my other brothers and sisters heard from him. We didn't know his address, or whether he had a job or was in a jail or a madhouse or what. We all secretly feared he was dead, but we didn't hire a private detective or anything to find out. Who could have afforded it? Sonia told me she prayed for his soul. I hoped that he would die as I used to believe my father had died, in his sleep. During the time when we didn't hear from him, I knew that he was in trouble somehow, that his life had gotten worse. I secretly hoped that one day he just wouldn't wake up. That was how I wanted him to die. I truly believed that Louis's karma would be better in his next life, and the next time he would come back as a creature whose heart and soul cannot be broken. Perhaps a monarch butterfly, a Canadian goose, or a caribou. Some creature that flocks or schools or herds. But it wasn't until Louis came home and killed himself that I realized how I had wished for this to happen, how I had wanted it.

I was visiting Sonia for a few weeks during a summer break when Louis returned. He called out of the blue, from a pay phone on Interstate 10 somewhere outside El Paso, and said he'd be in San Gabriel by that night. We went to the supermarket and bought wine and cheese, pasta and vegetables for sauce, and spent the day cooking dinner. It was late afternoon when he pulled into her driveway in the same beat-up VW he'd been driving since the time when he had been a whole and functioning human being. It now had bashed-in fenders and a coat hanger for a radio antenna. "That's my little sister standing there," said Louis, putting his head out the window. "With my little brother right next to her." Sonia stood in her front yard, wearing a sweater and jeans, smiling and waving both hands. Before he even got out of the car, I noticed how he combed his thin hair forward over his head the way some old men do. He hadn't shaved in days, and a cigarette-ash stubble covered his face and flabby neck. In his high school senior class photo, Louis looked like Treat Williams in *Prince of the City*, with dark bushy hair and thick eyebrows, square face and short, muscular neck. But as he had grown older, he had come to resemble a ragged David Jansen in TV's *The Fugitive*, who lived his life going from one town to the next, looking for the one-armed man who killed his wife. Sonia said, "We thought you were dead or something." She pushed his chest. "Why didn't you ever write or call?"

As Louis told us about never being settled in one place for long and being out of work for two years, Sonia tried not to cry, petting the roof of his Beetle as if it were an old dog, saying, "I remember this old thing." His floorboard was a jumble of swollen paperbacks and rumpled clothes. I shook hands with him and said, "Hey, buddy." He squeezed my hand so hard it hurt, then we hugged. He slapped me on the back.

"So this is where my little sister lives, huh?" He walked onto Sonia's lawn and looked around. "You're moving up in the world."

"It's just a house, Louie. But I like it."

"Hey Damon, Mom tells me you're going to get your Ph.D. anytime now."

"That Mom. She blows everything out of proportion. I still have a couple years left to go."

"I never thought of you as a professor." He smiled crookedly at me, and grabbed my shoulders. "It seems like you've grown so much. You're gigantic."

"I'm the same height as I've always been, Louie. It's just that you haven't seen me in a while."

"And I'm the same as I've always been," said Sonia. "Still working at the restaurant."

"There's nothing wrong with being a waitress. I bet if you stick with it, you could go on and become a manager or something."

Sonia wrinkled her nose. "Not in a million years."

"Sure. You can do anything you set your mind to." Louis

hugged her and patted her on the back again. "You won't count quarters all your life."

"Well I wouldn't want to be a manager. I don't think I'd be any good at bossing people around."

Louis picked up an acorn from the yard, stood for a moment as if he'd forgotten that we were standing there. He held it to his nose and smelled it. "That's what I really need. Some kind of job to get me back on my feet. I got to make some money."

"Did you get the Christmas presents we sent two years ago?" I asked. "Everything since then was returned by the post office."

"If I could just get a job," said Louis. "Then everything else would fall into place. Then I could get back on my feet."

I said he should probably be able to find something.

Sonia stood there looking at him for a long time, frowning. "You never called us or anything. We almost contacted Missing Persons."

Louis moved in with Sonia. There was no place else for him to go. But it wasn't until he had been staying with her for over a month that he told her about the voices. The voices he heard in his mind, that he had been hearing for years, that were getting louder and louder. Some were whispers, some deep and gravelly. They were warning him that we were all going to be killed. They told him that the neighbors next door—the short man who drove the Isuzu and his fat wife—were part of the plot and were watching Sonia's house. Louis told Sonia this after he had gotten a job at a fast-food restaurant and had already been fired. He kept splashing grease from the deep fryers on himself. His arms were covered with bubbles of blisters. He forgot too many orders, or let the food burn. He still smoked cigarettes constantly, and kept Sonia up at night with his coughing. He seemed to be in bed all the time, trying to sleep. Then he told her about the voices. Whispering threats, urging him to prepare, to watch out.

"And I see things, Sonia. I see people behind me all the time. I know they're not there, but I see them anyway. You can't believe what they tell me to do."

"What, Louis? What do they tell you?"

He shook his head. "I see and hear things that make me sick inside." He closed his eyes and rubbed his head with his hands. "I think maybe I shouldn't be walking around here on my own."

I was in San Gabriel the first couple of weeks that Louis was back in town, but had to return to New Jersey for a summer job, and wasn't around when he finally confessed to Sonia what was wrong with him. By that time she was calling me on the phone almost every night, telling me what had happened that day, how he was doing, asking me what she should do. I didn't know. I didn't want to see him in a state hospital. She told me things about the two of them I had never known. She said when she was seven and Louis was thirteen years old, he'd walked her to the bus stop every morning because she was afraid of a German shepherd that lived at one of the houses up the street, even though it made him late for school.

I told Sonia how Louis had protected me too. I told her how a hoot owl had lived in the oak trees of our house at Moonlight and Sunburst, and at night, the owl would hoot and frighten me, and I'd ask Louis if I could come sleep with him. He'd say okay, just don't take all the covers. "It's only an owl," he'd tell me. "Owls are good. They eat mice and stuff."

When I lay next to the warm body of Louis, I knew that nothing could harm me, that if I could just keep him from stealing the blankets I would be okay.

Now Sonia and I tried to conjure up what the best Blackout game of our childhood had been. Mine was when I was twelve years old. We had been eating watermelon after our favorite dinner of hamburgers cooked on the backyard grill, and Sonia, Lizzie, Tony, and Louis had been spitting watermelon seeds at each other, and especially at Melody, who didn't think it was funny. If they landed on your neck they would stick like a leech, only they were shaped more like a guitar pick, slimy and hard as a bean. All of a sudden Louis raced through the house shouting, "Blackout! Blackout!" He started off the game as It, but he found Sonia first. They rushed through the house together, finding all of our missing brothers and sisters, until the very last one, which was me. Then, a couple of rounds later, it was my turn to close my eyes and spin around fifty times. When I opened my eyes I was dizzy, the entire world still spinning around, and I stumbled slightly, until I stood underneath the white cotton net of our basketball hoop. I remember I wished the world would stop spinning. I was amazed at how beautiful the house and yard looked in the dark. The fig tree cast huge spatulate shadows on the concrete of the back porch, shadows cast from the light of the full moon, the air alive with lightning bugs, the sound of crickets and the smell of watermelon rinds in a bucket by the door. It was so beautiful I didn't want to go inside to find the others, because it was almost better to be there alone in the moonlit yard, knowing that all my brothers and sisters were hiding in the house, crouched among the shoes of the closet, their feet sticking out from beneath the pleats of the living-room curtains, whispering to each other in the dark.

It was now twenty years later, and Louis confessed that he'd been diagnosed as paranoid schizophrenic several years ago, in a community clinic somewhere in California. Now he'd begun to act like a retarded man. He would forget to close the door when he was using the bathroom. Sonia told him over and over again not to do this, but finally gave up, and would simply close the door behind him if she walked by. He couldn't keep his shirttail tucked in and got his buttons all wrong. He seemed to be getting worse, and Sonia was afraid for him, afraid that something would happen to him while she was at work, so I got a leave of absence from my department and moved back to San Gabriel in September to help take care of him. He was docile by this point, and didn't resist when we suggested that he take some tests and talk to the doctors at a psychiatric clinic. They immediately put him on haloperidol. When the doctor told us this, Sonia asked, "Will this make him normal again?"

It didn't.

Louis didn't seem to like anyone being around him anymore, and would just sit in the front of the TV and stare at it, or lie in bed. I went out one evening and brought home two paper bags of takeout Chinese for us. I stopped by his room, where he lay on the bed in his pajamas, one arm across his face, the other holding a cigarette. The room was stuffy and gray with the smoke.

"How are you feeling, Lou? I bought some Kung Pao chicken."

He sat up and rubbed his eyes. "Did you notice anyone following you?"

"No."

He told me he'd been calling our mother all day and there was no answer. He told me people were going to kill everyone in the family, and that they were waiting outside and watching the house, but don't look out the window, pretend you know nothing. He said that no one was safe, but there was nothing he could do about it, and that they were going to cut all of us up or strangle us or shoot us or stab us or throw hydrochloric acid on our faces or blow us up. And there was no way we could stop them.

"Maybe you should get dressed and have something to eat," I said. "Maybe you'll feel better."

Louis shook his head. "I think you better take me to the hospital, Damon. I think you better take me away." He stared at the wallpaper, with its pattern of pink and yellow tulips. A few nights before, he had said they looked exactly like people's faces, and they were laughing at him.

He was in and out of the clinic for five months. The doctors tried different kinds of medication on him, but he hated all of them. The only thing they did was make him lethargic and muted. After a while he refused to talk about his problems anymore, and we fooled ourselves into thinking that maybe he was getting better—maybe he was going to be okay—until one day he drove his Volkswagen to the intersection of Moonlight and Sunburst and parked it.

Right there, where we had grown up, he blew his head off with a shotgun.

The young couple who found his body told the police they'd been out for a walk. It had been a nice day and they wanted to go outside. They had passed the car once and thought Louis was a homeless man sleeping in the front seat, until the second time they passed, when they got close enough to see.

        This was January. As everyone arrived for the funeral in San Gabriel, Sonia and I stood in the kitchen of her house. She knelt on the floor and scratched one of her cats, which arched its behind in the air, purring softly.

"It was like he was in his own little world," said Leland. He leaned over the table spread with chips and dip, trying to dig a broken potato chip out of the guacamole. He was still tall and good-looking, but heavier now, wider. He had three kids, two of them in Little League. He worked as a computer systems programmer for a large corporation in Denver. Instead of football jerseys, now his standard casual wear was jeans, cowboy boots, a down vest. He was talking to Melody.

"I only saw him once in the last five years," she said. She was now forty years old, and had a son in the Marines.

"It's been longer than that for me. Every time I heard about him he was in a different city, and after a while, I just lost track."

Still petting the cats, without looking at Leland or Melody, Sonia said, "Could we maybe talk about something else?"

"Sonia," said Melody, "you know, you weren't the only one who loved him."

I got a twist tie from the knife drawer and tied up the plastic garbage bag under the sink, then started out the side door. It gave me a reason to get outside. My mother was in the living room, and it hurt me to see her. She wouldn't budge from the living-room sofa. She reminded me of a horse

The Fire Eaters

with a broken leg, whimpering in its stall, among the straw, rotten planks, pitchforks. So I took the trash bag out, got in my rental car, and just sat there. Tony's Ninja motorcycle had me blocked in. I didn't care. I only wanted to be out of the house.

I didn't know why we were calling this a "memorial service," except that Louis's body had been cremated, and I suppose you don't have a funeral without a body. No funeral without a cemetery, a casket, a tombstone. Just a crummy memorial service. Thinking about Louis's body being burned to a crisp and swept into a clenched gray fist of dust made me sick. It was too clean. Too complete. Too total.

Now there were seven children in the family, counting me. As we had grown older, the fact that we didn't share the same mothers and fathers, and that most of us did not have much feeling for each other—except perhaps vexation or annoyance—had become clear. Leland had driven down from Denver, picking up Melody in Tulsa on the way. Lizzie was stuck in Alaska. Agnes was in Santa Barbara, and had sent a card. Tony blew in from L.A. on his motorcycle, wearing biker boots and a black leather jacket with zippered sleeves and slanted zippered pockets. His black hair was slicked back, and he wore a silver hoop earring in one ear. No one recognized him at first. We didn't know what to say. He used to be so quiet. Leland asked, "Who are you supposed to be? The Fonz?"

Tony smiled, and said, "Arthur Fonzarelli, to you."

It was weirdly warm for January, like an Indian summer in the wrong time of year, and although the weather was almost like spring, the grass in Sonia's front yard was dead brown. Her neighborhood was full of old wooden two-story houses with piebald paint jobs, red brick chimneys, funky plumbing. As I sat in my old Datsun in the driveway, going nowhere, I thought about the family.

Leland walked out to his pickup carrying a beer. On the way back he knocked on my window. I cranked it down.

"Blocked in, eh?"

"I think so."

He leaned against the passenger-side door. There were three cars parked in Sonia's driveway, and two more on the street in front of her house. "Looks like a used-car lot here," he said.

"Uh huh."

He took a drink from his Budweiser. "You waiting for Motorhead to move his bike?"

I drew two circles in the condensation on my windshield. "I don't know," I said. "I think he's inside." I hoped Leland wasn't thinking about getting in the car. I didn't feel like a talk. Sonia's Bonneville was parked next to me in the driveway, and Leland squinted at it, kicked its tires. He rapped the roof of the car with his knuckles. "Sonny's paint job's a little rough around the edges." Huge flakes of paint had peeled off the roof and fenders; the dark brown primer beneath was now uncovered. "Looks like its time for Maaco."

I nodded, and leaned my head out the window of the car. "It's molting."

Leland started back inside. "You need anything?"

I shrugged, then scrunched myself down in the bucket seat. "A million bucks."

"Ha ha." Leland walked away. "Don't we all," he called over his shoulder.

A few minutes later Tony came out and said, pointing, "I'll just park it on the street." After he moved his motorcycle, I felt obligated to drive somewhere, instead of just sitting there. So I drove. There was no point in it, of course. There was no point in anything.

But I drove out to the old neighborhood and remembered how Louis used to take me hunting in the woods near there. Our routine was to walk slowly through the oak and juniper thickets, as quietly as possible, trying to sneak up on something and kill it. Once Louis shot a cottontail rabbit. The woods were full of these, and late at night, when we came home from drive-in movies, the headlights of our station wagon lit up the eyes of rabbits in our front yard. But that day, after my brother shot the rabbit, we stared at the blood sprayed on the brown grass, and the animal seemed to be looking up at us, to be accusing us.

Louis was seven years older than me, and had inherited my father's gun. I wondered if my father had used that same double-barrel twelve-gauge that we had used to hunt with. Would my mother have let us use it? I remember that gun, how heavy and hard it was, how it hung from the walnut gun rack in our room, with a fishing rod on the top rack, the red-and-white bobber still clipped to the monofilament line, the treble hook stuck in the cork of the handle, how the shotgun smelled of oil, the sound of the serious click of the broken breach. Whose lives were we going to defend with it? Whose lives were we going to take? To end?

I wondered if Louis had used the same gun he inherited from my father, but it's not a question that's easy to ask. And it's not a question you perhaps want an answer for.

When I returned from driving around I came upon Sonia in her garage, sweeping it out. It was cluttered with bicycles, bags of cat food, clay pots for house plants. Rather than go in, I sat on her washing machine and talked to her.

"You want any of this stuff, Damon?" She pointed with the broom at a stack of books and clothes, an old blow drier, a nylon duffel bag. "It's Louie's. Or it used to be, anyway. I don't know what to do with it."

"Maybe Mom wants it."

Sonia shook her head. "She won't even look at it. None of it's worth keeping. But it's Louie's. I can't just throw it away."

Sonia went back inside as I poked through the clothes and things. What was I supposed to do, wear my brother's clothes after he was dead? Pitch them in the trash? Hide them in the back of my closet? I didn't even like touching them, the weight of his life dragging me down with him. This was all that he had left behind. Some worn-out shirts, scuffed-heel shoes, a jumble of coat hangers. This was the summation of his life. Beneath everything I found two boxes. One of them must have been what passed for his desk. It was a green metal filing cabinet. It contained all the documents left in his life. An old California driver's license. A sheaf of job applications, some of them half filled out, some blank, as if he'd given up hope after a while, given up on everything. There were trinkets, junk. An old brass watchband. His high school ring. A token from an adult bookstore. An Indian-head nickel. Letters from doctors prescribing medication. My letters to him from Tulane. Sonia's letters. A stack of photographs from a trip he'd taken to Colorado, years before. Pictures of him holding a gray tabby cat on a rustic porch. Pictures of his Beetle in the snow. These were his memories. These were his souvenirs. His remains.

And at the bottom of the green box, I found something I hadn't seen in a long time. I wondered if Sonia had seen it. I figured she probably hadn't, and I took it, hoping she wouldn't return to the garage and catch me with it. The green metal box would be the only thing I'd take. This would also be the only thing of Louie's that I would hide, the only thing I would defend and protect. It was a small mason jar, still clean and clear after all these years. Louis had wrapped it in newspaper to keep it from breaking. Inside the jar was the gray half-moon of dried flesh I remembered—the piece of my father's ear—only it was smaller than I remembered —the jar itself was smaller. It looked so fragile. As if it could be anything. As if it could be nothing.

Yet it was my inheritance.

The night before the memorial service our family had a reunion at Luby's cafeteria. That way we would all have our own plates and saucers and our own choice of what we wanted to eat, and no one would have to agree on anything. I sat next to Leland and Sonia. He kept saying she needed to buy a car. He wouldn't shut up about it. "What you ought to get is one of these new Chevy Luminas. The body is completely plastic. It's kind of a cross between a minivan and a station wagon."

Sonia said she didn't have the money for a new car.

"What you should do is go to a police auction," said Leland. "I know a guy in Denver who bought a 1987 Pontiac Trans Am for twenty-four hundred dollars at auction. He could have turned around and sold the car that day for four thousand dollars profit, easy."

Sonia said, "But I wouldn't know the history of any of those cars."

"What's to know? Most of them come from deadbeats anyway. People who couldn't make their payments and left the state so their banks wouldn't get them. It's all perfectly legit."

"I don't know," I said, trying to take some heat off Sonia. She was picking at her peas on her plate, and looking like she would cry. "Her Bonneville is like an old buddy. She might feel like she was deserting it if she got something new."

"Yeah," she said. "Doesn't loyalty count for anything?"

"Loyalty? To a car? Earth to Sonia, come in Sonia. Your old buddy is falling apart."

Sonia drew fork lines in the lumpy mounds of her mashed potatoes.

"What if it won't start one morning? What will you do then?"

Sonia closed her eyes and set down her fork. "Leland?" Her voice quavered. "It'd be a wonderful thing, really. It really would. If you could please shut up."

"Okay, Sonny. I'm sorry. Geez." Leland looked around the table, but the rest of the family tried to stay out of it. "I was trying to help," he said.

After dinner, I rode with Sonia in her car, and we followed Tony on his motorcycle to a bar. We watched him speed down the freeway, with his leather jacket and helmet on. We talked about him as a cameraman in Los Angeles now, how we never would have figured it. At the bar he had ordered beers for all of us. "We don't need to go back to that madhouse yet," he said. "No offense."

Sonia said, "You shouldn't ride a motorcycle, Tony. It's not safe."

He nodded, offered her a Marlboro.

"You know I don't smoke," she said.

I took one and he flipped open his silver Zippo lighter. We laughed about how we'd all imitated our mother in our choice of lighters. I said, "I'm supposed to be quitting, but maybe today's not a good time for it."

"Hell," he said. "Maybe now's the time to *start*." He nervously spun the glass ashtray in the middle of the table, not looking at Sonia, telling a story about when I stayed over at Kit O'Hara's without telling them, and how pissed Louie was when he found out where I'd been.

I started talking about the high school football games that we'd watched Louis and Leland in, until Tony sighed and put his head in his hands, both elbows on the table. "I'm sorry. I just can't think about Louis anymore." He shook his head. "It's driving me loony." With his hair slicked away from his face, in the pale yellow light of a beer sign, he looked like a young and hungry Elvis.

Sonia took a cigarette from his pack of Marlboros and tapped the filter against the table, as she had seen us do. "I'm just going to pretend to smoke it," she said. "I'm just going to hold it in my mouth."

Only fifteen people attended the memorial service in the small chapel at St. Matthew's. I counted. Of the fifteen, twelve were family somehow, including step-relations—Glen's relatives—who had never even met Louis. The other three were Louis's only friend from high school, his friend's wife, and their six-month-old baby. He'd been the only person Louis still knew from high school, and somehow it disturbed me that he wore a hearing aid. It seemed like everything connected with Louis was damaged somehow. There was one floral arrangement. I didn't know what kind of flowers they were. I couldn't even tell if they were real or not.

I sat in the front row, next to Sonia and my mother, who held my hand fiercely. And since I couldn't bear to look up, I was keenly aware of the bones of my mother's fingers, the cordlike tendons, the wrinkled skin of her knuckles. She smelled of Jungle Gardenia, a perfume, cloying and heavy, that she used to wear when we went to church. And I wondered if she had gone through life with one bottle of perfume. The same way I wondered if the shotgun that Louis used was the same one that my father had used. My mother's short gray hair was curled and fuzzy as a poodle's. And she kept her eyes clamped shut, although they quivered, the mascara clotted in lumps on the lashes.

Tony sat on the other side of our mother. In his suit and tie and rockabilly hairdo, he could have been a defendant. He kept his head bowed throughout the service, holding his motorcycle helmet in his lap.

I hoped the Egyptians were wrong. I hoped that Louis wouldn't need his old body in his next life, because his jar of ashes would probably be passed from Mother to Melody to one of her kids and end up abandoned in a crummy apartment like at Villa del Sol sometime in the future. The priest explained that the Catholic church had changed now, that in the past suicides had not been allowed to be consecrated, but now it was okay, and I cried and cringed inside, breathing in the smell of my mother's perfume and the flowers I couldn't recognize, realizing for the first time that someone could actually blame Louis for what he did and how his life turned out, that everyone didn't believe that life is something that just happens to you, but something you order and direct, something you control.

A cold front had come in the night before, and for the first time in two years of unusually warm, greenhouse-effect winters, it was snowing. Since I was the first one to leave St. Matthew's chapel, mine were the first shoes to leave imprints in the snow-white front lawn as I walked down the sidewalk alone. I wanted to get away from everyone for just one goddam minute. The bells in the Spanish-missionesque bell tower tolled in the white air, tolled through the snow-flakes drifting down. In three months, I realized, it would be Easter. I would go to St. Matthew's wearing a suit and tie, and get Sonia to wear a lace cap on her head. She would wear a Jackie-O-in-mourning dress, with the black rosary our mother gave her over twenty years ago. The pews would be smooth and shiny. The grass would be green. The vestibule would be decorated with huge Easter lilies trumpeting and blooming like the throats of swans. And the priest would be saying a mass about the resurrection, and at communion we would eat the body of Christ. I would kneel and make the sign of the cross as I entered the aisle, before taking my seat. I would touch my chest, my stomach, my shoulders. They would pass the plate full of coins and dollar bills for the collection. I would pay for my sins, and for Louis's sins. And I would light a candle for his soul. Because if he isn't rein-carnated as a goose or a caribou, I know that somehow Louis will be given life again, that somewhere he'll be given an-other chance.

I remembered how Willi Unsoeld, the American mountain climber who made the first ascent of the West Ridge of Everest in 1963, saw a crow fly past as he down-climbed after his daughter Nanda Devi had died on the mountain she was named for, after spending five days at 24,000 feet. He had believed Devi's soul had been flying away in the body of that crow. I remembered reading how, weak and cold, Devi sat up in the tent and asked a fellow climber, "Take my pulse, will you, Pete?" But before he could do it she said, "I'm going to die," and pitched facedown. How did she know? How do we know? Did Louis reach that point, tangled in the spiderwebs of his voices and threats? I remembered this because as I left the church, an owl swooped silently past the snow-touched oaks in the yard of St. Matthew's.

And I remembered a wildlife film that showed an owl in a leafless, silhouette-black elm against a white winter sky, a gang of crows attacking it in the air, diving and flapping with raucous caws.

And I remembered that evening we played Blackout in my twelfth summer. I remembered walking through the quiet house, illuminated only by the moonlight in the kitchen windows, how the ring of the window sash over the sink was a dark circular shadow at the end of a faint string shadow line, and how, earlier, when I had been hiding and Louis found me, I had groaned and climbed out from under the kitchen table, saying I thought that he wouldn't look there because it would be too obvious. And there, in the dark kitchen, he pointed and told me, "Now you're It."